THE DECISION

John Rock

THE DECISION

Copyright © 2021 John Rock

ISBN: 978-0-6484388-2-3

For

My Tribe

I wish to add my thanks to my talented friend

Graeme Hindmarsh

for his creative design of the cover.

And to my gorgeously sharp eyed friend

Tim Waldock

for his advice and suggestions on edits.

Martin examined his image in the mirror while adjusting the Windsor knot on his tie until satisfied with it. The knot itself had to be perfectly symmetrical; the front tip of the tie should be just above the waist, and the smaller end a bit shorter and tucked neatly behind. It was the symmetry of the Windsor knot he liked; finding other knots such as the 'Four in Hand' irritating because of the lopsided effect. They just looked untidy. He craned his neck forward a little, turned his head slightly to the right, and lightly patted his well groomed hair. He was pleased with the total effect. Not in a narcissistic or smug way, but in a way that recognised the reality: he was 33 years old, a good looking young man of slightly more than average height, slim, with a fine bone structure. His hair was strong and a very light brown, almost a sandy colour. He kept it short because that way it sat well on his head, and was keen to present himself as well as possible. He paid rather more than average for haircuts and invested that money more often than most people.

Although not muscular he had a firm and well defined body, with slender hips, a flat stomach and a chest quite broad for a man of his stature, no doubt as a result of the swimming he had been forced to do as a child by his father. His well-developed buttocks rounded out his pants, a fact he was quite aware had caught the attention of the girls in his office. He had well proportioned features, small neat ears and nose, pale brown eyes, and a warm smile on rather sensual lips. His chin had a slight dimple; his neck was slender, almost elegant. He had been approached once to do some modelling for an advertising agency, but had declined.

He picked up the jacket of his rather expensive tailored suit of a light tan and beige material with a small hare tooth pattern. He chose it knowing that light colours went better with his complexion and hair colour. It was perfectly matched with the pale cream shirt, the red and brown tie and the Italian brown shoes. Slipping the jacket over his shoulders, he picked up his briefcase and walked down the passage to the front door.

The Paddington terrace he bought seven years ago had paid off well as Sydney house prices had skyrocketed in the meantime. It was small, with two bedrooms upstairs and a compact but well-appointed bathroom. Downstairs were a small sitting room, and a dining room that Martin had converted into a study. At the rear of the house was an open plan kitchen with a dining area that opened out onto a modestly sized patio-garden which was paved for tidiness and ease of maintenance. It was softened by so many pot plants that it sometimes seemed to Martin like a jungle. There was a small teak table and four chairs for outside dining or just sitting under the trees that sheltered the garden from prying neighbours.

Martin had decorated and furnished the house tastefully in a timeless style. It was comfortable, neat, functional and masculine. The floors were bare oak boards with oriental rugs, comfortable sofas, side lamps on small tables and walls covered with paintings. He favoured sketches and drawings, although there was one portrait – of the woman who had made it possible for him to buy the house and surround himself with his own statement. It was of his maternal grandmother whom he had adored as a child. She had been a formidable woman, strident and articulate, the daughter of a wealthy family of graziers. In her youth she had been a fiery advocate of women's rights, and had married unusually late for that time, at the age of 32, and 'below her station' as she put it to Martin. But she always kept her own money most of which she inherited when the farm was sold. She bore two children, Martin's mother and his aunt Renie. Martin was her only grandson and she spoiled him as a child. It was her death seven years ago that had given him the inheritance.

Martin opened the front door, ritually set the burglar alarm, closed and locked the door and walked the few paces up the street to where his car was parked. Even with residential parking it was often difficult to find a spot. On approach the central locking gave a crisp electronic beep; after getting in he adjusted the rear-view mirror to check his image quickly once again, just to be sure. After starting the engine he looked over his shoulder and carefully backed out of the parallel parking spot. He accelerated leaving a small hint of vapour behind hovering in the air for a brief moment as the cold engine awoke and commenced its duty.

Along the street, the terraces were standing quietly in the morning sunshine, some half hidden by the trees in the tiny front gardens. It was a November day, spring was well advanced, and there was even a strong hint of summer in the air. Usually Martin drove with the radio on, listening to something bright and invigorating to get him going, generally Triple J. He found the news too depressing, and as he could hardly do anything about all the misery, why get depressed early in the morning? This morning however, he did not put on any music, instead he listened for annoying car noises.

He hated the car, but realising that it was paid for by the company, had to accept it. The car did not have some of the items Martin considered essential, such as a good sound system, leather seating and electronic seat controls, let alone sensors. He would rather have had a Saab, Alfa, or even a sporty little BMW, but also knew that they were outside the company policy.

It was actually quite a good little mid-size Japanese car but just did not fit with the image Martin wished to establish. He had tried to negotiate to receive a car allowance instead of a car, and then he could have leased whatever he wanted. He had argued strongly that it would have absolved them of all other responsibilities. But they would not listen - they had their rules, no exceptions. To make his point, he sent the car to the garage at every single opportunity. If he was going to have to put up with a second rate car, he would at least make sure it was in first rate condition. This time there was a rattle coming from the front on the passenger's side. He leaned forward pressing bits of trim trying to locate it.

Without having identified the offending problem he returned his attention to the traffic for fear of causing an accident, and turned on Triple J to drown out the grating annoyance. He headed down New South Head Road towards the harbour tunnel on his way to the office in Chatswood.

****

3

Thelma Grant sat heavily in the sumptuous arm chair, moved the cushions into a more comfortable position, and looked out through the large French windows to the garden. She sighed almost imperceptibly. In another hour she would leave and catch the train to meet her younger sister Renie for lunch in the city. This was their periodic Tuesday arrangement. It was an opportunity to trade confidences and talk about their problems. As Thelma contemplated the well manicured garden, with the heavy foliage of trees which gave it such a feeling of stability and permanence, she reflected that there was a problem she wanted to discuss with Renie.

It was about Gordon. Theirs had been a satisfactory if not outstanding marriage all in all. He certainly had been a good provider. She, unlike many women of her time, had never been relied on to contribute financially to the household. She had taken the odd part time job, but mainly for want of something useful to do than to earn money or have a career. Even so, the 'pin money' as she called it had allowed her to buy more expensive clothes than she otherwise would have, and to put a little money aside. She wore clothes well, and even at the age of 57 still had a figure that many younger women would envy. Yes, it is true that she dyed her hair, but the auburn colour she selected looked natural, and many of her friends were still not quite sure whether it was dyed or not. Such was the value in paying well to have a professional salon do the job right.

She and Gordon had met at the twenty first birthday party of her cousin Moira. Gordon and Moira played tennis together at the local tennis club in Pymble in the affluent belt of Sydney. Whilst it was not the bolt of lightning love at first sight encounter, Thelma did admit in private moments that she had noticed him the minute he arrived; tall, self assured, with a degree of maturity lacking in other young men she had been out with. Even in those days he was solidly built, she supposed that he would have been an AFL football player, and indeed it turned out that he was. She would never have described him as handsome but she was attracted to his masculinity. His Anglo Celtic origins and pale blue eyes contrasted with her own deep brown eyes, inherited along with her fine bone structure from an Italian grandmother.

During the course of the evening she noticed him glance her way several times. Once when he looked at her he caught her glancing at him. He smiled a big smile, which she returned weakly and without enthusiasm. He walked over to where she was standing. She had a half empty glass of champagne in her hand, and he held a bottle in his hand, about to fill his own glass. Instead he topped up hers first, and then filled his own. To this day she remembers perfectly his first words to her. 'Champagne, a twenty first, let the world rejoice.' It was quickly established how they both knew Moira, and they talked a little about how much fun parties were.

The conversation drifted towards the theatre and he asked her if she would be interested in joining him for a play at the Nimrod Theatre the following Sunday afternoon. Thelma enjoyed the informality of the Nimrod, a small theatre where unusual works were often performed. It was a play she had thought she might like to see anyway, and she accepted. From then the relationship just seemed to develop, slowly, naturally, growing like a flower or a plant, steadily blossoming, becoming what it was destined to become. They got on well together, they seemed to like doing similar things, and what to Thelma was most important they seemed to have similar backgrounds and value systems.

They both lived at home, and when Gordon suggested a weekend away together in the Hunter Valley it was clear to Thelma that this would be the start of their physical intimacy, their physical union. It seemed right and it was time. They had been going out together for three months, and while they had managed some heavy petting in Gordon's car on many occasions, neither of them was the type to go all the way on a quiet headland or a deserted car park, misting up the car windows and tearing clothes on door handles and rear view mirrors.

They left early from work and arrived at a guest house renowned for its culinary arts in time for dinner. The meal was an exquisite work of art, accompanied by some of the finest wines the Hunter could offer. They retired to their room, and as naturally as if they done it many times before, without nervousness, hesitation or apprehension, they gave themselves to each other.

Their sexual relationship had not been one, at least from Thelma's side, based on a real passion. As for Gordon, she assumed that their sex life had been satisfactory enough for him although she had never asked. She knew that there were things that he liked her to do, but which she was reluctant to. Only once did she take him in her mouth when he quietly insisted by teasing himself around her lips and pushing gently but firmly. It was not as if it was something she objected to in principle, it was just that she never felt aroused enough to do it with Gordon; she reflected now that frankly she had never really lusted after him.

She looked abstractly at the hydrangea in the garden, and thought that it was quite possible that she never even really loved him, whatever love is.

She bit her lip inadvertently as she recollected the two men she had had sex with before Gordon. The first one had been when she was just 18 years old and she fell madly in love with Jonathan. But that came to a sudden stop and she did not even want to think about the circumstances that caused its bitter ending, it was just too painful. Then there was her brief and passionate affair with Sergei. She had met him a few months before that twenty first birthday party when she met Gordon. He had been in town for the Sydney Festival as part of a cultural initiative. Sergei was a photographer, a masterful photographer. His works in black and white depicting Russian rural life during the hardest communist years had been shown at the Art Gallery of New South Wales during the festival. She had been invited on opening night by a friend who worked with the organising committee. During the cocktail party that accompanied the opening she was introduced to Sergei. When, by way of introductory greeting, he took both of her hands in his she felt an electric pulse flow from their joined hands right throughout her body, a hot surge of magic. Thelma looked into his eyes and he smiled a broad smile that encompassed the compassion of the whole world. He held her hands longer than etiquette dictated, steadily holding her gaze, until his obligation required him to move to the next introduction.

But a short time later he came up to Thelma, and asked her questions about her and her life. She was astonished at how good his English was. She was also surprised that a man, especially a man as accomplished as he was, would prefer to talk about her and her life rather than his own.

He suggested that she should wait until the end of the cocktail party, and then they could share some supper; he did not know Sydney and she might have some suggestions as to where they could have a quiet meal together. She quickly agreed. Thelma was not a person given to impetuous or unpredictable behaviour. Even now she blushed slightly at the memory of that night and her uncharacteristic actions. She went back to his hotel, and they made wild passionate love until both of them were so sated, they melted into the same deep sleep, entwined as one. With Sergei there was nothing she would have not done. She was greedy for him.

But Sergei was married in Moscow, with a little girl. He had to return at the end of the month, and she knew from the very start that there would be no future to their love. When the end of the month came Thelma felt stunned, the energy drained out of her, leaving her emotionally void. As she left his room that morning at the hotel for the last time, she could not even look at him. She gently shut the door, and it was as if she had closed the door on passion for the rest of her life.

Even then Thelma realised that this experience with Sergei had implications for the rest of her life. She was convinced that search as she might, she would never ever find the same sort of passion for anyone as she had lived with him. And that is why it had seemed so easy to fall into marrying Gordon not long after. And now, thirty five years later, there were problems.

A bird flew across the window and started noisily calling to its mate as it landed on a branch of the small bush to the left of the crazed path. It shook Thelma from her reverie. She glanced at the clock; there was still plenty of time for the 10.25 train.

****

Gordon teed up for the third hole. He had arrived early at the club that morning. It was a perfect spring day, and he wanted to make the best of it. As was their habit in retirement, Thelma and he got their own breakfasts. His was easy in fact, a large glass of orange juice, a banana and two rounds of multigrain toast with vegemite. He made a cup of tea when he first got up, and then had a second after he had finished the toast. It seemed only fair to get his own breakfast as Thelma did the rest of the cooking. At his request they had discussed a change in their domestic responsibilities when he retired. Normally he would accept that it was his job to do the gardening and keep the pool clean and tidy, and attend to all those constant chores that a house of that age required. But the reality was that he was not able any longer to manage the heavy gardening. A lawn mowing service came in once a week in summer, less often in winter, and a gardener did most of the heavy work. He managed some tidying up round the garden, did some of the edging of the lawn, and kept the pool clean. Thelma after all had a house cleaner who came in once a week on Friday mornings to do the bathrooms, the kitchen and put the vacuum cleaner round. For his part he also washed both cars. So he felt that Thelma doing the shopping and cooking was not unreasonable. Yet, deep down inside he sometimes felt that he had got the better deal.

Golf had become an important part of his life. It was not so much because of the game itself, but rather the camaraderie with the other men at the club, and if he was honest the need to get out of the house and, dare he say it, away from Thelma for a while.

He had never imagined that he would retire at 58, nearly two years ago. He had always assumed that he would take over as CEO of the company when Reg retired, and serve out his time in that position until he was 65. Not that he needed the money, there had been plenty of that along the way, it just seemed that such a plan was in the natural order of things. Furthermore Head Office in Cleveland Ohio had indicated to him that this was the plan. Reg and he had even discussed it over a drink in the Boardroom on many occasions.

His illness had come as an awful shock. He had always led an active life. He may have been a bit overweight, but then what man close to sixty does not have a bit of a paunch? He had made a half hearted attempt to go to the gym a few years earlier, but to his dismay after several months of agony and sweat his stomach still jutted out. His belt sat low on his tummy, and he even contemplated buying some braces to make his profile, which he occasionally caught sight of with horror as he walked in front of shop windows, a little more flattering. He still had most of his hair, and there was only a slight greying at the temples. It is true that he had been on blood pressure medication for a while, but then most people in his family suffered from high blood pressure, and the doctor had assured him that as long as he kept on the medication and it was under control, there was really nothing to worry about. He ate a reasonably well balanced diet, thanks mainly to Thelma, and whilst occasionally the doctor frowned a little over his cholesterol, it was not really that high. He had a total blind spot as far as alcohol was concerned, and it never crossed his mind that his fat gut might in any way be related to the generous amount of alcohol that he had consumed, mainly in the name of company functions and social engagements that he considered as an integral part of his job. Overall he felt he was doing quite well for his age.

It had therefore come as a great shock when the results of his PSA test came through. He had never taken too much notice of all of the tests the doctor did. Michael, his GP, and he had been friends at the golf club for years and it was generally a laid back chat when he went to see him at his surgery rather than a formal consultation .Twice a year Michael ran some routine tests, Gordon had no idea what they were, and did not really take much notice.

One morning after such a routine round of blood tests, Michael called Gordon at work. 'Gordon, it's Michael here. I have just got back some of the test results from the blood we took last week, and I think we need to have a chat about them. When could you come in and see me?'

Gordon was a little surprised, but not in any way alarmed. He assumed that his cholesterol might have really taken a nudge after the visit from the American bosses and the mandatory wining and dining that had accompanied it, just a couple of weeks previously and before the tests were done. An appointment was made to see Michael for a couple of days later.

Michael looked a bit more businesslike than in previous appointments and came straight to the point. 'Gordon, when we did the PSA antigen test for prostate function last May there had been a further slight rise over the previous reading. This could be a normal variation but there has been a slight upward trend. And then this last test a week ago has shown a very large increase in the reading, and I think we need to investigate further.'

Gordon was taken aback, confused. 'What test is that? What are you trying to say?'

Michael explained that the PSA test was an indication of the activity of an enzyme. An increase could, but did not necessarily, indicate there was prostate cancer. It could also be lots of other things. Michael chose not to mention that another test that could also provide information was the digital examination. This would entail Michael inserting a finger into Gordon's anus and feeling the prostate for any abnormalities. He did not feel given his friendship with Gordon that he wanted to go down that road, and so he said nothing about that test and decided he would rely on further pathology work from a biopsy instead.

Gordon blanched. He felt his heart pump. 'But it would be curable?' he enquired hesitantly.

'I am not even saying that you have prostate cancer at this stage. The test is only an indication and not a foolproof predictor. But if it should turn out that it is cancer, the chances are that we would have got it in time. But I cannot promise you that. We need to arrange some further tests as soon as we can.'

The next few weeks had been a time of great anxiety and stress; the initial exploratory operation to take the biopsy samples that he found so undignified, the waiting for the biopsy results and the confirmation of cancer. He had tried during this time to keep working normally, believing that at least it would take his mind off things. But the fact was that he found it hard to concentrate. His mind drifted off in meetings and he was depressed. He confided in Reg, as he felt that he deserved some explanation for his rather distrait demeanour.

Of course he had had to tell Thelma. He had been surprised by how calmly she took the news. They went to see the specialist together to talk about treatment options. There were several, and Gordon found it confusing. He had spent his life making what seemed at the time important decisions. He now reflected that they were in fact not. Or that if they were, their human effect was far enough removed for him not to be aware of their impact. They certainly were not a matter of life or death. This was, and it was possibly his own life or death he was being asked to decide on. The specialist gave him the options and the statistical history associated with them. It seemed like a game of roulette in the casino. In his work there were always some risks, but they were quantifiable, controllable in many cases. Here there were just numbers of years on average without a recurrence. Percentage risks of possible side effects. What did that mean? Nothing could tell him with any certainty what his own outcomes would be, only average statistical outcomes. He found that particularly hard to deal with. It seemed to him that the more radical the intervention was, probably the more likely the cure. But would he then face loss of ejaculation, no more erections, and possibly incontinence? They agreed to go away and think about it; but not for too long.

****

Martin carefully watched his speed through the tunnel. He started to think about the day ahead. A product strategy meeting at 9.00 a.m., a meeting to discuss environmental impacts with the EPA at 12.00 which they were hoping might drift into lunch, and no meetings scheduled for the afternoon. Martin worked for a German multinational plastics company in marketing for the largest and most profitable line of plastics raw materials. After graduating from Sydney University majoring in Chemistry he had taken a couple of years off to go travelling around the world, and then returned to think about making a career. He joined the company as a sales executive. He did not really enjoy the job, but at least there was not as much sales pressure as in some industries; the sales role was mainly to visit customers, keep them happy, provide them with technical information on new products and report on the activities of the competition. He would have hated a job where he was pushing potential customers to buy something they neither wanted nor really needed, and even worse if his income would have depended on how good he was at doing it. That would have been utterly soul destroying, and frankly he did not think he would have been capable of doing it.

He had seen his future as being in marketing rather than sales, and so he enrolled to do a Masters of Business Administration as a good way to gain a foothold. The strategy had paid off, and after several years of hard slog part time in the evenings and at weekends he obtained his qualifications and he was promoted to the position of Product Manager. Two years ago he was promoted to Market Manager for a product group, reporting to the Marketing Director, a good position for his age. The job kept him engaged, paid well, but at times he was not so sure that this corporate world of multinationals was where he really wanted to be. On the other hand it offered him stability and predictability that gave him a certain peace of mind.

He enjoyed the many meetings he was required to attend and the battle of wits that often emerged in them. He was a good debater who had always been a favourite for the debating team at Uni, and was able to express himself clearly and logically. He

12

suspected this was one of the reasons he had got so far so quickly. The position also entailed customer contact where his main role as part of the team was to 'build relations' and provide information on the market. It also gave him the opportunity to engage in discussions on the product application technologies without having to go down to a factory floor and get his hands, or even his shoes, dirty.

But most of all he enjoyed the analytical part of his job. He loved working through the figures, market trends and analyses, trying to decide which products to manufacture, which to import, and which to abandon to the competitors. His father was after all an accountant by training. Maybe despite everything, he had after all inherited something from his father. If it were to be anything he would have preferred it to be this.

He headed out of the tunnel towards Chatswood. At least with his promotion he had been allocated a permanent parking spot. The office was in one of the more recent high rise developments which had erupted in Chatswood in the last few years, filling no doubt the demand for north shore executives to have offices within shorter commuting time from their leafy suburbs. Martin had to admit that the offices were comfortable. He parked the car and took the lift to the fourteenth floor. It was eight thirty and the office was slowly coming to life. Most of the managers were already at their desks. It was still a rather male dominated workplace, with women achieving management level in only the legal department and in Human Resources. The other women in the office were all support staff. There were of course no secretaries any longer. There was a departmental administrative assistant, Debbie, who in fact was a sort of PA for everyone, and a marketing assistant, Suzanne, who reported to Martin. Martin chose to keep his distance, although Ted, the National Sales Manager, had told him late one night after a few drinks that he knew for a fact that Martin would only have to say the word, and Debbie would be there. Martin had surmised as much himself. On several occasions he had caught Debbie looking at him with more than casual interest, in particular his rounded arse. But he had made it known quite publicly that he never ever got involved with girls at work, simply as a matter of principle.

However it was Suzanne who used to probe his love life, maybe on a mission from Debbie, as the two of them were close friends. She would ask what he had done over the weekend, who he went on holiday with, who he played tennis with and so on. He always found a way of avoiding a direct answer without sounding offensive. He preferred his social life to be a mystery. Martin had various components to his life, all of which he tried to keep discrete and separate. He spent very little social time with his work colleagues. Not that he was standoffish, he just chose to not socialise with them. He did go jogging with a few of the other managers sometimes at lunch time, and occasionally, if there was a birthday, he would go to The Oaks with the group for a drink after work. He knew that in the long run this might prejudice his career, as 'getting on' with the right people and being part of the clique was important. He hoped that he would make it by simply being good at what he did and not getting anyone off side. He had managed quite well so far.

He placed his briefcase and laptop on his desk. He always took the laptop home with him, not because he did much work at home, he did not believe in that, but because he wanted to make sure he knew where it was and who was looking at it.

Debbie popped her head round the door of his office, 'Good morning Martin, you're looking gorgeous this morning.'

'You too,' he retorted, 'it must be the hint of summer in the air.' It was said in the tone of voice which ensured that it was a throw away conversation.

'Ready for your meeting?'

'Yes, I think so, unless Production have managed to dream up another reason why they can't make the products we most want to sell.'

They both laughed. 'Want a coffee while I am going past the machine?'

'Thanks, I will get one in a minute to take into the meeting with me. I might need all the stimulation I can get!'

14

He thought about making a phone call before the meeting. He pulled his iPhone out of his briefcase and pulled up the number, toyed with it for a few minutes, then thought better of the idea, and put it back.

****

Thelma crossed her legs and looked again at her watch. She might as well wait here in the comfort of her own sitting room rather than at the station. She would walk the five minutes or so to the station, it was quicker than taking the car and then having to find somewhere to park; the car park at the station was usually full with commuters who left their cars there all day.

She sometimes thought about getting another little part time job. She had let the previous one go when Gordon had his operation, anticipating that she would need to care for him. She regretted it now. She did not really need to be there all the time to look after him when he came out of hospital, and within a couple of weeks he was out and about again, leaving her without her part time job. She resented that. It had been a good little job, just three days a week, from ten until four, looking after the local bookshop. She knew when she told the owner Hilary that she was going to have to stop work to look after Gordon that the job would not be there if she ever wanted it back. She hardly expected to want it back so quickly. She went to see Hilary, who was surprised at her request so soon after she had quit. She explained that the job had been filled and in all fairness she could hardly ask the person who had taken the job to leave. Of course not, Thelma had agreed, although she had been disappointed. That had been two years ago.

She reflected on Gordon's undelivered promise that they would start to do together in their joint retirement all those things that they had wanted to do for so many years and had not because Gordon was always so involved with work. They had talked about lunches out together, mid week escapes to the Central Coast or the Blue Mountains, afternoon movie sessions. None of it came to pass. He had his golf, and spent time with his mates in the club house after the game. As far as she was concerned they were a bunch of heavy drinkers using golf as an excuse to get to the nineteenth hole and exchange dirty jokes over a beer.

Gordon seemed to busy himself, but on the other hand she observed that he did not seem to live his life with any relish. The previous year they had taken a trip together to Europe. They had never travelled much together while he had been working although Thelma loved the idea of going overseas. Gordon had had a lot of work-related travel including the twice-yearly business meetings in Cleveland for the last fifteen years after the company had been bought out, but he never took Thelma with him. When holidays came round he refused point blank to get on an aircraft. Instead they would go to Nelson Bay or Hawks Nest, rent a beach house and do little at all. When Martin was young it was alright. He enjoyed the beach and there were other families they met there over the years, so that he had company his own age. This was important to her, as she always felt that Martin missed out somehow being an only child. She felt that he was a rather lonely and distant child. At least at Hawks Nest there were other children he could play with.

Part of the post retirement plan was the trip to Italy. Thelma had always loved art, and Italy was a place she had often dreamt of going. They took Qantas Business Class to London and then to Rome; a few nights there, and then Florence, Assisi, Venice, Verona. Gordon had insisted on hiring a car as being the best way to get around. But he was not used to the traffic, had rarely driven a left hand drive car, and had not driven a manual car for years. He did not speak any of the language, and was incessantly bad tempered and frustrated with the driving. Or at least that is what he said was the reason for his bad mood. In reality Thelma suspected there were other issues. To start with Gordon seemed to have lost any interest he had in art or history. After they got married they were always going to plays and concerts and Gordon used to read a wide variety of books. The trip demonstrated to them both how very far apart they had grown over the years. She knew that Gordon felt that being in

16

such a romantic destination as a hotel on the Grand Canal in Venice would normally require that he make mad passionate love to his wife. As a result of the operation he couldn't, and she knew he hated it. Frankly Thelma was indifferent, or even rather relieved that sex was no longer part of their lives. For men sex is so much more of an issue, a central part of their self identity. Thelma and her sister had often laughed over lunch that men were support systems for their cocks! Thelma had always thought that penile size was far more important to men than it was to women. She suddenly thought of Sergei, wondered where he was, what he had become and what had been his life. She did not often think of him nowadays, and the memory jolted her back to reality.

Their life had worked while Gordon was working, as they had each been able to pursue their own agendas and own interests. But being forced to spend more time together was a strain.

She glanced at the clock; it was time to catch the train.

****

Gordon had never faced the concept of his own mortality before his discussion with the specialist that day. Death had been something that was there of course. Every day in the newspapers as more and more awful crimes were committed and every night on the news there were shootings and stabbings thrust in front of your eyes. In wretched third world countries it was the way they seemed to carry on with their despotic leaders and chaotic society. There was always terrible loss of life in natural disasters. Then there had been the death of his parents. They were old, and it seemed a natural part of the way the world is. But all of those things were remote from his own mortality. He had successfully managed to place his inevitable death in a completely different compartment. Until that day. As he thought about it, he was frightened, frightened for himself. He had never been a religious man, and had never thought about existential problems like the meaning and purpose

17

of life, or death and what it meant. Only now did he start to ask the question about what death meant, and what followed it if anything. It scared him.

When he discussed treatment options with Thelma after the initial diagnosis, she had simply said that the course of action that would most likely get rid of the cancer was the one to take. That must be the only consideration. It quickly crossed his mind that his inability to get an erection and have sex would be totally inconsequential to Thelma, and indeed he suspected that maybe she even considered that it would remove her obligation to satisfy him from time to time. Their sex life had always been a pleasure for him. He knew how lucky he was to have a wife who at her age was still so young and attractive looking. He knew that most of his work colleagues and friends had cheated on their wives on occasions. But Gordon generally had not. He had been attracted to other women, of course. There was nothing wrong with him! But he did not feel that it was the right thing to do. Only twice had he strayed, and both times had been far enough away that he was able to totally divorce these events from the context of his marriage with Thelma. One occasion was a company convention in New Orleans, when after a few rounds of toxic looking fluorescent blue hurricanes he had been propositioned by a young girl on the next table who was fascinated by his accent. They ended up spending the night in his room. The sex was not even that good as far as he could remember.

The other occasion had also been on a business trip. This had been a more serious lapse of morality, to the point that he had felt guilty about it. Pat was the Administration Coordinator at the Cleveland Head Office. After the Americans had bought out the company he had his first trip overseas on business, and Pat was the person who made all the arrangements for his stay and was his contact point. She was a free spirit, a few years older than Gordon, and enormously extroverted. He had felt a bit like the country boy when he had first met her, fascinated yet at the same time self conscious. At the end of the second day of meetings she had suggested they have a drink while they reviewed the implications for Australia of the sessions that day. He was naïve enough to believe that that was her actual intention. Shortly after they sat down she asked him if he was married. He had told her that he was married and had a son. It was only afterwards that he realised that she was not at all interested in his reply or his family arrangements; it was just a way of opening up the conversation for her. Inevitably he did what was intended of him, and asked her if she was married. She told him she had been married three times and was now separated, about to get divorced again. She followed this up by confiding in him that she was awfully horny, and it had been several weeks since she had had sex. She paused for a second, and when Gordon did not respond, sitting there absolutely struck dumb, she went on to say that she had a reputation of giving very good 'head,' as she called it. He laughed nervously and said, a little late on cue, 'Maybe I can help you out?'

'Great!' she had responded, 'Let's get going.'

Gordon had had a few casual relationships before he met Thelma, and part of these sexual initiations had been oral sex. He had loved it whenever it happened, and it was a regret of his that Thelma did not seem to be interested in giving him pleasure that way, and seemed to derive absolutely none herself. Since Pat was as good as her word about her expertise in this area, Gordon went wild. He thought that he had never been so hard, never had such powerful orgasms, never produced so much ejaculate, which to his amazement Pat consumed completely and with enormous enthusiasm.

When he got home to Australia he gently tried to pursue this activity again with Thelma, but she made it quite clear that she was most reluctant. In fact at one point she said to him, 'Have you gone all American since that business trip of yours?' For fear of her coming to the right conclusion and stumbling across his secret, he never mentioned it again, nor tried to pass the no go zone of her lips.

In coming to a decision about treatment, the bottom line was from a practical point of view, he really did not have much option. None of the treatments gave much optimism for a continued normal sex life anyway. He decided to opt for the surgery, the removal of the prostate and with it the cancer. And his manhood.

. Gordon had never talked seriously or openly about sex since his operation. There had always been the risk of incontinence let alone virtually guaranteed impotence. Gordon was lucky that he had not suffered incontinence, but he no longer had erections, even in the morning with a full bladder. He had been reluctant to discuss it with Michael his GP, not only as they were close friends and Gordon felt embarrassed, but also because Michael had just fathered a child at the age of 52 with his recently acquired second wife twenty years his junior. The comparison was just too galling to contemplate for Gordon.

He went along once to a sex clinic, where they told him the only way he could get an erection was to use an injection into the shaft of his penis. This did not appeal to Gordon in the least, and he did not know how he could ever broach the subject with Thelma. After the sex clinic visit Gordon had just said to Thelma that it was never going to work, and that had been the last anything had ever been said.

He wondered whether his concern was one of missing the pure pleasure of sex, or whether it was more to do with his identity as a man. He remembered all the jokes about men not being able to 'get it up'. His life as a virile male was over, and his identity as a real man died with the removal of his prostate.

****

Tony stretched and yawned. It was nice and comfortable in bed. He had been putting it off for an hour or so, but the aching of his erection told him that he was just going to have get up and go for a pee. He touched himself with a certain amount of satisfaction, and then got out of bed, and walked through the kitchen to the bathroom. He relieved himself, and then contemplated going back to bed. He had rehearsals in the afternoon at 2.00 p.m., Grieg's Fugue in F minor, for 2 violins, viola and cello, and he was one of the violins. A glance at the clock told him it was five to ten. The dishes from last night were still on the dining room table, looking sordid. He managed to look past them as he had so many times before. His flat mate Phil had had a few people round for a 'bowl of spag,' and they stayed rather late. Tony was not even sure what time they called it a day as he had gone to bed, but supposed it would have had to have been around two. He marvelled at how those with more conventional lives than his as a violinist managed to get up and go to work in the morning; like Martin for example. He liked Martin, and was half expecting him to call. It was a week since he had seen him and that was somewhat unusual. He would wait a few more days and then think about it again.

Tony decided that he would go and have a coffee and read the paper at the local café in Glebe Point Road, just round the corner. He liked living in Glebe. It was close to the city, full of university students and other less main stream inhabitants. It was much cheaper than Paddo and less yuppie. He had teased Martin a few times about his yuppie surroundings, but did not insist too much as he felt that it made Martin feel a bit uncomfortable.

Phil had gone to work. He worked in the Flight Centre office at Bondi Junction, and must have felt less than well when he left for work that morning. He had shared with Phil for a year or so. It suited him fine. Phil had a job, paid the rent reliably and was honest. Tony had learned not to expect much more than that from a flat mate. He was able to ignore the untidiness, and the dirty dishes. Eventually Phil got round to clearing up, and if the truth be told, Tony was not exactly house proud himself. He might have preferred to rent on his own, but being a musician never pays that well. Tony occasionally did some casual waitering to supplement his meagre income from music, but even then he was tight on money so sharing was the only option.

Tony pulled on a pair of tracksuit pants and a T shirt, one of his old favourites from the Huntington Estate Music Festival of 2012. The material had become rather thin, and it was the soft comfortable worn feel about it that Tony liked. He slipped on his sandshoes, grabbed a twenty dollar bill and some change from his bedside table, his keys, and went out into the street closing the door gently behind him.

Glebe has some wonderful old federation homes. As he walked up to the main road he reflected how much he liked living in this suburb. The trees were old and established, and the houses looked as if they belonged there. Many were federation in various states of repair. Some had been bought by loving and quite well off owners who had carefully restored them to their former state, even improved them considerably. Then there were others, like the smaller worker's cottage that Tony rented, in need of a lot of work. He knew that his landlord had bought the house for a song and was simply waiting until the top of the market before he sold. Tony might have done the same if he had had the money. Meanwhile the landlord had not the slightest intention of spending a cent on the place. Tony accepted this in return for a rent that was certainly on the low side for Glebe.

He reached the top of his street and turned right onto Glebe Point Road. It had a comfortable mid morning feel about it. The rush hour had passed and the street was full of local shoppers and delivery vehicles. The local butcher was receiving a delivery of meat. The traffic was for the most part fatalistic about the truck blocking half the street. Tony liked that about Sydney. People accepted that the streets were narrow and tended to be far more patient about the consequences, unlike his experiences in Adelaide and Melbourne, not to mention how he imagined various European countries where the mid morning torpor would have been shattered by hooting impatience. At least Glebe did not suffer from that aggressive race of young women who mainly inhabit the Eastern suburbs, and who delight in cutting up male drivers, and then double parking while they pop into a shop for some trivial need. They often have a screaming brat strapped in the back seat. He thanked god that that would never be a part of his life, and felt sorry for straight men whose accommodation with women for company and sex forced them into marriage, as he saw it. He was very much aware of the recent trend in advertising that portrayed men as stupid or in some way subservient to women in a kind of vindictive reversal of perceived history, but which Tony felt added nothing to the justified quest for equal rights for women. For him it was populist and distasteful.

He greeted the middle aged woman from further up his street as she scuttled out of the greengrocer and into the newsagent on the corner. He followed her in, exchanged a few pleasantries, bought the Sydney Morning Herald and picked up a free copy of the Sydney Star Observer, Sydney's gay newspaper. Then he went next door to the café where he usually had breakfast, ordered a flat white and a croissant, and sat down at a table on the pavement. It was warm in the spring sunshine, and he liked the feel of the heat on his body through his T shirt.

****

Martin closed his computer down, shut the door to his office and walked down the corridor to the staff kitchen. In these days of equality, it seemed to him, nobody wanted to take responsibility for keeping the kitchen area clean. It obviously had not been cleared up the previous night, and there were dirty mugs all over the sink, and spills of coffee and tea on the table. Given his obsession with order and tidiness, this was very challenging for him. He glanced at his watch and decided he had time to at least put a few of the mugs in the dishwasher. People were too self absorbed to even bother to put a dirty mug in a machine! This act cleansed his conscience and he felt a small surge of indignant self satisfaction at his socially responsible action.

Then he tapped the jar of instant coffee gently on the bottom until the right amount of coffee had transferred itself to the bottom of the mug. He had been teased about this habit of his, and always retorted that that was about the chemist of old that was left in him. In fact he hated the fact that the spoons were all dirty, and just preferred to use a wooden paddle to stir his coffee. He added some hot water and then topped it up with milk. He took a wooden paddle, gave the coffee a quick stir, let it rotate for a few seconds while the remaining granules of coffee all dissolved and then took a quick sip to make it easier to carry to the meeting room without spilling it. Why couldn't they get a Nespresso machine and some half decent coffee instead of this instant shit?

He opened the door to Meeting Room 2. The four grey Formica tables had been placed in the centre with chairs around the central rectangular arrangement. Len Scipione, the Production Planning Manager, was already seated in the middle of the long side of the rectangular shape. Martin wondered quickly whether he should sit next to him, opposite him, or on one of the shorter sides. He expected that there was going to be some conflict between Len and Pat Henry, the Operations Manager, and he figured that he might be better off sitting between the two, and so chose one of the seats on the shorter side, at a 90 degree angle to where Len was sitting, assuming Pat would sit opposite Len. The two men were cordial to each other without being particularly friendly. Len thought Martin was rather pretentious and poncy, and Martin thought Len was rather ordinary and boring. But they both had a basic respect for the other to do their job correctly. They exchanged greetings, and affirmed to each other that they were both well, and busy.

Ted, the National Sales Manager was the next to arrive also armed with a cup of coffee, but one from the coffee shop on the ground floor of their building. He sat down opposite Len, and sat a little closer to Martin than the middle of the longer side of the setting. He provided a cheerful greeting just as Pat came in, looking flustered and sitting down without comment on the only available last side of the rectangle, on the other short side opposite Martin. So much for Martin's assumptions!

The others expected Pat to provide a greeting of some sort, but he did not. Instead he said abruptly, 'Well, let's get going. I have this report that shows that to make T566 is going to disrupt the whole cycle on reactor three, and frankly it just can't be justified.'

Martin looked up at him, and said slowly, 'Pat, let's just wait for Richard before we start, as it will be his assessment of the financial impact of your report which will indicate whether we should make T566 ourselves or import it.'

Pat shuffled his papers, looked up at Martin, and said nothing. Ted set the scene for the impending argument by saying, 'What we cannot do is to carry on much longer without it, we are being cruelled in the marketplace as we have no equivalent to Marvex 700 without it, and we are already losing market share.'

Pat had just opened his mouth to utter a counter sally, when the door opened and Richard, the accountant, came in apologising profusely for being late, muttering about a breakdown on the Anzac Bridge holding up all the traffic. Martin reflected for a second how awful it would be to live in those suburbs that required the Anzac Bridge to be crossed to get to work. Richard placed his laptop on the table, pulled up a chair next to Ted, and looked up expectantly. Len sat quietly as always. That was the problem with Len; he just was not strong enough to mediate between the usually opposed forces of sales and marketing on the one hand and production on the other.

****

The front door closed with a firm solid sound. Thelma turned the key and walked down the path from the front door to the gate. She turned right after carefully closing the gate and walked briskly up the slight slope towards the station. Not that she was short of time, but she tended to do everything with deliberate and quick movements. It was, she reflected, a magnificent day, clear and crisp, with a hint of warmth from the sun. Very few people in this area walked along the street, and she was quite alone as her steps echoed on the neat footpath, edged by well cared for grass strips. Large substantial homes slumbered behind thick hedges and under yawning old trees, often with only their tiled rooves or an occasional upstairs lattice window visible between all the foliage. The only sign of life was the odd car that purred quietly along the road.

Thelma suspended her previous musings as she walked to the station, instead letting the thought pass through her mind that maybe one day their house would be just too large for her and Gordon, and they would be obliged to move into something smaller and more manageable. She dreaded the day. She loved her house and living where they did. She was determined to manage there as long as she could, even if it meant that they would need more and more help with the house and garden. A friend of hers whose husband had died a year ago, had just sold the family home and moved into a new unit in a modern block in Manly. She visited her recently, and although she did the right thing and said how wonderful it was, Thelma in fact hated it. She hated the small rooms, the lack of a garden, the loss of privacy and the awful walls made out of board. Not only did they allow the transmission of all sorts of sounds one would rather the neighbours keep to themselves, but you could not even hang heavy paintings on the walls. Thelma was horrified. The thought crossed her mind as to what she would do if Gordon were to die. She tried to banish such disgraceful thoughts immediately from her mind. But she had to face it; there were no guarantees after his operation. Things seemed alright, but one never knows.

She turned the corner and glanced up the street. No, she would continue on in her home as long as she possibly could, with or without Gordon. In any case Martin would probably want to move in to the family house eventually, once he got married and had children. That would be the time for her to move somewhere smaller, alone or with Gordon, of course. She recognised another nagging concern at the back of her mind. When was Martin going to meet a nice girl and settle down and have a family? He was starting to leave it a little bit late. Now was really the time for him. He had a good job, still his good looks, and had so much to offer.

The lights suddenly started their rhythmic chuckle indicating to sight impaired people that it was safe to cross, and woke Thelma from her reverie. She crossed the road, walked through the station entrance, took out her Opal card, and walked down the steps to the platform below. She noted with some satisfaction that it was spotless, not a paper or piece of plastic in sight. She sat on one of the benches for a few minutes, and then the train arrived. She sat upstairs from where she had a more expansive view of the leafy North Shore gliding past. The harbour sparkled in the morning sunshine, a glint of light reflected off the roof of the Opera House, and suddenly she was at Wynyard station.

She easily climbed the pedestrian mall to David Jones, where she had arranged to meet her sister, Renie. They always met there, went for lunch first and then always took a stroll round the store. Renie was already waiting at the main entrance when Thelma arrived. They embraced, and Thelma asked,

'Oh, am I late?'

'Not at all,' Renie replied, 'I got a lift from a neighbour and arrived earlier than I had planned. In fact I just had a quick look round David Jones. They have some exquisite glassware from Slovakia I want you to have a look at after lunch.'

'Fine, where shall we have lunch?'

'The café, Level 1?'

****

Gordon looked up the fairway, squinted slightly against the sun, and took aim, slowly and deliberately. His first two shots had been ordinary. The third really needed to be a bit better. He brought down the iron, and watched the ball soar into the air, quite satisfied with the result. He set out slowly up the slight incline towards the ball and his next shot.

Suddenly he felt a slight twinge in his lower groin. It brought him back to his worries again. So far everything had been clear since the operation. Two years. But they had told him that only after five years could he rest easy and assume that the cancer would not recur. He wondered whether the twinges that he felt from time to time was due to processes going on that would carry him off with a painful death, or if it was just old age. Or maybe even they were just in his imagination. He just did not know, and did not like this uncertainty in his life.

One thing he was certain of, however, was how he felt about the way they got rid of him from work. Once he had decided to have the operation, he told Reg what was going on. He and Reg had had a drink in the Boardroom after work one evening, just the two of them. Reg had been very supportive, told him to take as much time as he liked, not to worry about work, getting well again was the only thing he should concentrate on. Gordon told him about the likely consequences of the operation with respect to his sexual function and incontinence. He deeply regretted later having done so, as he felt that it had put him in a vulnerable, weakened position. But at the time Gordon had not expected Reg and the company to do what they did.

Gordon assured Reg that he would only be off work for a week or so, and then depending on whether there was any other treatment prescribed, he would be back at work, as good as new. Maybe there would be a further period of radiation, depending on what they found, in which case he would need more time off. In fact the surgeon advised against it after the operation, and he would not have needed more time off. Gordon was hoping that Reg would say something along the lines of how glad he was to hear that, given that he, Reg, was still planning to retire at the end of the year, and he wanted to make sure that Gordon would be well enough to take over the reins by then. But he did not.

Reg did not visit Gordon in hospital, but there was a beautiful arrangement of flowers from the office, with good wishes for a speedy recovery, delivered to his private room in the North Shore Private hospital. It was signed by his secretary on behalf of all the staff.

Gordon was home again after a week. The surgeon told him before he was released that the operation was a success, they had got all the cancer, and that he was hopeful that there would not be any problems of incontinence. In fact there had not been, Gordon was relieved to find. But, although he had harboured a tiny illogical hope that in his case, maybe he would still have erections and a normal if 'dry orgasm,' it was soon apparent that was not going to be the case.

After another week at home, Gordon had been given the all clear to return to work. He called Reg to give him the good news. To his surprise Reg had sounded a little strange on the phone, distant, very distant. Gordon had detected in his voice a degree of tension and nervousness that he normally never showed. After Reg had asked him how he felt, and Gordon had told him that he expected to return to work the next week, Reg said, 'As a matter of fact I was thinking of coming round to see you. What are you doing this evening? Say around about six?' Clearly, Gordon was not planning on going out, and so they agreed to meet at Gordon's house at six.

Right on the dot of six, Reg pulled up outside in the street in his brand new Jag. Gordon saw him from the sitting room. He got out the car carrying a large box. He balanced the box on the old wall at the front of the property while he put his keys in his pocket and then walked up the drive. In a few moments the door bell rang. Thelma opened the door, they exchanged greetings and then Thelma showed Reg into the sitting room. Gordon noticed that the large box was no longer under his arm; he must have placed it in the entrance hall. As Gordon rose to his feet, Reg strode with exaggerated energy across the room and greeted him with an exuberant handshake.

'My, Gordon, you are looking well for someone who has just had major surgery.'

'Well, not that major, really, Reg. The operation nowadays is not anywhere near as intrusive as it used to be.'

'Even so, Gordon, even so.' Reg certainly did not want to get involved in any of the details of all that sort of thing; better left well alone.

Gordon felt that he was being patronised. He had been a little surprised when Reg had suggested visiting him at the house, which was not really Reg's style. But now that he saw how ill at ease Reg was, he began to feel anxious himself. Gordon offered him a drink.

'Reg, a drop of the usual? I have some Glennfiddich. With just a little water?'

'Oh, er, alright, Gordon, just a small one. I can't stay long.'

Gordon poured him a Scotch with water, and a gin and tonic for himself.

'Are you sure that you should be having that, under the circumstances?' Reg indicated with his hand the gin and tonic Gordon had just poured for himself.

'Of course I can, I am fine. Raring to go actually, ready to get back into things. Work next week!'

'Ah, yes, Gordon,' Reg said, suddenly becoming very serious, 'I wanted to talk to you about that. You probably don't know, but David was out here last week from Cleveland. I did not tell you, with everything that you would have had on your mind with your health and all that. But, anyway, there was a special meeting, and it was decided that with your health problems, this changes a lot of things. It was felt that you should be given the very best chance of dealing with this, and the company decided that you should be allowed to retire now without all the stress of executive life.' He took a large gulp of his scotch and water, and looked out of the window, avoiding having to look at Gordon. He was just about to start talking again, when Gordon interrupted him.

'Reg, I am perfectly alright. I have always dealt with the stress of the job without any problems whatsoever, and I am certainly up to the demands of my current job, and beyond, at the time that you retire yourself. I thought that was the agreement. I was going to take over the top job when you go at the end of the year. This is what David himself again confirmed when I was in Cleveland last year.'

'Well, that had been one of the options, originally, yes.'

'One of the options, Reg, what are you talking about? It had been agreed. We talked about it on several occasions. Don't have the audacity to tell me that you have forgotten!'

'Gordon, I am sure that you will see that this is the best for you in the end.'

'It is absolutely not the best for me, either now, in the end, or whenever.' Gordon had become angry. 'This is what I have been working towards for the last several years and there is absolutely no reason to change the arrangement now.'

'Gordon, I am sorry you feel that way. But the decision has been made. David is quite adamant. It also has the support of the Board. You will be looked after.'

'Looked after, Reg, looked after?' Gordon interrupted, 'Don't be patronising.'

Reg took up the theme again, 'I am not being patronising in the least. The fact is that a generous package has been prepared, in recognition of the long years of valuable service you have provided.' He now had returned to the script he had prepared and he felt on firmer ground. 'You will retire with the same entitlements and package as you would have had you worked through to the age of 62. In other words, four years paid holiday! And although the company has no obligation to do this, it was decided to buy the lease out on the Merc, and let you have that too. Now....'

'Fuck the Merc, Reg!' Gordon cut him off; he was furious now, and his face had turned white and he was shaking with rage. 'And fuck your so called generosity. How dare you do this to me? I always thought that we were friends. How wrong I was. You wait until you have an excuse and you shaft me. You bastard!'

Reg had anticipated that Gordon would not take this calmly, but he had not expected such a violent reaction. He was keen to get out as soon as he could. He was also pleased that he had brought all Gordon's personal things that had been removed from his office and were in the box he had placed by the front door in the entrance hall. That way he would be spared a scene in the office.

Reg stood up finishing his scotch in one large gulp, and placing the empty glass heavily on the side table next to where he had been sitting. He said, 'Gordon, I am sorry that you feel this way. I had hoped that you would recognise that this would be an opportunity for you to give yourself the best chance of recovering from this awful illness, and for you and Thelma to spend a happy retirement together.'

As he walked to the door he said, 'All the paperwork has been prepared and will be handled by Tom Casey of Casey, Casey and Stroud, to save any problems. All the documents to sign have been already sent to them together with the settlement cheques and so on. Your personal effects have been collected, and I have them in the entrance hall for you. Just call Tom and make an appointment when you are ready.'

Gordon was also on his feet now, looking narrowly at Reg. The whiteness had given way to a red rage of boiling blood that crept up from his collar. 'Reg, I am going to fight this,' he bellowed.

Reg opened the door from the sitting room, and turned to Gordon and said quietly and sternly, 'I am really sorry that it had to end this way, Gordon. Really I am. But there is nothing to fight. Your termination is quite legal, the offer we have made is beyond any legal requirements that we have, and there is nothing you can do. We have checked it out. Now please, calm down and do yourself a favour. Go and enjoy a very comfortable retirement. A far more comfortable one than most people could ever aspire to.'

With that he walked through the door, across the entrance hall, opened the front door and without even looking at Thelma who was standing in the doorway from the kitchen into the entrance hall, slammed the front door behind him, walked with long strides down the garden path, and with relief passed into the neutral territory of the footpath, jumped into the Jag and roared away as fast as he could.

Thelma rushed into the sitting room, to find Gordon standing there crumpled, as if drained of life, sobbingly quietly and helplessly. The pillar of strength that she had married was broken. She felt that at that moment the baton of being the strong one in their married life had been passed to her. And she really did not want to take it.

****

There was rarely much significant news in the Sydney Morning Herald on a Tuesday Tony mused, as he leafed through the pages. There was an interesting crit on a play he had managed to get free tickets to the previous Sunday. He agreed with the assessment that the play dealt with a valid and interesting theme (adoption of children by gay couples), but that it was not well scripted. He agreed that the acting was excellent, but did not like the character portrayals, which he found rather hackneyed and stereotyped.

There was even less substantial reading in the Sydney Star Observer. He glanced at the photographs of delirious looking half naked men supposedly having tremendous fun at some of the many gay parties that abound in that city. There was just one man that he felt attracted to. He supposed that he was on with the young gym type that he had his arms round in the photo. He looked at the personal ads at the back of the paper, and mused how all of those offering massage services were lucky to be so well endowed. He had always taken the view that there was more bullshit talked about dick sizes by gay guys than virtually any other subject in the world.

He folded the papers, slipped them under his arm in case he felt like reading a bit more later that day, paid his bill, and set off back to the house. He had about an hour before he needed to set out for the Opera House for rehearsals and thought that he might try to develop a few ideas he had for a piece he was composing. He knew it was not enough time to accomplish much before he had to leave, but just felt in the mood.

Music was his life. He had been brought up in a working class family in Tamworth, a town in New South Wales. His father had worked for the local mill in the quality control department. It was a reasonable job, and allowed him to bring up a family of three boys and a wife, well, if modestly. Tony was the youngest of the boys and had worn the clothes of his elder brothers as they grew out of them, until he was 15 years old. This never worried him much. He had never been brought up to feel any attachment to possessions. As a family they had few anyway.

The only thing he had cherished as a child was the violin that his maternal grandfather had given him when he was 10 years old. He still had it now, eighteen years later. When he was 10 his eldest brother went out to work, and that freed up a little extra cash for Tony to have violin lessons. His parents felt perhaps as the youngest he had been a little deprived. Just one example was his brothers' cast offs. So they were pleased to try to make amends by paying for weekly lessons.

They were a little surprised when Jean Swanningham, the violin teacher called Tony's parents to ask them to come and see her after he had been taking lessons for a couple of years. She told them that they might not be aware, but she felt that Tony had a great gift in music, and that he was by far the most talented student she had even seen. She felt that they should know this, as it would be sad to waste such a talent, and he should really follow a career in music.

This came as quite a shock to Tony's parents. They had never imagined him to be anything other than a country boy like his brothers. Although it is true that Tony's grandfather, the one who gave him the violin, had said to his daughter, Tony's mother, at the time, 'Watch this boy. He has the capability to go places. That is why I am giving him my violin.' And it is true that Tony's mother had noticed how happy he was playing the violin. He never missed a lesson and seemed happy to spend hours practising. His brothers had wanted to go out and play with the local kids or kick balls around, but Tony seemed to prefer to stay at home and play the violin.

After the meeting with Jean Swanningham, Tony's parents discussed the conversation as they walked home to the red brick house in Tamworth. His mother was quite enthusiastic, and said that they should encourage him at school, and maybe he might manage to get to University in Sydney. He was a good student, better than the other two boys, and it would be nice to have one of their boys with higher education.

But his father was less enthusiastic. He did not think music was an appropriate career for a young man. There was something he could not quite put his finger on, an uneasiness about the whole idea. In his mind's eye he could not see a son of his poncing around a concert hall. Without giving verbal expression to his concerns, he simply said, 'Very few people ever make a decent living out of music. I would not want to see him condemned to a life as hard financially as we have had.' Tony's mother slipped her arm through that of her husband, and squeezed him affectionately.

'I know,' she said, 'but I think we should allow him to make some of those choices himself. We never had the chance to make choices in our lives. I would like him to be able to do whatever would make him happy. After all, we have been happy compared to most families. And that certainly has not been due to the money we have made.'

They walked arm in arm in silence for a few minutes, and then Tony's mother took up the theme again. 'Why don't we wait and see if his interest continues? Let him continue his lessons with Jean. He is 13 years old now. If in another year or so he would like to take his studies in that direction, then we will do whatever we can to support him. But he must realise two things. The first is that we do not have money to send him to university; he would have to take out a loan which would need to be repaid. And the second is that to get into university he would have to get good marks in all subjects, and that he must work hard in all subjects not just music.'

That is what Tony's parents did. When he turned 15, they sat him down and told him what Jean Swanningham had said and what they had agreed on two years earlier. They also made a proposition to him: if he would take a weekend job at the local supermarket to earn some money, his parents would equal what he earned and with that money they could afford to send him to Dr Ralph, the director of music at the local college. Jean Swanningham felt that Tony needed to go to someone better able to develop him than she felt she was. Dr. Ralph was an acquaintance of hers, and she had already discussed Tony with him. In fact, she had invited him to one of Dr Ralph's lessons, introducing him to Tony as simply a friend of hers from the college. Afterwards, Dr Ralph and Jean had discussed Tony, and agreed that he needed more tuition. Dr Ralph was ready to assist.

Tony could hardly believe his luck, and agreed readily to anything that would allow him to follow his heart into the world of music. His father did provide one parting shot, however. He warned, 'Don't get so absorbed into all of this that you forget who you are. I would like to see you play football, just like your brothers Brian and Angus did, and still do. I don't want you turning 'funny' or anything.'

Looking back Tony felt that he had been very fortunate. It is true that he had to work very hard to earn money to make it all happen, to get the marks he needed at school to get into Uni, and to develop his musical talents with Dr Ralph. But he enjoyed it for the most part, and because the goal was so worthwhile, he never minded giving up a lot of things the other boys of his age did. In fact, if the truth were told, Tony found it hard to identify with them on most levels. He got on well with his school mates, but kept for himself the fact that he felt different in some way. He could not explain it, he could not describe it, he just felt it.

He had more of an inkling what it might be that was different one weekend that he went to Armidale to play in a youth concert. They stayed on the campus of the University of New England, and he had to share a room with one of the older students who was from Melbourne. Simon was 18 at the time and Tony was 16. When it was time to go to bed Tony watched as his roommate undressed, and was intrigued by the feelings he had. His heart was slightly pounding, and he was aware that he was fascinated by the young man's body. In fact, he did not seem to be able to take his eyes off him. He watched as he loosened his sandshoes and then kicked them off, then his socks, and next his jeans. He peeled off his shirt over his head, revealing a broad chest and a small line of hair going from his navel to the top of his underpants. At that point Simon threw back the bed clothes and literally jumped into his single bed.

Tony watched him closely and then started to take his own clothes off. But he did not stop at his underpants. He took them off too revealing a hard and eager erection. Simon sat up in bed, staring at Tony with a certain amount of surprise, but no discouragement. Then he threw the blankets back, revealing by the bulge in his own underpants that Simon was not averse to investigating a little further.

Tony walked over to Simon's bed, lay down next to him, and put his arms round his neck and kissed him passionately and deeply. Tony had no idea how he knew what to do, but he knew. He closed his eyes and thrust his tongue deep into Simon's mouth. Simon responded in like fashion, and they spent most of the night discovering each other's bodies, and for Tony this was his introduction to sex, at least with another person! For Tony it was natural, it was normal, something about which he never had to think twice. He felt no guilt, no remorse afterwards, just a warm all encompassing feeling that he had become what he was always meant to be.

Tony and Simon in later years used to joke about the fact that Simon could easily have gone to prison for that night. Tony was only 16 years old, and while it would have been legal for him to have sex with a female, at the time it was not with a male. Tony pointed that out to Simon when they met again a year or so later,

'That would hardly have been fair,' Simon objected, 'you were the one who seduced me.'

'Doesn't matter,' retorted Tony, 'I was under age and you should not have been party to leading me astray.'

'Under age? With a horn like that! And you waving your stiff cock around was hardly me leading you astray. Please!'

'Under age in the eyes of the law. The principle is that being gay is a matter of choice. At such a tender age, a guy should not be allowed to have sex with another man in case he likes it, or thinks he likes it, and gets converted to something nasty, like being gay. Such recruitment must be stopped.'

'Recruitment!' Simon laughed. 'It is not like a club you join, like tennis or bush walking. Or the Young Liberals! I know that in my own case I always knew that I was different, from maybe six or seven years of age. It is not a question of choice. It is not negotiable. My sexual orientation is so much an integral part of me, that I just cannot imagine it being any other way for me.'

'Me neither,' agreed Tony. 'But the people who set the laws and the voters in elections just did not understand that. And so we have to suffer a discriminatory difference in the age of sexual consent. We just have to keep fighting for our rights, Simon, nobody else is going to do it.'

Tony found it hard to believe that just a few years after he had had that conversation with Simon, the laws had been amended and even same sex marriage had come to pass. But, he reflected, it was because of the efforts of a vocal few. Those who put their freedom on the line at the first Mardi Gras in 1978, for example. And he reflected on the larger, much larger number of those comfortable mature gays who have benefitted from the advocacy work done on their behalf by others, and yet remained silent in the old days. He understood their need to preserve the comfortable lives they had. But he just hoped that they now appreciate what others did as they sit back and enjoy the freedoms, get married, hold hands when they go to the opera and kiss each other when they meet at dinner.

Tony and Simon had remained in contact and stayed firm friends, even if they did not see each other very often, usually when they performed in concerts together.

****

Thelma and Renie sat down, signalled for the waiter to bring the menu, and then ordered lunch. This was always the signal to start exchanging their confidences. While they were waiting for their lunch to arrive, they would use the time to talk about things they both felt they could not easily talk to other people about.

'So, how are things with Gordon?' Renie started. Thelma let out a deep sigh, one of those sighs that came from the bottom of her soul.

'I think he's alright. He went off to golf this morning as usual.'

'That's not what I meant, really.'

'No, I don't suppose it is.' Thelma paused for a few moments, and then started to talk again.

'The thing is Renie, I think that Gordon and I are just drifting further and further apart. And the worst part of it is that I really do not care. I feel relieved when he goes out and I can repossess my territory, as it were. All those years while he worked it was fine. In the day time I had the house to myself and I led my life for most of the day as I wanted. I did not feel that I had to account to anyone. I was there in the evening, if Gordon was at home, but often there were meetings and dinners. Sometimes he would take me along, but at least one or two evenings a week I could do as I pleased. But now I feel sort of trapped. He expects me to be there. And then when I am, he ignores me. How on earth am I going to manage if this goes on for years?'

'Well, Thelma, you are not even 60 yet, so it might well go on for years.' Renie interjected.

'Yes, I know, and that is part of what frightens me. How are we going to live our lives like this?

Thelma neglected to say that sometimes she found herself secretly hoping that something would happen to Gordon, and then she could have her life back again. Then she would feel guilty for ever having being capable of producing such disgusting thoughts, to want your husband dead, for god's sake! And when she thought about it of course that is not what she wanted. But just on one level, it would make things much easier for her. She would never dare admit to anyone that she had had such awful thoughts, not even to Renie.

She continued, 'I don't know, I just get so confused. All I know is that I am miserable.'

'How do you get on when you go out together?' Renie enquired.

'That is part of the problem. We don't go out very much. You see when Gordon was working, that was his whole life, dinners and so on that were both business and social. We never really had that many friends we went out with outside of his work. He had his business colleagues and dinners, and I had my friends through the Bridge Club and the library, and we tended to lead our own lives. Now that all the business contacts have just gone, Gordon has his golf, and I have let some of my socialising go, because I feel I just can't leave him alone and go out. Bridge is not his scene and so most evenings we tend to stay in. We watch some television, and I often read as I am not that keen on television. Gordon likes his sports and watches a lot of that. Frankly, he also has started to drink more than he should. It started off with 'a G&T before dinner' and a glass of wine with dinner. And it has expanded beyond that to two G&T's before dinner, a bottle of wine with dinner, and a night cap. Or two!'

Renie was listening carefully but said nothing. Thelma continued, 'Somehow all those years I was never confronted with how far we have drifted apart, or in some ways grown apart. It was partly a process which I fostered by developing my own life while he was working. I think that I have in some ways continued to grow, but I sense that Gordon really has not changed emotionally since I married him. And that is partly why when they got rid of him from the company, he took it so hard. For him there was nothing else in his life. Now he is trying to make up lost time and create it. But it is a bit late, and he is left with golf and drinking! It is sad really because when we were younger we did go to plays and concerts and he had a much broader range of interests. I suppose that is the penalty of being devoted to a job. '

'And sex?' Renie came straight to the point. Renie had always been a lot more forthright than Thelma.

'Well, of course there isn't any, I told you that. After the operation, that was the end of it. Gordon could not handle those injection things, and to tell the truth, I was relieved.'

'Yes, I realise that. What I meant was, for you?'

'For me Renie, how do you mean?' Thelma was taken aback, wondering what was coming next.

'What I mean Thelma is sex without Gordon. If you want a sex life, just because Gordon cannot perform, you should not deny yourself one.'

'Don't be ridiculous! Take a lover? Even if I wanted one, where is a woman my age going to go and have a sexual adventure?

'I did. After Bill died, for a few months. I never told you, because I thought you might disapprove. I met this guy through the local Catholic church. Ironic really, isn't it. Sin on the doorstep, as it were!' Renie laughed. 'It was wonderful while it lasted. But I was not interested in living with him, and in the end he went to Brisbane to live with his sister. Maybe he just wanted someone to wash his underpants and iron his shirts. I certainly was not going to do that. You can send out for that sort of thing!'

'That was different. Bill was dead. Gordon is still very much alive and I am married to him. In any case, sex is not an issue for me. It never has been. Well, not for a very long time.' She remembered Sergei again, and instinctively bit her lip, as she always did when she thought of him. 'So, why did you never tell me at the time?'

'To start with given it was with a Catholic priest I had to be careful it did not get out. In a sense the fact that nobody knew about it was part of its attraction. You know, clandestine meetings made it more exciting. You can imagine how scandalised the church would have been had anyone found out! He was fun, he showed me that I was capable of a human response after Bill died, and it was good for my self esteem. I absolutely do not regret it, even though I did miss him when he went to Brisbane. Well, I missed having the company rather than him, the relationship itself, I guess. If it had really been him I missed, maybe I would have washed his dirty underpants for him after all.'

They both laughed.

The waiter brought their food. They both took a mouthful, with appreciative sounds of satisfaction. Serious again Renie suddenly said, 'Thelma, the other thing I wanted to ask you about is Martin. What is happening in his life?'

****

Martin closed his files and looked up. 'So, we are agreed then!' he stated more than asked. It had been a frustrating even if predictable meeting. Richard had distributed the costings on T566 based on the figures that Production had provided. But Martin knew exactly how Pat operated. There would have been several assumptions that could be, and indeed should be, questioned. Martin had done his homework, and had other actual production figures of other products that were made at the plant on the western fringes of Sydney, and also similar comparisons from the German and the Brazilian plants.

He now presented these in a very logical and convincing way. It showed, or at least strongly suggested, that Pat had exaggerated the expected amount of transition material that would be produced in the reactor as they transited into and out of the prime base product for T566. This had been costed by production at no revenue, which also was not true. It had some value. And Martin was able to show that the amount of such material produced would be about a third of what Pat was claiming, unless the plant were to be significantly less efficient than either the German or Brazilian plants. Not only that but he had added in two transitions, in and then out of the base product; clearly it was going to transition into something anyway, so only one transition should be costed to T566. Pat knew he was on dangerous ground. If he claimed extenuating circumstances that would cause costs necessarily to be higher in Australia, he was risking an argument to close the whole manufacturing operation in Australia. He knew that had been discussed in Hong Kong as recently as the last strategic planning meeting the previous year. He was not going to give people ammunition for that argument.

Reluctantly, Pat had agreed that some of the assumptions should be changed, Richard reworked the figures on his laptop, and they came up with another figure altogether for what it would cost to make T566 in Sydney, one that was a significant amount lower than the one based on Pat's original assumptions, and which would return a very nice profit to the company.

Len mentioned that it would be better to have the costings done on a low and high estimate of sales, whereas Ted had only provided one set of figures for the next three years estimated sales. Ted explained, rather patronisingly, that there had indeed been a high and a low sales estimate, but the lower figure had been used for the calculations. If that lower one showed that the project would make money, then a higher figure would be even more cost effective.

Pat interjected, saying that he did not have rubber reactors and that there was clearly a limit on how much could be produced without prejudicing the manufacture of other products.

Martin could see, even feel, the tension rising, so he intervened.

'Look, there is plenty of spare capacity taking all the reactors together, something like 17%, Pat right?' Pat reluctantly nodded, but said nothing. Martin continued, 'In that case it becomes a production planning issue as to which reactor you use to make which products, and surely that can be sorted out between you, Len and Pat?' He looked from one to the other, waiting for a response. After a few seconds they both murmured their agreement.

Martin held centre stage for a few minutes more. 'I have looked through Ted's figures and compared them to demand in several other countries, and the expected Australian growth rates in that industry segment. If anything, on this occasion, I think Ted's lower figure may be a bit conservative. But what it shows is that manufacture here of T566 certainly is viable, and should go ahead.'

There followed some negotiation over the timing by which Production could have the product ready for sale, and Martin suggested that they import T566 from Brazil in the meantime. The fall in the Real would make it cheaper than importing from Germany. He made a note to talk to the Brazilians and then the Purchasing Department.

The meeting was over and Martin felt a sense of satisfaction. This is what he enjoyed about his work. He was also aware that he enjoyed winning. Overall his life was under quite good control. The goodbyes were brief and he walked back to his office, but as he did so, on further reflection he was aware at some kind of subconscious level that despite his feeling of satisfaction with the meeting, in fact his life was not altogether under control, only certain parts of it were. Again he thought about making that call, but decided that he could justify postponing it until later when he could be assured more privacy.

****

The jacarandas were in full bloom, the intensity of the mauve colour was starting to wane and in a few days the petals would drop a delicate carpet on the greenness of the grass at the edge of the fairway. As Gordon looked up towards the horizon he could see that over the tops of the gum trees at the end of the fairway, the sky had turned quite dark. In a little while it would rain, but by then he should be well inside the club house.

He felt comfortable there. He was amongst friends. He suspected that some of them also had had their career disappointments, but it was never talked about. The secrets of their working lives were kept in boxes at home, and never brought into the club house.

His life had changed after Reg's visit. Gordon was in shock. All the things that he had identified as being himself were crumbling away. He felt that as they fell away from him they revealed that there was nothing left at the core. His life had been one of superficiality. What was he really other than the second in charge at work, a husband who provided? A man who had done the right thing by his family and the world? When he had to fall back on what was inside, he found that there wasn't much at all that he could feel or see, or be. His identity had been taken away in such a way that he was not able to prepare himself for another phase of his life, suddenly wrenched from him, like a beating heart.

He had been aware that evening in the sitting room as Reg's car roared away into the distance and to safer ground, that he was quietly sobbing and as Thelma approached he instinctively turned towards her, although it was not what he really intended to do. She led him to the armchair, and sat on the arm of the chair with her arm protectively round his shoulder. She had heard enough, and did not need to say anything. She just tried to comfort him as he gave in to his grief.

Thelma had realised that there was nothing that could be done. The die was cast; there could be no talk of court cases, challenges. They just had to learn to accept the situation that had been presented to them, and learn to live with it as best they could. Although she was trying very hard to understand what this meant to her and her own life, her actions were directed towards Gordon. In reality she did not see too many positives in the situation, but knew that whatever ones there were she had to dress up and try to use them to lift Gordon up.

She tried to reassure him that she was sure by the way that Reg had reacted that this had been forced on him by the Americans. He was himself virtually powerless as he was retiring in a few months. Who knows what drives those people in Cleveland? Would he really have wanted to be part of that? At their time of life was it in any case wiser to avoid such tensions, and stress? After all they should count their blessings. They had more than enough money to live a very comfortable retirement and do those things that they had not had time to do all these years. Maybe they could find a way of getting closer again. Privately she tried to think of some things that Gordon had said he wanted to do and never had time for. But she could not think of any. With increasing alarm, which she hoped he would not pick up on, she realised that in fact he had no other interests than work, and it was going to be very hard to fill the void of the career vacuum. And impossible to do so without impacting on her own life, which had really been in quite good order until all this happened.

She talked about taking a trip together, planning a few weekends away, decorating the interior of the house and making it fun rather than a drudge. She talked about golf. But she was struggling, and they both knew it.

Gordon heaved a sigh as deep as the earth itself, and asked Thelma to get him another gin and tonic. Thelma was grateful of the opportunity to do something more or less constructive, and she made one for herself too. They sat down opposite each other in silence and sipped their drinks. Thelma had a horrible premonition that this was a symbol of her life to come. She suddenly regretted some of the decisions she had made so many years ago.

It took a while for Gordon to internalise the fact that he was no longer on sick leave but rather that he was retired. He signed all the paperwork, took charge of his considerable payout and had the Mercedes transferred into his own name. In some ways this was pseudo work, and almost like the mechanical processes one goes through when a loved one dies, of registering death and starting on the lengthy legal and documentation processes that death entails. In the same way Gordon was putting to rest the identifiable part of his own life.

He wondered whether or not he should think about taking a job, maybe a directorship of a company. But he realised that the only contacts he had were through the company he had given nearly forty years of his life to, and he did not have the stomach to revisit those relationships. If someone approached him he would consider it, but he was not going to lower himself to seeking such a position and then face the high probability of being rejected. He also knew that once a person has been dumped, there is a kind of animal instinct for the pack to leave well alone. He would not be approached.

He considered donating his time to worthy voluntary organisations. Surely he must have some skill that they could find useful. But when he stopped and thought about it he was not quite sure what those skills might be. Perhaps as an accountant, but that would be too demeaning for him, and besides he recognised that community based organisations might operate in very different ways from what he was used to. The bottom line was that he just did not think that he would ever be able to get on with a load of airy fairy do-gooders who had never had to face the hard life of commercial reality. They would probably all be Labor voters, or even worse, Greenies.

Instead he decided to take life day by day, get stronger after his operation, and then consider, as Thelma suggested, some more social activities and making the odd trip. But as he idly flicked through magazines and scanned the titles of books in the book store in the local shopping centre, he was uncomfortably aware that there was nothing in all of that to really interest him. And that was how golf had become such an important part of his life.

There was a flash of lightning and a clap of thunder that seemed almost overhead. He hurried the last few metres to the club house and got inside just as the deluge broke. It was cooler inside, and a couple of his mates were already at the bar.

'Just in time!' he said as he approached them.

****

Thelma was pleased at Renie's question about Martin, as Martin was at the centre of her existence. They were very alike she and Martin, Thelma realised that. The fine features, the ability to wear clothes well, the style, the good looks. On the rare occasions she went to his house in Paddington, and saw the neatness and cleanliness, she could see a reflection of herself.

'Oh, Renie, he is just doing so well. He never says anything specifically, that is not his style, but reading between the lines, they seem to be very pleased with him. I wouldn't be at all surprised if there was another promotion in the offing.'

'Actually, Thelma, I was not asking so much about work, as about his life in general. Is he happy? Does he have someone in his life?'

'Well, not as far as I know, but you know what young men are like these days. The parents would be the last to know. He will probably turn up one day, say, 'this is Fiona' and we are getting married on Saturday!' Thelma laughed a little nervously.

'And if he doesn't?'

'I have to confess that I would like grandchildren. It might be the very thing that would get Gordon back into the world other than golf! And in that case, well of course I would hope that Martin would marry. I just think it makes life, sort of, well, less complicated later on for the children. These modern relationships where people are de facto or whatever it is are just not right in my book. And he is getting to the age where he needs to think about this. I have never believed that it is good to leave having a family too late, nobody should still be putting their kids through university when they are in their late 50s.'

'No, I mean, if he doesn't meet 'Fiona'.'

'Everyone meets someone, surely. And Martin is very eligible'

'And what if it is Fred rather than Fiona?'

Thelma glared at Renie who was leaning forward a little intensely. 'Don't be ridiculous. Not Martin. There is nothing wrong with him. I'm sure of that.'

'How old is he? Thirty three, with never any sign of a girl friend. Thelma you have to be prepared for the possibility that he might be gay.'

'Gay?' she almost screamed. The woman at the next table looked round. Thelma leant towards Renie, and lowered her voice. 'Of course he has had girl friends. Look at that nice girl he used to go out with and took to Gordon's Golf Club dance.'

'That was several years ago, and there was no evidence at all that I noticed that they were in any way intimate or that they were having a relationship. I am just mentioning it because I think it is a little odd. And frankly, Thelma, and please don't take this the wrong way, judging by your defensive reaction, I think that the possibility has also crossed your mind too. I am trying to help not to attack you. I love Martin and I always have. And if it turned out that he is gay, it would not make the slightest bit of difference to how I feel towards him.'

Thelma looked into the layered deposits of the tiramisu on her plate. Her face was flushed.

She sounded angry now, 'No Renie you have got it totally, totally wrong! I know my own son for heaven's sake and

I can assure you there is absolutely nothing wrong with him. You are wrong, just plain wrong!'

'Am I?'' Renie said gently.

They sat in silence for several minutes. And during that silence all sorts of thoughts and memories started to course through Thelma's head. It was true that Martin had never mentioned any girls, ever. She remembered that once on a rare visit to his house she had glanced at a magazine on the coffee table and Martin had quickly whipped it away, but she was a bit surprised that it seemed to have a naked man on the front cover. She remembered Gordon saying once to her that he wished Martin was a bit more like other young men with an interest in sport rather than arts and concerts; it had been a comment between disgust and exasperation. She thought back to his childhood when he would stay at home during the holidays and read rather than go out and climb trees like the boys up the road. He hated school sports and was dismayed every time he got mud on his knees. She put it down to him being an only child, and rather sensitive in the same way she imagined herself to be. With a kind of anxiety bordering on panic she began to wonder if Renie was right.

'What do you want for him, Thelma?' Renie asked. She could see that Thelma was a bit distressed and obviously deep in thought.

Thelma was startled by the question, and looked up at Renie. Slowly she said, 'I want him to be happy, to get married, have a family and be happy the same way Gordon and I have been.' As soon as the words came out of her mouth she wondered whether Gordon and she really were that happy and whether that was what she wanted for Martin after all. She bit her lip involuntarily again. Renie noticed.

Renie said, 'Let's split those into two parts. You want him to be happy. Of course! But Thelma, let him decide what being happy is for him, rather than impose what you think it means on him.

Thelma ignored Renie's comment and said, 'There's nothing on our side of the family.'

Renie looked at her a little puzzled.

Thelma continued, 'Gordon had an uncle who never married and who he always said was a bit strange. I only ever met him once. It has to be on his side, it is not my fault.'

'Thelma, Thelma, this is not about fault. In fact it is not about you at all! I could be wrong, Martin may be straight. But whatever he is doesn't matter. I suspect he may be gay, and I have thought so for a very long time, and if he is then I think you should think about it and be prepared to handle it the day that it comes out, and one day I am certain it will.'

Thelma stayed silent and made a decision to find out one way or the other. God knows how Gordon would take it; it would probably be the end of him. Our only son 'like that,' how could the world be so cruel?

****

Tony picked up his violin, put a few things in his backpack and was ready to head off to rehearsal. As he picked up his phone he checked again to see if Martin had called. He hadn't. They had had a great weekend together and he was hoping they were going to get away together the weekend after next. He was free from rehearsals and they had been planning on a weekend away in the southern highlands at a kind of farm stay. It had been Martin's idea, and it sounded like fun. But the Saturday of that weekend was also Martin's birthday and he was supposed to be working out how he could manage to get away for the weekend and not have dinner with his parents on his birthday night, which was what he normally did for his birthday. It seemed that Martin's parents had no idea of Tony's existence, or even that Martin was gay.

Tony and Martin had been seeing each other for a few months. He almost never went to the Oxford Hotel at Taylor Square. But one evening after he had been to visit a friend of his who was in St Vincents hospital just down the road, he decided on the spur of the moment to go and have a drink. It was a warm night and he was thirsty. He wasn't even sure how they got talking, but he and Martin somehow got into conversation. It turned out that the previous week they had both been to a Brandenburg Orchestra concert at Angel Place Recital Hall. They both enjoyed similar music it seemed and they chatted a while about one thing and another. Then Martin had to go somewhere and they exchanged phone numbers. Tony rang Martin the next day and they arranged to meet the next Friday evening. Things just developed from there and they started going out regularly. Tony found Martin easy to be with in general, although his pedantic tidiness could be annoying; he enjoyed his company and the sex was good. It was not for him the *coup de foudre* that Roger had been, but then neither did he want to relive all the drama that followed with Roger in the turbulent relationship he had had with him. He teased Martin about his yuppie life style which was so different from his own, but he actually liked the stability and cautiousness in Martin.

Roger had been a disaster. It is true that he was just Tony's type physically, blue eyes, solid rugby build, with thick legs, a broad hairy chest and short blonde hair and a strong masculine face. They ended up living together, but there were always arguments. Roger was impetuous, fiery, and above all passionate in bed. In fact sex was the cornerstone of their relationship. Roger worked in landscape gardening and drifted from job to job, but somehow managed to just about make ends meet most of the time. It had been alright despite the stormy interactions, until Roger had suggested they spice up their sex life with drugs. Tony had tried ecstasy a few times and enjoyed it, and he had smoked dope on and off since he was a teenager, but Roger wanted to try crystal meth. Tony had not heard much about it when Roger had suggested it, but that was after all quite a few years ago. He agreed to go along with it and try it out. Until that time for the most part Roger had fucked Tony although sometimes the tables were turned. The first time they tried crystal meth was a Friday night at home. They smoked it through a glass pipe. Tony had never felt anything like it. There was a sudden surge of amazing sexual energy. He felt like an animal and was desperate to feel Roger fuck him as hard as he could. And he did,

51

like a mad man, but then Roger pleaded with Tony to fuck him. Tony had never known Roger like this, just hungry to take it as hard and deep as he could. The sex seemed to go on forever and Tony felt exhilarated, invincible and so hungry for cock that he barely cared whether it was Roger or anyone else. It took them all weekend to recover and by Monday Tony had had time to reflect. It certainly had been an amazing experience and in some ways he wanted to do it all over again and in other ways he was scared. Roger and he never discussed that first experiment but Roger wanted to repeat the experience two weekends later, and this time at a friend's place with a small group. Tony had misgivings but in the end decided to go along with it. He experienced exactly the same feelings of voracious appetite to get fucked, and he ended up having bareback sex with several of the other guys in the group. He was shocked at his own behaviour as he was normally not so uninhibited and hungry for cock, and in the background he was aware that he was at some level dismayed by seeing Roger turn into such a bottom whore that he hardly recognised him. The comedown was miserable and he felt depressed and wretched. He decided that he would not be repeating that experience. There was something evil about it, yes exciting and intense, but dangerous, something that took away the person and replaced it with animal lust and nothing more. He was also scared about whether he might have contracted HIV during the wired frenzy and the unprotected sex. Tony went to the clinic despite feeling awful and got himself onto a month's course of PEP (Post Exposure Prophylaxis) to minimise the risk of HIV infection. He encouraged Roger to do the same but he said he didn't really care, which Tony interpreted as him feeling too down to bother.

Fortunately testing over the next few months showed that Tony was still negative but the whole experience was enough for him to swear off ever doing crystal again. However for Roger it was different and he kept trying to persuade Tony to join him in taking crystal. That was how their relationship broke down. Tony insisted on using condoms on the few occasions he and Roger had sex after that, and they drifted further and further away from each other. Roger started to go out on Friday nights and often did not come back until Monday looking dreadful. He began to miss work and his health declined. By this stage the feelings Tony might have had for Roger had waned but he still felt a sense of responsibility towards him and tried desperately to get him to stop. It was useless, and Roger's life fell more and more into disaster until Tony reluctantly gave up. The last straw came when Tony found a large amount of drugs hidden in Roger's bedside table and he realised that he must be dealing to try and pay for his habit. Tony confronted Roger and told him he had two options. Either Roger would go into rehab and stop using or Tony would move out. Roger agreed to go into rehab, but never turned up for his first appointment and Tony decided at that stage that resolving the situation was beyond his capability and he left. He had heard that Roger ended up in hospital a few months later and eventually had been forced into rehab. He had no interest in knowing what happened after that.

When he met Martin he knew that here was a man who would never do drugs, he would be too scared of losing control! He was stable, centred, honest, straight forward, intelligent and kind of wholesome. Yes he was a bit stitched up, but they shared many interests such as music and theatre, despite being from quite different backgrounds. Sex with Martin was not the all consuming experience that he had had on crystal, but it was satisfying, connected and Martin was very affectionate which he also liked. He felt that he had grown up after Roger, and it was time to build his life into something.

****

Renie paid the bill while Thelma continued to sit there deep in thought. She stood up with a slight sigh as Renie walked back to the table and they took the lift to the fourth floor to look at the Slovakian glass that Renie had mentioned. Thelma was not really in the mood for browsing shops any longer and just felt she wanted to get home and be on safer territory to think over what Renie had said. After spending what Thelma found an irritatingly lengthy time poring over the glassware, Renie decided she did not need any after all, and so they walked towards the station. Renie had a few other things she wanted to do in the city and so Thelma kissed her lightly on the cheek as they went their separate ways.

'Be kind to yourself Thelma, whatever it is, it is not such a big deal,' Renie said.

Thelma looked at her and said, 'He is not your son. You don't have children, how could you possibly know?'

With some relief Thelma took out her Opal card, swiped it and went through the barrier and up to the Northshore line platform for the train back home. As she stared out of the window without seeing anything at all, Thelma's mind oscillated between thinking that there was no way that Martin could be gay to trying to persuade herself that she could cope with him being gay and that it wasn't a problem. In the middle of that she was already partially grieving about not having grandchildren, and wondering whether she should mention it to Gordon or not.

Thelma got off the train and walked down the tree lined street to home. The neat grass verges were just the same, the well established trees stood unchanged casting their welcome shadows on the footpath, large comfortable homes snoozing behind the walls with flowers and bushes partially obscuring their generous dimensions. Everything was normal, comfortable, Northshore correct. But now it wasn't somehow correct and Thelma felt edgy.

She turned the key in the door; Gordon was not home yet, but she had already surmised that as he would normally leave his car on the drive, and it wasn't there. She loved her comfortable home and right now it felt like her security, the one thing she knew and that was right in her life. She went into the kitchen, put on the kettle and made a cup of tea. She let it steep for only a minute, added a dash of light milk and then went into the sitting room and sat in her favourite chair looking out into the garden.

She was wondering how she might approach finding out what the truth was about Martin. Did she really want to know?

On the one hand she didn't, but she knew that she could not just ignore the issue now. Should she ask him? If she was wrong he would be offended. If she was right he might deny it. However she need not have worried about how she was going start the dialogue, that was about to be taken out of her hands.

****

Martin was quite aware that he had been procrastinating over making the call to his mother about not going to their place for dinner on his birthday. He knew that it was going to invite all sorts of questions that he was not sure that he was ready to answer. But he fully intended to go away with Tony for that weekend. He could not really confirm that until he had spoken to his mother just in case things turned difficult, and he knew Tony was waiting for his call to confirm. He was very happy with the way his relationship with Tony was developing. He had not seen anyone on a regular basis for a long time. Maybe he was just too picky or maybe he was looking in the wrong places. He had tried some of the gay apps but found that many of the guys he met were into drugs, and he was not, or that they had various hang-ups or other baggage. But somehow Tony was different. They had met in a way that Martin often thought fell into the category of 'meant to be'. Neither Tony nor Martin frequented the Oxford Hotel regularly at all. But one evening several months ago now, Martin had arranged to meet a friend in Taylor Square for an early dinner. The friend called to say he was delayed by an hour or so. Martin went into the Oxford to have a beer and kill time until his mate arrived. Tony meanwhile, he understood, had been visiting a friend in St Vincents hospital. They both approached the bar at the same time. There was a brief exchange of 'after you,' and somehow they got talking. They had both been to the same concert the previous week which at least suggested they had some interests in common. After an hour Martin had to leave for his dinner arrangement and they exchanged phone numbers. Martin was pleased when Tony called the next day and he did not need any persuasion to agree to meet the next Friday night.

Tony was olive skinned, had blue eyes, and was shorter than Martin, but like Martin was slim. He had dark brown hair and just a little hair on his chest. Martin had asked him if he was of Italian descent, but Tony said that he was a mix of Irish and English, and had no idea where his dark looks came from. He was very much Martin's 'type'. Martin also liked the fact that Tony led a kind of artistic, almost bohemian, life in comparison to his, and that gave him a well needed perspective on other demographics of gay society than his own. The fact that Tony did not work a conventional week did make it hard sometimes for them to get together. On several Friday and Saturday nights he had concerts and had to work. Martin liked classical music and often bought tickets. On those nights he would meet Tony afterwards and then they would go back to Martin's place in Paddo to sleep. It was early days, but he could see himself settling down with Tony. He enjoyed his company, loved going out with him, looked forward to seeing him at weekends and sometimes during the week, and enjoyed sleeping with him, both the sex and being cuddled up with him in bed. He wanted to let the relationship develop and see where it led. Part of that was going to be the weekend away on a farm in the Southern Highlands. It would be so different from city life and a good break where the two of them could just be together. Fortunately it was not a weekend when Tony had a concert and would have been working.

Martin had never mentioned to his parents that he was gay and had in fact avoided telling them anything that might alert them to the fact. He had been aware as a teenager that he was attracted to men. At school he used to look with interest at the prefects who were a few years older than him, and wonder what they looked like naked. He enjoyed looking at the other guys in the showers, and imagined himself touching them. Despite this awareness he had not acted on these urges and put them to the back of his mind thinking that perhaps this was just normal curiosity and there was nothing 'wrong' with him. It had been at university that he had had his first sexual experience, and it changed his life, fleeting though the experience was.

He had been passing the Carslaw Building at Sydney Uni and decided before heading home he would go for a pee. As he went into the toilets a very good looking guy came out, no doubt another student. Martin went to the urinal and was just starting to urinate when that guy came back into the toilet again, and went and stood right next to Martin. There was nobody else in the toilets, it was quite late, and Martin realised that it was with intent that he had returned. The guy got his dick out with a bit of trouble as it was already half hard. He stroked it a bit and in seconds it was rock hard. He was aware that Martin was looking at his dick and he turned towards him so he could see it in all its glory. Martin's dick was still out and it too got as hard as a rock. The young man knelt down and took Martin's dick in his mouth. Martin loved the feeling but was terrified that someone would come in and catch them. 'This is too dangerous,' he muttered in a hushed voice.

Yes, OK,' the other guy said, and got up, his dick still out, and walked over to the stalls behind. He opened the door to one of them, went inside and then motioned for Martin to join him. Martin followed him and shut and locked the door behind him. They both pulled their pants down. The student knelt again in front of Martin, and took Martin deep down his throat deftly running his tongue around the head of Martin's cock. He had never felt anything like it and was just so aroused he felt he was getting close to ejaculating. The other guy stopped sucking his cock just in time and they reversed roles. Martin felt that he had suddenly discovered the secret of the universe and finally realised why people raved about sex. They again reversed roles, and this time Martin was not able to control himself any longer and ejaculated down the guy's throat in the most powerful orgasm he had ever had, one that went on and on, as the guy greedily swallowed every last drop of his seed while he masturbated himself to orgasm at the same time. Martin was still spasming from the orgasm when the other guy smiled and said, 'I think you quite enjoyed that.'

'Oh god!' was all Martin could summon up.

They pulled up their pants, carefully unlocked the door and made sure that nobody was there, and then both left.

This was not the most romantic introduction to sex that Martin could have had but it was earthy, real, urgent. It clarified something for Martin that had been lurking in the shadows for years. He was gay. He had had dates with girls, ended up kissing, and felt nothing. He had wondered what all the fuss about sex was. He had never had any desire to take it any further with girls which he recognised had frustrated them on several occasions. He knew that he was supposed to play with their breasts, and gradually sex would unfold. But he had had no desire to do so, and so he never took it that far. Now he knew where he belonged. His erotic dreams, his fantasies when he masturbated all came into focus. He felt no guilt or remorse, he just accepted it. It was in some senses as if a burden had been lifted, and it never occurred to him that another burden had replaced it, that of being gay in what is predominantly a straight world.

Martin was not prone to taking risks and those who knew him would have described him as being a bit preppy and quiet, even in his student days. It was therefore surprising that Martin continued to pop into the toilets at Carslaw Building to see if there was any action. One day he met a guy who suggested that Martin should join The Pride Network at uni, a gay organisation for students at Sydney Uni. That had been Martin's introduction to gay society, and he never looked back.

While Martin was quite comfortable with his sexuality he did not wear it on his sleeve and was discreet in situations like work and with his parents. He had some straight friends and some of them knew and some of them didn't. He played it according to the reaction he thought he would get. His mother was always dropping hints about him settling down and giving her the long awaited grandchildren she aspired to. But he never took the bait and just ignored it, saying nothing in response. She had never dared to ask a direct question, that was not her style, and so he never had to give a direct answer. Conversations with his father were distant and very general and never touched on anything personal. Martin recognised that this could not go on forever especially if he met someone and wanted to settle down with him. And he did want that. He did not want to spend all of his life on his own and felt that now was the time to be in a relationship as he approached his 34th birthday. He wanted to share his life, to have someone to eat dinner with, to go to the theatre with, to travel with. He wanted someone in his bed, someone that he was happy to wake up with every morning, as more than anything he craved affection.

He was not sure how his parents would take his being gay. They were not religious, that was not the point. But he recognised that they were very conservative in their views, both politically and socially. His father had made typically 'anti-poofter' remarks in a derogatory and dismissive way over the years, but then so did most straight men of his era. It did not necessarily mean anything, he thought. His mother was a bit more flexible in her ideas whilst certainly not being progressive. He imagined that for her the issues would be grandchildren and maybe what the neighbours and friends would say. He could not do anything about either of those. He did not intend necessarily to tell her today, but he was trying to prepare himself in case it did come up.

He went into his office and closed the door, picked up his mobile and rang the home number in the hope that she would be there in the late afternoon, rather than catch her out somewhere on the mobile. It rang three times before his mother answered, 'Seven six four three, hello.' She always answered with just the last four numbers of their phone in what Martin thought was almost a strange affectation.

'Hi, Ma, it's me,' he said.

'Oh Martin, I was just thinking about you.'

'I am at work and so I can't talk for long.'

'That's alright. I understand.'

'Look, I thought I should just let you know that I won't be able to come for dinner the weekend after next, for my birthday.'

'Why not? You always come for dinner on your birthday, we have always done that.'

'I know, I am sorry, but I am going away that weekend. To the Southern Highlands.'

Thelma was in a state between annoyance, indignation and panic. 'Is it a work do, a conference or something?'

'Well, no, not really.'

'So why are you going away that weekend, of all weekends?'

'It's some special deal; a kind of get away from it all weekend.'

'Get away? Who from?' She felt stupid as soon as she said it.

'Not from anyone, Ma. But it is my birthday and it is an opportunity for me to do something I want to do'. Martin raised the tone of his voice just a notch.

Thelma paused for a second and then asked, 'Are you going on your own?'

'No with a friend.' Martin was trying to be ambiguous.

Thelma was not going to let him off the hook. 'A girlfriend?'

This was the question Martin had been anticipating. He had turned this over in his mind and had been half prepared to tell her the truth, but now suddenly he backed away from it, again. 'No, a mate.'

'A mate? Who?'

'He's just a mate I hang out with sometimes.'

'You never mentioned a mate you hang out with. What is his name? Do I know him?' Thelma's voice was a bit caustic and pointed.

'No you don't know him. It's no big deal Ma, I just wanted to let you know I won't be over that weekend.'

There was now a frostiness between them and Martin did not want this to be the way he explained to his parents that he was gay, he would rather do it face to face. He continued, 'Ma I need to go now I have a meeting to go to.'

'Martin, are you sure there is nothing you want to tell me?

She knows or at least suspects something, he thought, but right now is not the time. 'No, Ma, look I really need to go. See you one evening during the week after maybe?' He put the phone down without even waiting for an answer. He was both relieved and at the same time a bit anxious.

Thelma was annoyed with herself at how she had conducted the call and with Martin for not answering her questions. She thought that the conversation was further evidence that Renie was most likely right. Martin was gay, or at least spending time with some unknown mate rather than a girlfriend; it did not look good. It seemed as if this weekend was going to be something a bit special for Martin, and she had not intended to spoil that. But it was something special with a 'mate' and not a girlfriend. At his age that was suspicious. Even more so because she could tell he was being evasive. Perhaps what upset her most was the fact that he did not feel able to be open and honest with her. Was she so judgmental that he was afraid to tell her if he was gay? Well, maybe she was, and it suddenly struck her that she certainly had not given him any signals that it was okay. And it was indeed not okay for her, she absolutely did not want her only son to be gay. She had been confrontational rather than accepting and understanding; it was after all his birthday to enjoy as he wanted. She wished that she could pick up the phone and rerun their conversation. But it was too late for that and she would have to wait until he came round. Maybe if Renie had not said anything, and the issue of him possibly being gay was fresh in her mind, the call would have been different.

Would she share her concerns with Gordon? She had never talked about such things with him. He had always been very conservative in his approach to life. Neither of them was religious really, they never went to church except at Christmas and Easter, and it would not be religion that would inform his reaction. But she supposed he would not want any son of his, especially his only son, to be less than a full blooded Aussie man. As it was he had already commented about Martin being precious and a bit 'poncy'. She would bide her time and see what

61

happened. But if there was going to be a conversation with Martin the next time he came round, she would just have to speak to Gordon first, whether she liked it or not. They needed to have a united front.

Her cup of tea was cold now. She looked at it with distaste and decided to pour herself a gin and tonic instead.

****

Martin picked up his phone again and dialled Tony.

'Martin, I am just on my way to practice, just waiting for the bus now. Did you speak to your parents?'

'We are on. All confirmed for the weekend.'

'Good! So how did the conversation go?'

'Not that well. She was upset and I am sure that the penny has dropped. She was asking all sorts of questions about who I was going with and if there was something I wanted to tell her.'

'And you chickened out!' Tony laughed.

'It wasn't the right time.'

'Your call! But we should confirm the booking at the farm.'

'Yes I will do that now.'

'See you Friday. The bus is coming.'

****

Gordon walked up to the bar and ordered a schooner of Super Dry for himself, and looked to see if his mates were ready for another drink.

'Stan, Frank, ready for another?'

Frank said, 'Gordon, we just arrived and got a drink, we are both right for the moment, thanks. Looks like a bit of a storm coming.' To reinforce his observation there was a sudden crack of lightning followed only a few seconds later by a robust roll of thunder.

'That was close. At least I won't need to water the garden,' Gordon commented. He sat down on a stool at the bar next to his mates, and took a long swig of his ice cold beer. 'Ah,' he said, 'I always think the first mouthful is the best.' Stan and Frank murmured in agreement.

'So how is retirement going, Gordon?' asked Stan.

Gordon sighed. 'I suppose I will get used to it. It was not what I was expecting, not what I wanted, at least not yet, and I am not sure how to handle it. I just get bored. I didn't have time to prepare for it.'

Frank said, 'I was the same initially. It took me quite a while to settle into a new routine. I fixed up a few things round the house, and then got stuck into the garden, and suddenly I realised that my focus had changed and that my whole pace of life was different.'

Gordon responded, 'The problem is that I am no good at fixing things and I have never liked gardening. We always paid for people to take care of that sort of thing. But I do think I need some sort of hobby or activity of some kind to get involved with. Otherwise I am just going to go potty.'

Stan offered, 'We find we get very busy with the grandchildren. Fiona and Barry both have very full on jobs and they rely on us to look after the children, sometimes too much I think. We pick them up from school, look after them in the holidays, take the boy to footy, and the girl to ballet and stuff. Those kids have such full lives nowadays and getting on buses like we used to as kids is not an option any longer, it seems! They come and sleep over if Fiona and Barry go out at night, which they often do for dinners and meetings. Fiona takes her career very seriously. I am not sure how they would manage if we were not around. But I am not complaining, we love the grandkids, and it is great to watch them grow.'

Frank agreed, 'Yes we spend a lot of time with our two grandkids as well. I would never have been able to do that if I was still working. My wife adores them and I get a kick out of them too. How about you, Gordon, do you have grandkids?'

The description of their retired lives and grandchildren was not helping Gordon at all. 'No, I am afraid not.' Gordon paused. 'My son is not even married yet.'

'Oh, how old is he?' Stan asked.

'He is 34 next birthday. He is just like his mother. I think she indulged him a bit too much. Doted on him as an only child, mollycoddled him in my view. He is a strange boy in many ways. He has a good job and has never got into trouble or anything, it's just that somehow he is different from most young men his age, and I find it hard to understand him. He is nothing like I was when I was young. He isn't interested in football or cricket, or the sorts of things most men of his age are interested in. I wonder sometimes where he came from.'

Stan and Frank exchanged glances, probably both thinking the same thing, but neither of them was game to make any comment or go further into the issue. They waited to see if Gordon was going to say anything else.

After a long pause Gordon said, 'So no grandchildren on the horizon.'

There followed a silence as the three men sipped at their beers. Stan then ventured, 'Gordon, you must have some hobbies, something that you like doing that you could get more involved in now?'

Gordon thought for a moment or two before replying. 'I guess I never really had many interests outside work and the family. I used to when I was younger, but then I threw everything into my work and never seemed to have time for anything else. If I had my time over I would never have devoted so much time to that bloody company, damn them. It was those fucking Americans. They just have no sense of honour or commitment, just money, money.' He stopped for a second realising he was getting flustered and had gone off track from the question. 'Sorry. Hobbies? Well no, not really. I used to read books but don't have the appetite now. I tried decorating once. Paint ended up everywhere and it was a disaster and I had to get a painter in to finish it.'

'Well what sorts of things appeal to you?' Frank asked.

'I quite like watching sport on Foxtel, but I can't watch TV all day. I think Thelma would complain. And I feel I need to get out and do something.'

'Well, there are walking groups for seniors you know. Or what about bowls, that is a more gentle kind of activity.'

'Bowls, maybe, but it just seems like an old codger's game.'

'Not really, Gordon,' Stan interjected, 'not any longer. There are quite a few young guys playing bowls nowadays. What about photography, or things like films or history, or even art? What sort of music do you like?'

'I have never been very interested in art, I leave all that to Thelma, she loves all that stuff. We went to Italy and she dragged me round all those monuments and galleries. I was really bored shitless. Thelma goes to the galleries and stuff with her sister sometimes, and when she wants to go to a concert she asks Martin to go with her. She says he appreciates it and I don't, so why not go with him?'

Frank was desperately trying to come up with a useful suggestion. 'Have you ever thought about doing some of those courses at the WEA? They have some amazing stuff. They have everything from learning Mandarin to history, learning how to write, all sorts of things.'

Gordon sighed and said, 'Yes you are probably right, I should look at them.' But with a tone of voice that suggested he wouldn't.

Stan ordered another round of beers, and the storm rumbled on. Stan and Frank had run out of suggestions and Gordon felt more dejected than ever.

****

Martin had prepared on Thursday night everything he thought he would need for the weekend away and packed it into a light-weight medium size suitcase that he used for short business trips. He left the suitcase open on the table in the sitting room and in the morning after he had shaved and cleaned his teeth he put his toiletry bag in the case, and closed it. It was typical for him to be so well organised. He had already printed out the confirmation for the farm and he had placed that in his briefcase. He had loaded the address and directions onto his phone and had packed two chargers for the phone in case one of them failed – he had been caught like that once before on a work trip to Melbourne. On Friday morning he got ready for work and the only thing that differed in his routine was putting the suitcase in the boot of the car.

Martin had organised his day so that they could leave a bit earlier with the intention of getting out of the city before the weekend traffic got too bad. He drove to Glebe to pick up Tony. At Tony's place he changed out of his suit into more casual clothes, slacks and a checked short sleeved shirt that he retrieved from the suitcase. He hung his suit up and left it in Tony's bedroom. Tony had a canvas bag with a couple of changes of clothes; he always was very casually dressed in jeans and T shirt. Martin had always liked how tight Tony wore his jeans accenting both his rounded buttocks and showing a noticeable bulge at the front.

'Did you pack something warm just in case?' Martin asked.

'Yes, a sweater. I know it is a bit cooler in the southern highlands,' Tony reassured Martin. 'I also packed some lube and stuff just in case you didn't.

Martin laughed. 'Well, I did as a matter of fact.'

Tony kissed Martin on the mouth, and Martin could feel his erection growing. 'Come on, we need to get on the road, we will have plenty of time for that later,' Martin said.

The journey to the southern highlands was a bit slow but uneventful. Once they got onto the M5 the flow of traffic was good and they made good time. The young men chatted away and both were clearly happy and looking forward to their weekend away in the country. They located the farm without too much trouble; the last kilometre was down a narrow dirt road leading into an open area in front of a quite imposing stone house. Martin took the booking confirmation out of his briefcase, got out of the car, walked to the house and knocked on the front door. It was opened by a middle aged woman with greying hair, and somewhat over weight. She introduced herself as Margaret Branston but did not offer her hand. Martin noticed that she had some kind of skin disorder that left red blotches on the left side of her face. She showed him into the accommodation which was in an independent building separated from the rest of the house by a small garden. The room looked very comfortable and the en-suite bathroom was almost sumptuous. Martin was glad that their quarters were quite separate from the main part of the house.

By this time Tony had picked up their bags from the boot and followed Martin into the house through the still open door. Margaret Branston looked at him in surprise as he walked into the bedroom.

'And who are you?' she enquired in a less than friendly tone.

'I am with Martin,' replied Tony.

'I don't understand,' she said and turned towards Martin. 'There is only one bed, you booked a double.'

'Yes, that is right,' Tony said smiling.

'There must be some mistake.' Margaret Branston was now angry. 'I am not having any of that nonsense in this house. We are God fearing people and I will not tolerate having perverts in my house.'

Tony could see Martin flush red, partly with embarrassment and partly with anger, he suspected. Tony decided to take matters into his own hands. He walked up to her, looked her right in the eyes and said through gritted teeth, 'Martin and I are a couple. This is the twenty first century, not the nineteenth. Furthermore by law you are not allowed to discriminate against people on the basis of their sexuality.'

Margaret Branston stood firm and said, 'My husband and I are good Christians. I don't care what you think the law says, I am not having disgusting behaviour prohibited by God happening under my roof. Now get out.'

Martin, put his hand on Tony's arm, and said gently, 'Tony I don't want to stay here anyway. Not now.'

'Fair enough, neither do I.' Tony turned to Margaret Branston and said 'Alright we will leave, but I am warning you that this is against the law and it will not be the last you hear of this. You have no right to refuse same sex couples service based on their sexuality. The Act of 1984.' Tony picked up the bags and he and Martin retraced their footsteps back to the car, got in and they drove in silence back down the unmade road to the tarmac of the main road. Martin pulled over to the side and looked at Tony.

'I am so sorry, how was I to know that?'

Tony cut him off. 'You couldn't know and I am just amazed that people like that even exist nowadays, but we are better out of there. What are we going to do?'

'Find somewhere else if we can, maybe a hotel or something. It is going to be hard so late on a Friday, it is already 7.30.' Martin started to look for possible places googling 'Accommodation in the Southern Highlands'. The first three places he tried were all booked out. They were both a bit despondent, and neither liked the thought of having to drive back to Sydney and abandon what they had planned as a special weekend. But with the fourth one they got really lucky.

'Can you believe we just had a last minute cancellation? I just put the phone down, something to do with a parent being rushed off to hospital. If you give me a credit card to secure it, it is yours.'

Martin had the phone on loud speaker so Tony could hear. It was somewhat more expensive than the farm, but Tony nodded and Martin gave the woman on the other end of the phone his credit card details. She said, 'Dinner, bed and breakfast and dinner finishes in an hour.'

It was about 15 kms away and Martin told her they would be there within twenty minutes or so. Neither of them felt like talking, each one turning over in their mind what had happened. Tony was determined to not let it go but decided to wait until after the weekend before he discussed with Martin whether they should initiate a complaint under the Act, knowing that Martin would probably prefer to just let it go and not have any chance of publicity. They were both a little anxious about what the place they had booked would be like. As they approached the house their concerns lifted. It was a huge two storey country mansion with ivy covering the old stone walls. Several rather expensive looking cars were parked outside. Through the windows they could see a well laid out dining room already full of diners. Their host was waiting for them.

'Welcome,' she said, 'you boys just drop your things in the room and then go and enjoy dinner. We can fix all the paperwork up later.' They just had time to take in the room, cosy with a comfortable looking king size bed, heavy solid decor with deep reds and browns, and a well equipped bathroom, even though it was a bit small. The room was on the upper floor with a view down the garden to the bush beyond. Tony went up to Martin, kissed him and said, "All's well that ends well. I am starving, let's go and eat.'

The dining room was cosy and there was just one spare table. The other diners, all presumably house guests, were well through their meals. There were about ten tables, mostly couples including at least two who looked as if they were gay.

Tony looked around once they sat down, and turning to Martin observed, 'Well, this might not be the secluded get away with just the two of us together that we planned, but you know what, it suits me fine!' The meal was excellent, a set meal with just a couple of choices. They both ordered the chicken dish for main course. Martin ordered a good bottle of red wine and the two men started to relax. By the time they had finished the other diners had left and the dining room was empty.

'Before we go to bed, and I am looking forward to that,' Tony reached across the table and squeezed Martin's hand, 'let's just go for a walk, I want to feel the country night.' They walked down the path towards the road. The house was out in the country and as soon as they had walked a few minutes it was absolutely dark, with no street lights, but just the wondrous sky to light their way. It was a clear night with just a tiny sliver of a moon. The warmth of the day lingered and there was not a breath in the air. To save craning their necks to see the stars they laid down on a grassy verge staring up at the sky.

'How amazing is that,' Martin almost whispered, 'it is like a carpet of stars. We just have no idea in the city what is above us.

'I find it a bit frightening,' Tony commented, 'so vast with numbers that are so huge I could never comprehend what they mean. I feel on the one hand that we are so inconsequential in the vastness of it all, and yet at the same time I am the centre of at least what I experience from my place in the universe. I don't know how to bring those two things together.'

'Maybe they are already together, they are one,' Martin said.

'That sounds very deep.'

'I did a course in Buddhism once,' Martin offered, 'I spent ages trying to understand what 'oneness' meant.'

'And did you work it out?'

'No, not really.' They both laughed.

Tony said, 'Well it certainly puts into perspective that bigoted woman's refusal to have two men sleeping together in one bed!'

'Talking of which...' Tony rolled over and kissed Martin. 'Let's go to bed."

****

Thelma felt better, calmer once the first few mouthfuls of the gin and tonic started to work their magic. She sighed as she watched the bubbles dance to the top of the glass. She started to reflect on her life, and was not very happy with what she saw. In a moment of truth as if a veil of mist had been gently blown away, her life came into focus, crisp and defined. She suddenly felt a bit frightened and alone. It was not so much that she and Gordon had grown apart since his forced retirement but rather that they had grown apart years ago and only now was that unmasked so that she could not avoid it any longer. At some level she had been vaguely aware that their relationship did not satisfy her for a long time. It was hard to say when it happened. In the early days of their marriage they were always out at dances, plays, all sorts of events. As Gordon got more and more involved in his work, and as Martin was young and needed to be cared for, those outings gradually stopped. Nowadays they lived a life of habit; there was a certain functionality of sharing a home, a routine of established patterns and protocols. Long gone were the days when she looked forward to him walking through the door, wanted to kiss him, feel the stubble on his cheek, smell his manly presence, please him. She suddenly remembered those nights when she was keen to go to bed, to turn off the light and reach for him, both of them full of eagerness. For god's sake she used to seduce him! Even if it was not the passion of Sergei, she was keen for sex in those early days. How things had changed!

Time was ticking by, and soon enough they would be old. She thought of some of the health problems already besetting some of her friends. If only he would do something with his life instead of moping around at a loose end, with occasional trips to the golf course. Maybe she should take up some sort of activity to get out of the house, out of the routine; a painting class? Actually she felt more like getting on a plane and going somewhere where she could immerse herself in culture and escape all the problems at home; away from Gordon and away from having to pursue the question of Martin's sexuality. She wanted to escape from her current life.

An overseas trip was impractical, but at least she could find an art class and join it. The more she thought about it, the more it appealed to her. She reached for the local newspaper to see if there was anything advertised there. She scanned it from the first page to the last but could not find any references to art classes at all. She then remembered that her former colleague at her part time work used to go to art classes. She called her and indeed Pat was able to recommend a group that operated out of Chatswood, just down the road. She determined to call them up and see if she could join. It would have to wait until the next day as it was after 5.00 p.m. and Gordon would be home soon and looking for dinner. Thelma decided to have another gin and tonic, this one just a little bit stronger.

****

Both young men had been looking forward to this moment, getting to bed; their first real trip away together in a hotel. It seemed to them both that this was making more of a statement about being together than the weekends they spent at Martin's house. They were staying publicly as a couple. Martin was quite surprised to find that he liked it.

'Well, Mister, and what would you like tonight for your birthday?' Tony reached down to Martin's cock that was already hard. He took his hand away for enough time to deposit some saliva on it, and then put his hand back rubbing the saliva slowly round Martin's bare glans. Martin shuddered a little and then whispered in Tony's ear.

'I think you know.'

Tony smiled. 'I think I do.'

In the morning they awoke cuddled up together as they had fallen asleep, with Tony's arms round Martin's chest, both on their sides like two spoons together. It was overcast, and a weak sunlight filtered through the heavy chintz curtains. There were some birds chattering away as the day got underway, and other than that just silence, apart from the odd noise from somewhere inside the house as guests awoke and the staff started to prepare the day. No cars, no bustle of the city. Martin reflected that for him there could be no better way of starting his birthday.

'Happy Birthday Mister,' Tony said as he saw Martin open his eyes. He reached for the drawer of the bedside table and took out the small wrapped parcel he had put there the night before. He handed it to Martin and gave him a kiss on the cheek. Martin unwrapped the parcel. Inside there was a small case and inside that a Montblanc Pix manganese orange rollerball pen with Martin's name engraved on it.

'Oh my god, a Montblanc, are you crazy? They are so expensive.'

'Do you like it? I wanted you to have something that would remind you of me when you are at work, perhaps imagine us fucking every time you make notes in meetings.'

'Like it? I adore it! Imagine us fucking indeed, naughty boy! And I love the colour, it is so striking.' Martin turned to Tony and kissed him strongly and passionately on the mouth. 'Thanks so much, it is a really wonderful and very extravagant gift, and I will cherish it every time I use it.'

The boys had a latish substantial breakfast, the sort of indulgence that occurs only occasionally on holidays. It was a traditional full English breakfast down to the black pudding. They headed to Bowral and mingled with the local Saturday morning shoppers. It had started to rain, a gentle and reassuring light rain, and they were glad they had taken their rainproof jackets. They had a coffee and cake in one of the many little cafes along the main street, having decided to skip lunch, and as it was still raining they decided to go and visit Retford Park National Trust house and gardens.

Martin was imagining what it would have been like to have lived there in those days early in the 1900s. In some ways he felt it would have been idyllic. Tony would have preferred something smaller and more modest.

'In any case we would have had to have been very, very discreet in those days or we would have been hounded out of the area or worse,' Tony observed.

'I could have been your butler or manservant,' Martin said.

'You would have been hopeless at that. No I think I would have needed to have been your gardener.' Tony laughed.

They went back to the house where they were staying in the late afternoon, and laid down for a late siesta before dinner, but they ended up having sex again.

'I don't know why I enjoy sex in the afternoons so much,' Tony observed when they laid back in each other's arms.

'You like sex any time and all the time,' Martin said as he squeezed Tony's now limp dick.

'Complaining?' Tony asked.

'Never,' Martin reassured him.

'I will remind you of that after dinner,' Tony threatened.

They went down to the restaurant a bit later than most of the guests, and ate a thoroughly excellent dinner, accompanied by a good pinot noir Hayden from the Cherry Tree Hill estate that Martin chose in order to support local industries. They both found it a bit light compared to the Coonawarra reds they were used to.

In the final event they were both too tired and too mellow for sex again, and they started to drift off to sleep, when suddenly Martin said,

'Oh fuck. I forgot to call my parents. They were expecting me to call for my birthday.'

Tony laughed. 'Too late now honey; you will have to call them tomorrow. You can just say that you were so engrossed in getting fucked by your boyfriend that it slipped your mind.'

'That is what I should say. But won't.' Martin was pensive for a moment, and then added, 'I wish I could.'

'One day. Now forget it and let's sleep.' Tony kissed Martin on the lips.

Martin held the back of Tony's head in his hands and said, 'Thanks for the best birthday I ever had.'

****

Gordon drove into the driveway, a little relieved that he was home without any incident. He knew he must have been over the limit but as the distance between the Golf Club and home was less than two kilometres and he always took the side roads, he figured he would be alright, as long as some idiot did not run into him. He supposed Thelma would have the dinner almost ready and then they would spend the evening in front of the television. At least there were more options to select from since Martin had got them on to Stan and Netflix. He did not like to admit it, but he really struggled with the new technology available nowadays. He accepted Martin's offer of help, and pretended to understand everything he said about how to access the various programmes. He could get Netflix and Stan alright but still had no clue how to get photos from his phone onto the TV screen, even though Martin had shown him.

Thelma was in the kitchen. He noticed with a bit of surprise that there was one of the large cut glass tumblers empty in the lounge room, with a tired slice of lemon in the bottom of the glass. It looked as if she had had a gin and tonic already. He decided to get himself one while Thelma prepared dinner.

'How was golf?' Thelma enquired without the slightest interest in his answer.

'Alright, the usual. I had a chat with the boys afterwards in the bar.' Gordon wondered if he should tell her about the conversation, but decided not to. Thelma did not pursue Gordon's comment.

'Dinner will be in twenty minutes,' she said, 'just a steak and some chips, and a bit of salad.

'I will get the wine.' Gordon went to the wine rack which he kept full of good quality wines that he chose after considerable deliberation. He chose a Riddock shiraz.

By this time of their lives there was not much to talk about over dinner, just the few things that each of them had done during the day. On this particular day neither of them felt like sharing much of what had happened or what they had been thinking about during the day.

There was one thing though. Thelma said, 'Tomorrow is Martin's birthday and normally he would have been with us for dinner tomorrow evening. I half wondered whether he might call before he left for the Southern Highlands, but I expect he will call tomorrow.

'Yes.' said Gordon. 'What did you say that was all about, this weekend away?'

'I wish I knew. He was really cagey about it, very unlike him really. He said he was going away with a mate.'

'A mate you say? Who?'

'I asked him that and he just said that it was someone he hangs out with a bit.'

Gordon decided it was time to share some of his thoughts after all. 'You know today they were talking at the golf club about their kids and their grandkids, and it brought home to me that Martin doesn't seem like most men of his age. Stan and Frank both have grandkids, and here is Martin turning 34 tomorrow without even the sign of a girlfriend on the horizon.

'I know,' Thelma said, 'I have been thinking about that recently. To be honest I had lunch with Renie last Tuesday and she said something that upset me. But then it got me thinking. She said that Martin is homosexual, well gay was the word she used. At first I was angry and dismissed it. But Gordon, the more I think about it I wonder whether she is right.'

Gordon sighed. 'It had crossed my mind too. It wouldn't surprise me and if he is, it is all your fault for having indulged him so much as a child and exposing him to all that cultural stuff. You should have supported me when I wanted him to join the cadets. It would have knocked all that out of him and made him into more of a man.'

Thelma was now a bit angry and she spoke sharply to Gordon. 'Gordon, don't blame me. If he turned out to be like that it is not my fault.'

Gordon was also getting angry. 'Well it is someone's fault and certainly not mine. I don't know if he got into the wrong crowd at Uni, or whether someone we don't know got at him. He is our only child and I don't want him to be like that. What will people say? I can remember the looks that Stan and Frank exchanged at the golf club when I was talking about Martin. It would be so embarrassing, so demeaning, a nancy boy as a son.'

'We don't even know for sure that he is.' Thelma was clutching at straws.

'Well, we have to confront him and ask him what he is going to do about it.'

Thelma softened her tone a bit. 'All I want is for him to be happy. To get married, have children and have a family who will support him and care for him. I know that there is a lot of talk about this gay thing nowadays and saying it is alright. But not in my books. It is not natural. I want something better for

Martin. God knows why they call them gay, when it must be a miserable life.'

'When did he say he would come round?'

'An evening next week he said, but he didn't say which day.'

'When he comes we will confront him and get this sorted out.'

They fell into silence each with their own thoughts and fears. This was the most animated conversation they had had in years.

****

Martin and Tony had decided to take a longer drive back to Sydney via Kangaroo Valley and then up the coast. They took the back way to the road that leads down to Fitzroy Falls. They got out and walked along the paths to look at the falls from both sides. There was much more water than they expected given there had not been significant rain in a long time. They stood there leaning on the railings for quite a while in silence just taking in the views and the sheer beauty of Morton National Park. They were delighted to suddenly hear a lyre bird with its extraordinary vocal performance.

As they drove down into the valley they both marvelled at exactly how beautiful this valley is; a kind of Shangri-la hidden away in a hollow of the escarpment. As they drove over the Hamden Bridge Tony said, 'Isn't this the most out of place construction imaginable here right out in the country? Gothic Revival with crenellated turrets.'

'How the fuck did you know that?' Martin asked with raised eyebrows.

'Aaaah. Well, I did a course on architecture once and this bridge is considered a classic of suspension bridges.'

'I am impressed.' Martin offered.

They decided to have lunch at the local pub in Kangaroo Valley village and then set off along the back road to Berry, climbing from the green and fertile valley floor, twisting and turning round steep curves up the escarpment. The road then follows the top of the ridge between some wonderful ferns and with spectacular views back over the valley. They drove through Berry dodging the tourists as they wandered across the street. After Berry they were on the highway pretty much all the way back to Sydney. Both of them had really enjoyed the weekend and were sorry it was coming to a close. Their mood changed as they thought about the week ahead.

It was Martin who broke the silence. 'It has been a wonderful weekend and I had the best birthday I ever had.'

'Yes me too,' Tony added, 'we don't have to wait for another birthday or any other excuse to do it again.'

'Yes, we should do it again soon.' As his mind turned to home he suddenly remembered his parents. 'Oh fucking hell. I forgot to phone Ma again. She will be either worried or furious, or most likely both. I will call her after I have dropped you off.'

'I'm sorry, I meant to remind you and then I completely forgot too. What excuse are you going to give?'

Tony grimaced as he was driving. 'I don't know. If I say I forgot it sounds bad. I could say that the signal was too weak and there was no reception. And I could say that where there was a signal there were too many people around. I will think of something. I said I would go there one night this week for dinner anyway. I think that might be the night we all have deep and meaningful conversations.'

Tony looked at him knowing how hard this was going to be and yet at the same time it was inevitable. 'Are you prepared? Do you know what you want to say?'

'Yes I think so but I need to think it through a bit more. I don't know which one will be more difficult, Ma or Dad.'

They entered the Sydney greater area and now the traffic was more dense. Martin dropped Tony off at his house in Glebe and then headed home to Paddington. He called his parents' number on the way using hands off and bluetooth.

****

Around five o'clock on Sunday afternoon Thelma said to Gordon, 'It really is not right that he hasn't called us all weekend. It was his birthday yesterday after all. I am a bit angry with him. Sometimes he can be so thoughtless and selfish.

'Did you try and call him?' Gordon responded, 'After all it was his birthday and normally you call people on their birthday and not the other way round.'

'Don't make excuses for him Gordon, you know very well he was going away and it would have seemed a bit wrong for me to call him. It was up to him to call me.'

'Us.'

'Well, yes, us,' she conceded.

It was after six o'clock that the landline phone rang. 'Seven six four three, hello.' God, it annoyed Martin the way she answered the phone. He was not quite sure why, but it did. She put the phone on loud speaker and Martin correctly guessed that his father was listening.

'Hi Ma it's me.' He tried to sound as relaxed and upbeat as possible.

'At last, Martin! She always called him by his name when she was angry with him. 'And why didn't you call me yesterday so that we could wish our only son happy birthday?'

'I am sorry Ma, I was out in the country and there was no signal, and then today there were too many people around and it would have to have been on loud speaker and I was not going to be comfortable with that. I am on my way home and this is the first chance I have had.'

Gordon indicated to her by waving his hand in a downwards motion to cool it. He could just see this was going to get out of hand and he was afraid Thelma would say something they both might regret.

'I am sorry Martin but that is not good enough. We are your parents.'

'Ma I said I was sorry. So, are you going to wish me happy birthday?'

Thelma felt she was trapped. 'For yesterday, yes.' There was long pause until she added, 'Yes happy birthday darling from us both.'

'Thanks Ma. And Dad. I said I was going to come round for dinner one night this week. How about Tuesday? I could come straight after work.'

'Yes I think that would be alright.' Thelma looked at Gordon and he nodded.

'Okay, see you around 6.30 Tuesday.' Martin knew that that had been the easy part.

****

'So have you decided how you are going to tell them?' Tony was chatting on the phone with Martin on Monday evening.

'I have been rehearsing sets of words in my mind, and I am still not sure. I think I will just wing it depending on how the land lies when I get there.' Martin sounded apprehensive.

'When I told my mum at the age of twenty three she just said she already knew and she couldn't understand how it had taken me so long to work it out. She said she was aware when I was a teenager that I was different. My dad was really laid back about life in general, nothing seemed to faze him and so in the end it was not an issue. They were both really supportive.'

'Your mum is very different from mine, far more socially progressive. With my dad, he is very traditional but he is harder to pick. Anyway, we will see tomorrow.'

Tony said in a very caring voice, 'I hope it all goes alright. However it works out try not to get upset and don't say anything you will later regret. Let me know.'

Meanwhile Thelma and Gordon had had a similar conversation about Tuesday's meeting with Martin. On Tuesday afternoon, they sat down for a coffee. Gordon had been reluctantly doing some light work tidying up the garden. The gardener was due later in the week, but now he had so much time on his hands he would sometimes get the blower/vacuum to suck up the leaves, and potter around tidying up the pot plants outside the French doors of the sitting room.

Thelma had been preoccupied thinking about that evening and had not done much all day. She was going to prepare a meal that she knew Martin liked, homemade beef and kidney pie, correctly surmising that it was not something that he would bother to cook for himself. In the morning she made a pumpkin soup that she knew Martin liked and in the afternoon she got the pie ready to bake in the oven.

Thelma put Gordon's mug of coffee on the side table and said, 'I think you should broach the subject.'

Knowing exactly what she was referring to Gordon responded, 'No it is much better coming from you. You are far better with that sort of thing than I am, and in any case he is much closer to you than to me.'

'Do you think it better to approach it by asking about the weekend, or just ask him straight out if he is homosexual?' Thelma was addressing the question as much to herself as she was to Gordon.

'I wouldn't use that word.'

Thelma ignored him. 'I could just ask him why he hasn't got a girlfriend and see what he says.' She was beginning to prefer that approach.

Gordon was tiring of this conversation and it was something in any case that he did not want to confront and found distasteful. 'I am sure you will find the right words when it comes to it. Maybe wait until after dinner.'

It was with a lot of apprehension that Martin headed up the Pacific Highway after work on Tuesday. Yet he was determined to have the conversation about being gay. He wanted to tell them about Tony. He pulled into the all too familiar drive through the substantial open gates painted green to blend in with the garden, remembering the crunch of the stones beneath the tyres. He parked in front of the large bay window. He could see a figure inside move, presumably to let him in. He locked the car and the front door opened as he approached before he even had time to ring the bell. His mother greeted him with a kiss on the cheek. But she did not say anything.

'Hi Ma.'

'Your father is the lounge reading the paper.' She wondered why she had said that as soon as she said it. They walked into the lounge room, Gordon looked up from his paper, stood up and he and Martin shook hands.

Thelma asked Martin, 'Would you like a G&T? We were just going to have one.'

'No thanks, Ma, I am driving, but go ahead.'

Martin noticed that she was a bit heavy handed with the gin and figured that they were both a bit nervous and not their usually relaxed selves.

'So, how is work?' Thelma chose a non controversial topic to start off with.

Martin was prepared to play along with what seemed to be evolving as the plan and suspected that questions would come during or after dinner. 'Fine. Busy. We are in the middle of doing budgets and then the plant had a hiccup and so everyone is running around trying to find stock to get out to customers.'

'They always seem to have problems at that plant,' Gordon observed.

'Yes, well it is a bit old and they try and run it hard and don't make enough time to do maintenance, and so that is what you get. It is very short-sighted but that is how they operate.'

Gordon felt on safe ground now. 'I always used to insist that they did their annual maintenance over Christmas. I know many of the plant maintenance people did not like it, because it meant they could not take holidays with their kids during that time. But it was important for the business and so I insisted on it. It caused a bit of friction.' He laughed.

'Do you miss work?' Martin also felt this was safer ground. Thelma looked sharply at Gordon interested to see what he would answer.

'On some levels I do and then others I don't. I am glad to be free of all the politics that started when the Yanks started to get more involved. It changed the culture of the firm. But I do get a bit bored. I guess that is to be expected. I haven't quite found the right path into retirement yet, even though it has been almost two years.'

Thelma saw her chance. 'I wish he would find some interest or occupation. He spends far too much time moping around the house.'

Martin could feel the tension between them.

There was a silence of a few moments and then Thelma said, 'I will go and get dinner ready. It is just about done; your favourite, steak and kidney pie with some pumpkin soup to start.'

'Thanks Ma. I could smell it when I came in.'

Martin and Gordon engaged in some small talk about the garden, the house, Martin's work, Gordon's phone plan with which he was not happy, until Thelma called from the dining room.

'Dinner is on the table.'

They went into the dining room, Gordon and Thelma sitting opposite each other and Martin between them on the other side of the rectangular table.

'Nice glass of red? It is a Coonawarra,' Gordon offered.

'Just the one. I am driving and I don't take risks.'

Gordon poured the wine. Thelma raised her glass and said, 'Here's to your birthday, belated though it may be.' They clinked glasses. Martin felt that the word 'belated' was a little barbed. As they ate they exchanged small talk again. It was as if there was an elephant in the room everyone was trying to avoid. Thelma recounted the various miseries besetting people Martin barely knew, such as neighbours and distant relatives Martin had not seen in years.

As they finished the main course Thelma asked, 'So how was the weekend?' They were getting down to business.

'Superbly excellent! The best birthday I can remember.'

Thelma was taken aback at the animated exuberance Martin displayed. It was quite out of character, and it was not the response she expected. Even Gordon raised an eyebrow.

'Oh, I am happy that.....'

Martin interrupted her. Now was the time, at last. 'Look there is something you need to know. I am gay. I went away this weekend with Tony. He is a wonderful guy and we have been dating for quite a while.'

Thelma and Gordon exchanged glances. Thelma said, 'Don't be ridiculous Martin of course you are not a homosex...er gay. You look completely normal; there is nothing odd about you at all. You just have not found the right girl and have lost your way a bit.'

Gordon added, 'Martin this has to stop. Now. If you need help from a psychiatrist to get you through this period, I am happy to help out with the costs. But I don't want to hear any more about that man or about you being a homosexual.'

Martin was taken aback; denial was not one of the scenarios he had worked through in his mind. While he was sorting out how to respond, Thelma took the floor again. 'I am your mother and I know you better than you even know yourself. I have always said to you that you will only be happy once you get married, have a family and settle down. This drifting around is no good for you. You are 34 now and it is time you got married.'

Martin went entirely off script now, his planned speech was redundant. 'Let me repeat it, I am gay. I have always been gay and I always will be. This is not something I chose, it is something that I am. I am never going to marry a woman and have children; it would ruin at least two lives, mine and hers. I am perfectly happy with who I am. I am asking you please to accept me as I am. Nothing has changed; it is just that you know a bit more about me. There will be no wife, no grandchildren, and I am sorry that you will be deprived of that because I know you would have liked to have had grandchildren.' Then he added, 'And no psychiatrists.'

Thelma tried another tack. 'Are you saying that you have never had a girlfriend, that you never, you know, made love?'

Martin was now getting angry. 'I never ask you about your sex lives, and I shudder at the thought. And I don't expect you to ask me about mine. Suffice it to say that I am only attracted to other men and I always have been.'

Gordon shuddered. 'This is utterly shameful. It is wrong. It is not natural. I can't believe I am hearing this from a son of mine.'

'In what way is it wrong? Who says so?'

Gordon snapped back, 'You know very well that this is not in the natural order of things. Men and women are supposed to get married and have children, that is how the human race survives.'

Martin countered, 'There are already far too many people on earth and a few less is no bad thing. The human race will still survive. Gay men and women have been part of society from the beginning of history. We may not be the majority, but we are neither unnatural nor wrong or shameful.' Martin could not believe how in control he must have appeared, while inside he was shaking partly with anger and partly in fear.

Thelma reflected that Martin had always been bright and mounted strong arguments. That had not changed. He could also be quite single minded. She decided to take another approach again. 'All I want is for you to be happy. This is not a life that could ever be happy. You will not have the comfort and support of a family, it might affect your career, and people will discriminate against you.'

'To start with Ma, this is not something where I have a choice. It is what I am. Just like the colour of my hair or eyes. I was this way from the day I was born. Secondly this is the twenty first century now, and attitudes have changed, especially in places like Sydney. Maybe thirty years ago, yes, it would have been more difficult, but nowadays it is not an issue.' Martin thought about the B&B where they were turned away, and added, 'Generally.'

Martin continued, 'I am happy. I just want you both to accept me as I am. I know you are disappointed, but I can't help that or change that. Only you can.'

'You risk being lonely in your old age, nobody to look after you, no family,' Thelma said.

'Even those with children can end up lonely and in homes. Nothing is guaranteed in this world.' Was this a veiled threat that Martin was delivering to them?

Thelma suddenly thought about her own old age. Would Martin be there to look after her? Probably not, especially if there is no wife.

'I know lots of guys who have been in long term relationships. Nowadays I don't think gay guys are any more lonely than anyone else.' Martin was countering all of their arguments.

Thelma was doubtful, she could just not see how any man could be happy unless he had a wife and children. But suddenly she was gripped with fear. It had only just come into her mind. 'What about this AIDS thing? You are alright aren't you?' she asked.

'Of course I am. Both Tony and I are very careful. You should know me better than that, I am always careful,' Martin reassured her. Thelma still looked concerned.

Gordon realised that there was not much he or anyone else could do about this situation. 'Well, son, let me say I don't like this at all. And I certainly do not want any of your funny friends round here.'

'You need to know that Tony is an important part of my life. He is a wonderful man, and I would have liked you to meet him.' Martin was standing firm.

'I don't think so!' said Thelma somewhat acerbically.

There was a silence of what seemed like minutes, while they each considered their options.

Martin broke the silence, 'Well I think I should go. I have quite an important meeting in the morning.'

'Thanks for coming.' Thelma regretted the words immediately as she could see how meaningless and stupid they were, but she had to say something. Martin stood up first and then Thelma and Gordon; he gave his mother a light peck on the cheek and went to shake hands with his father. Gordon, thinking that to shake hands might give the impression that he was accepting any of this withdrew his handshake.

Martin walked to the front door and opened it. He strode to the car not looking back. Thelma and Gordon stood silently in the doorway and watched as Martin got in the car and headed quite fast down the drive without waving.

****

Thelma headed to the table where the gin was. 'I need a drink. Do you want one?'

'I'll get them. You sit down. Gin and tonic? I might have a scotch.' Gordon poured the drinks and they sat down in the lounge chairs.

Thelma sighed. 'I sort of knew this was coming,' she said resignedly.

Gordon was reflective, 'We should have picked it up before. Then we could have stamped it out early on, and it would never have come to this. When I think back there were signs. You always mollycoddled him.'

'Don't blame me,' Thelma protested. 'Look at that cousin of yours, James, he never got married and I always thought there was something odd about him. I think it probably comes from your side.'

'Does it really matter?' Gordon was a bit edgy. 'What are we going to do about it?'

'Well, if he won't go and see anyone, there is nothing much we can do. He was adamant that he is not going to change. He is 34 now, an adult, and we can't force him to do anything he doesn't want to.' Thelma sounded resigned. 'I always wanted grandchildren and it looks as if I will never have them.'

'There is nothing much you can do about it, I agree. We just have to accept that there will be no grandchildren. When I hear Frank and Stan from the golf club talking about their grandchildren I must admit I feel a bit envious.'

There was a silence between them for a few minutes, each resting with their own thoughts and preoccupations.

'Thelma broke the silence. 'What actually do they do?'

'What do you mean?'

'Homosexuals, what do they do with each other?'

Gordon blushed a little; he was not used to such talk with Thelma. And when he thought about it he found the whole idea distasteful, especially the anal thing. But surely Martin would not do that disgusting sort of stuff. He thought about oral sex and for a second he almost felt envious. Thelma had never liked it and he suddenly thought about what he had missed. He did not feel like getting into talking about oral sex with Thelma now.

'I suppose they fool around with each other, I prefer not to think about it.'

'Do you suppose they kiss?' Thelma felt quite sick at the thought of Martin kissing another man, it just was not right.

Gordon was annoyed now. 'How would I know what they do? I am not an expert in perversions. Frankly I am over the whole thing; it is like I lost a son. If you want to know ask him, or google it.' Gordon pondered on the lost son theme. 'I did think about whether we should cut him out of the will.'

'Oh don't be ridiculous. He is still our son after all, and who else would we leave it to? The dogs' home?'

'I suppose you are right. And what good would it serve anyway? We could hardly use that as blackmail to force him to stop this stuff. That might be tempting but I don't think it would work.' Gordon was still toying with the idea, but as he worked it through it did not really make sense. Yes he was angry about it, but cutting Martin out of his inheritance would not really serve any useful purpose. It might make Gordon feel better, that he had made a statement. But after consideration, it was too harsh.

Thelma continued the theme, 'Knowing Martin he would probably dig in even more. He can be very single minded, even stubborn actually. No, we can't cut him off.' She waited a few moments. 'Gordon, what are our friends going to say? Or your brother and sister and Martin's cousins?'

'We don't tell them.' Gordon made a decision.

'Well Renie already knows. Somehow she worked it out. She brought it up when I had lunch with her a few weeks ago.' Thelma thought for a moment. 'Actually it did not seem anything surprising to her really. But it is not her child. I am sure she would feel different if it had turned out that she had a son like that. It is easy to be liberal in your views when it is about other people and not your own.'

'So what are we going to do?' asked Gordon wanting to bring this all to a close.

'Nothing. Just live with it, I suppose. But I don't want to meet Tony or any of his other homosexual friends for that matter. He will not pass the threshold into my house.' Thelma was totally sure about that. That decision was clear and firm at that moment in time but would confront her again in due course.

'Agreed. I am going to bed; I have had enough for today.' Gordon got up and walked to the kitchen to get a glass of water before he retired.

****

Martin headed down the Pacific Highway, barely concentrating on the road. He called Tony using his Bluetooth and hands free.

Tony picked up immediately. 'How did you go?'

'Not brilliant. I had not anticipated that to start with they were just in total denial. They kept saying that I wasn't gay.'

'They should have asked me, I would have told them.'

'I don't think that would have helped! They were very upset. The only thing I can say is that they did not throw me out. But they do not approve and what probably hurt me the most is that they refused to meet you.

'You told them about me?'

'Yes of course. That is one of the reasons I told them I am gay. I wanted them to meet you.'

'It will take them a while to get used to the idea, especially if they had not really already worked it out. You are their only son. In my case there are my two brothers and they will provide the grandchildren I won't.'

'I think part of the problem is that they just don't understand it. I think they believe it is a choice that I made. So if I wanted to I could unmake it. And to be honest, especially

89

knowing my mother, they will be scared about what the neighbours will say.'

'So how did you leave it?'

'They told me how much they disapproved and in the end the conversation sort of came to a halt and I told them I should go as I have a meeting in the morning. My mother gave me a peck on the cheek and my father refused to shake hands with me. And that hurt.'

'Yes it would. That is exactly why he did it.'

'Do you want me to come over or do you want to be on your own?' Tony was always considerate.

'Can I pick you up? I need to go to work early tomorrow but I just feel like a hug.'

'Okay. I don't have rehearsals until late tomorrow and so I can sleep in while you go to work. I suppose I might get you breakfast.' Tony laughed.

Martin changed lane to get into the right lane for the western distributor so that he could pick Tony up in Glebe. 'Be there in ten.'

Tony was waiting outside when Martin got there. He jumped into the passenger seat and leaned over and gave Martin a kiss. Martin was as perfectly presented as he always was, hair in place, his clothes immaculate, but pale and Tony thought he looked shaken and sad.

Martin looked at him and gave him a faint smile. 'I am just so disappointed.' His voice sounded thin and full of emotion.

Tony placed his hand on Martin's thigh as they drove off into the traffic. 'I know you are,' he said, 'but I also think that eventually they will accept it and it will work out.'

'I hope so. But I am not going to change, I am gay and there is nothing I can do about it, or would want to. They are the ones who will have to change.'

****

'Good morning, my name is Thelma Grant, a friend of mine Pat Stuart gave me your number, and I am interested in joining an art class. Pat told me that you are running art classes.' Thelma had not slept well after the disastrous dinner with Martin, but she was determined to get on with her life. Rather than drawing her and Gordon together over Martin, she felt that it had pushed them apart even further. She was not sure why, because logically they would have had their concerns in common. Gordon somehow did not seem to be as upset about it as she was, or at least not in the same way. Maybe they just showed their emotions in different ways, and in essence she thought that was the nub of the problem.

'Yes, Thelma, we do; at the Art Craft School in Chatswood. We have classes for most people. Have you already got some expertise and experience?'

'Well, no, not really. I used to draw when I was younger and people said I was quite good.'

'I would suggest our adult classes for beginners, and you can progress from there. Those classes are every Tuesday from 2.00 pm until 4.00 pm or also on Saturdays. If you are able to come in the week, I think it better as there are fewer people and you get more intense tuition.'

Thelma did not hesitate, 'Yes Tuesdays suit me fine. When can I start?'

'Come next Tuesday. Your tutor will be Sebastian. He is very experienced and I am sure you will enjoy it. Should I just run over the fee structure?'

'No it doesn't matter.' Thelma regretted saying that the moment the words left her mouth. It came across maybe as if she was so wealthy it did not matter. 'She added, 'I am sure the rates will be fine. Do I pay class at a time or do I pay for the whole series?'

'You can do either. Let's sort it out if you come in a bit earlier next Tuesday. Do you know where we are?'

'On the Pacific Highway near the school?'

'Yes that is right. Not far from the station.'

****

Gordon felt even more depressed than ever. His life was a mess. He didn't understand how Martin could have turned out to be a homosexual. He went online a few days after Martin's visit to try and understand more. His business career had taught him that he needed as much information as possible to deal with difficult situations and he recognised that while there was a lot of popular comment about the subject, he did not know the educated thinking about it. He cringed at the thought that people would call his son a shirt lifter, or a pillow biter.

What he found came as a bit of a surprise. With some horror he read about conversion therapy and how most of the negative attitudes towards homosexuality came from the religions. He had never had much time for religion and so he tended to discard what people thought the bible said about it. The two salient things that came from his several hours of browsing were that the percentages of homosexuals seemed to be more or less the same irrespective of nationality or race, and the fact that people seemed to have no choice in the matter. It appears that this was something that was pretty much set when children were very young, and that there may be a genetic predisposition or possibly some hormone or other influences during pregnancy. It was clearly a complex thing, but what all serious researchers seemed to say is that it is not a choice that people make; their sexual orientation is part of them, they cannot change it. That was exactly what Martin had said, and it seems he was right. What that also meant was that Martin being gay was not in any way their fault. Come to think of it he had always at some subliminal level known that Martin was not quite like other boys when he was growing up. He didn't get into trouble, he didn't climb trees, or even seem to enjoy playing cowboys and Indians. He never kicked a football around the yard. It was so obvious now, but at the time those things subconsciously annoyed him, and he took it out on Martin, and blamed Thelma for cosseting him too much. Suddenly he felt sorry for Martin, and was especially regretful for some of the things he had said to

92

him that evening. He had always assumed that it was a choice that people made, and now he understood that it absolutely was not. The choice was made for Martin, not by him.

He suddenly felt very lonely. He did not think Thelma would listen or really understand. She did not want to understand. And it was not something that he could discuss with his mates at the golf club. Maybe he should think about having dinner with Martin one night, just the two of them, and perhaps he could make amends. How did he feel about Tony? That was going to take a bit more time getting used to. .

A few days later Gordon was still turning things over in his mind. He had not yet discussed with Thelma what he found through his online research. He had been to golf a couple of times, but could not bring himself to bring up the subject of Martin with his mates. Thelma was out somewhere or other, he was not quite sure where. Had she told him and he had not really listened? He could not be sure.

It was a beautiful Sydney day, clear blue sky, the air sparkling and full of brightness and colour. It was warm with a slight breeze. What a wonderful climate, he thought. He remembered his visits to the USA this time of year with grey depressing and oppressive skies and how he would come home and be struck by how sharp and bright everything was in Australia. He decided on the spur of the moment to walk down to the local park. He needed the exercise and it had been ages, years even, since he went there.

The park is about fifteen minutes walk along the tree lined streets of the suburb where they lived on the north shore. It was quite a large park, natural with trees and grass and only a few flower beds. It looked neat and tidy and he recognised that the local council kept it in good order. He walked slowly along the path towards the centre of the park. There was a bench seat under a huge fig tree. He sat down intending to just take in the tranquillity of the surroundings. He closed his eyes and listened. He could hear the slight breeze tease the leaves on the tree; it sounded almost like water. Then he realised that there were lots of birds; they must be around all the time but he never noticed them. All this had passed him by him by as he had spent his life climbing the corporate ladder, and he was wondering what really was important, and regretted all those years he had missed out on just being.

His reverie was broken as a voice said, 'Do you mind if I sit down?'

He looked up and saw a young woman with a child aged maybe about four or five by her side.

'Yes of course.' He moved up slightly to give her more room. She smiled and sat down beside him, her legs crossed. To Gordon she looked as if she would have been late twenties, maybe even thirty. She was casually dressed in a shirt and jeans, a nice neat figure, he observed. She had dark hair and looked as if she was from some none Anglo background.

'Now not too far, Anton,' she said to the child. He sat down on the grass seemingly inspecting it and the clover growing in it.

'He seems happy enough,' Gordon ventured.

'Yes he is a really good child, and is so interested in everything.'

'How old is he?'

'Anton tell the gentleman how old you are,' his mother said to him.

Without looking up Anton very deliberately said, 'Four but more like four and a half.'

Gordon addressed Anton directly, 'So you will be going to school soon?'

But Anton was engrossed in the grass and left it to his mother to answer. 'Yes he starts with the new term. He is looking forward to it, but I'm not!'

'Is he your only child?' Gordon asked.

'Yes he is. I will miss him when he goes to school, and it sort of marks the start of their growing up and eventually leaving home. They are never with you ever again in quite the same way.'

'No but they are with you in deeper ways.' That was simply a platitude and Gordon reflected that was perhaps how it should be and thought about his relationship with Martin and how they had just seemed to grow further apart as he got older.

After a few moments of silence the young woman said, 'I love this park. It is like a haven of peace in the middle of houses and suburbia, a kind of oasis. It is almost like being in the bush.'

'Yes it is lovely,' Gordon agreed, 'I must admit that I have not been here for years. I have lived in the area pretty much all my life and I can't remember the last time I came here. It hasn't changed much, and I think that is because they have just kept it natural. I was at a bit of a loose end this afternoon, I am retired now, and I just decided on a whim to come here and see if it had changed.'

'I must go,' she said, 'Oh I am Natalia,' offering her hand.

He shook her offered hand saying, 'Gordon.'

'I often bring Anton to the park in the afternoon, so I might see you around again.'

They walked away down the path with Anton holding his hand up for the security of his mother's hand.

Gordon felt a pang of regret. How he would have loved to have had grandchildren, so trusting and innocent. Maybe he would have managed to be a better grandfather than he had been as a father. He mused again about Natalia, thinking it was not a very Aussie name. He liked her, and was wondering what her story was. Is there a husband? She did not mention one. Did she work, did she live locally?

Gordon decided to go to the park again a few days later. He had done the few odd jobs round the house that needed his attention, and he had been to golf again twice, and now he wanted a change and to get out of the house again, and the exercise walking to the park would do him good. In reality he was bored. He mused that he was perhaps deluding himself a bit, and if he was honest, he hoped he might meet Natalia and Anton again; in some strange way he was fascinated by them. Thelma looked a bit surprised when he said he was going for a walk, but she made no comment.

He felt good, even had a spring in his step as he walked to the park. The same bench was free and he sat down taking in the grass and trees as they fell away down the slight hill. After a while he heard a 'hello,' and as he looked up there was Natalia, with Anton at her side.

'Oh Natalia, hello, come and sit down.'

Natalia sat down next to Gordon on the bench and Anton looked at Gordon.

'My name is Anton,' he said.

'Yes I know,' Gordon responded, 'and you are four and a half years old.'

'Yes and I am going to school soon. You must have gone to school a very long time ago.'

'Oh Anton, you shouldn't say that,' his mother admonished.

Gordon smiled. 'You are quite right Anton, it was a very long time ago. But I still remember it.' In fact it was the first time for years that Gordon had thought about that little boy at Pymble Primary, so innocent and a bit timid.

Anton had a toy truck and he set about playing with it on the grass.

'Do you have children?' Natalia asked.

'Yes, I have a son, Martin, about your age I guess.'

'And grandchildren?'

'No I am afraid not. Martin is not married.'

'Oh!' was Natalia's response.

And suddenly Gordon wanted to talk about his sadness and Martin, and Natalia seemed so approachable and it would be an anonymous conversation; that was the best part of it. She would not know anyone who knew him, and in any case she did not know him or anything about him.

'You see, Martin is homosexual, you know, um gay,' he blurted out.

Natalia's response was totally unexpected. 'Oh, my father was gay,' she said in a very matter of fact way.

'Your father?' Gordon was incredulous, 'How can...'

Natalia laughed, and started talking, getting Gordon off the hook. 'It is a long story. My parents were Hungarian; I was born in a refugee camp in Austria. My parents met at university in Budapest in the 80s, they both were studying law. I think my mother fell deeply in love with my father, and I can understand it because he was a wonderful man, handsome too. They got on extremely well and spent a lot of time together. In the end my father told my mother that he was gay and he couldn't marry her. If he had not been gay he said he would have married her. In those days in Hungary being gay was exceptionally difficult. In the soviet times it was frowned on and then after the changes in 1989 and the end of communism the Catholic Church started to flex its muscles again. Perhaps even worse it was very heavily stigmatised by most of the population even if it wasn't exactly illegal. My mother suggested that despite him being gay they should get married, that she was prepared to accept him exactly as he was.'

'At first my father told me he was reluctant because while he did love my mother in one way, he did not feel he could be a complete husband to her. She appeared not to care, as she was more interested in the non sexual aspects of relationships. As she used to say, we spend more time out of bed than in bed, and mostly once in bed we sleep. I think it was actually a very happy marriage for the most part.'

'But you came along, so it must have worked at least sometimes.' Gordon was now a bit puzzled.

Natalia laughed. 'Yes, I guess so. Maybe he was bisexual with a strong leaning towards men. Many gay men are biological fathers. It is just that that is not what really satisfies them. Today I am sure they would not have got married, things have changed and it is so much easier for gay people to lead their lives true to who they really are.'

Gordon was wondering what the implications of hearing this were for Martin. 'So you think it is possible for a gay man to get married and live a normal life?'

'Well I wouldn't say my parents were in any way normal, they were actually extraordinary people in their own way, both of them. It was very unusual, and it only worked because at the time it was just too hard for my father to come out and be gay. So in those days the alternative would have been for him to live in the shadows, possibly a lonely but certainly not a fulfilled life. I know my parents had an understanding when they got married. Just from something my father once said I think that in Hungary he used to go to the public baths sometimes, Budapest is famous for them.'

'So how do you feel about your father being gay?'

'They told me when I was about 16, both of them together, holding hands, I remember it so well. As you might imagine they had brought me up to have very liberal values anyway. I had asked them why they slept in different rooms, because most of my friends' parents seemed to sleep together. They never really answered that when I was younger. They explained their decision to marry by saying that they loved each other, and reassured me that they both loved me, and made it quite clear that they had both known all along about my Dad and had made their decision to marry anyway. And they both said that it was a decision that neither of them had ever regretted. It was presented as no big deal for them, and so that was also the way I took it. If they had lived at a different time and in a different place, everything would have been different. And I would not have been here.'

'That is an amazing story.' Gordon smiled at Natalia. And then serious again he asked, 'You kept saying 'were,' are they still alive?'

Natalia looked down. 'No, neither of them. My father died in an accident and I lost my mother two years ago to cancer.'

'That must have been very hard for you.'

'Yes it was, and hard for Anton as well. He has no grandparents, no brothers and sisters and no cousins. I wanted a child and was determined to have one. Anton's father sort of did me a favour, no obligations and so he has never been part of Anton's life.

Gordon looked at Anton busy playing on the grass, and suddenly he felt a surge of compassion or some such emotion sweep over him. He had never felt anything like it before. He wanted to pick him up and hug him and tell him he was not alone. But of course he didn't, he just sat there looking at him. It was as if he had fallen from the sky into another world, one he did not know and was trying desperately to understand. .

****

There was just something about Tony, the way he seemed to understand Martin, and was always there for him, especially when he needed him. Tony had a kind of intuition about how Martin felt. Within a few seconds of a phone call, if there was something wrong or something on Martin's mind, a problem he was trying to deal with, Tony immediately knew. The night of the dinner with his parents, after Martin had picked him up on the way home, when they got to Martin's place Tony was watching him closely and tried to comfort him the best he could. Martin made a tea for them both and they sat on the sofa, side by side, close together in silence. Tony put his arms round Martin, but did not say anything; he felt it was better to wait and see if Martin wanted to talk or just stay with his thoughts. Then Martin said he just felt like going to bed. Once in bed, Tony turned Martin on his side and put his arm around his chest holding him tight, and just kissed him lightly in the nape of his neck and then nuzzled his ear, their naked bodies spooned together. Martin felt so secure, so loved, and that was all he wanted right then and Tony seemed to know it. Martin held Tony's hand and squeezed it and within a few minutes they were both asleep.

Martin was still asleep when Tony gently extricated himself from him and quietly got out of bed. He made some coffee, and poured a glass of orange juice. He got out the toaster and two slices of wholegrain bread, and the butter and vegemite. He then woke Martin with a kiss on the forehead and told him breakfast was virtually ready, handing him the orange juice. This was Martin's habitual breakfast, Tony knew well. Tony normally did not eat breakfast but he poured them both a coffee and they sat together at the breakfast bar in the kitchen.

'I need to get ready and go. Reluctantly.' Martin said. 'What are you going to do?'

'I might leave with you if you can drop me at the bus stop and then I will head home to do some practice.'

Tony finished his coffee while Martin had a shower and dressed. In the car on the way to the bus stop Martin said, 'I am so grateful that you came over last night, it is just what I needed. I am okay, a bit sad, but I am so glad I have you in my life.'

'The feeling is mutual. See you Friday?' Tony kissed Martin lightly on the cheek and got out of the car.

As he drove off Martin thought that while he felt bad about how the dinner with his parents had gone, overall his life was pretty good. He and Tony just got closer together; he was very comfortable in this relationship and he had no plans at all to change it. They were very different in some ways, but their differences seemed to complement each other, and most importantly of all they had similar value systems.

Martin parked the car and walked to his desk. He had hardly sat down when his boss David came into his office. It was not David who appointed Martin, but his predecessor Noel, with whom Martin had had a very good relationship. David was in his 50s, good at marketing and knew the business well. He was savvy and astute. But he was not a good manager, and it was typical of him to leave things to the last minute and then cut corners to get them done. They had a cordial but not very warm relationship; Martin respected his abilities but he did not like him very much, and suspected that the feeling was mutual. David was very much the Rugby League, sporty man's man kind of person. He was married with three teenage children but he never seemed to spend much time at home.

'Oh Martin, are you busy for half an hour or so?'

'There is nothing that can't wait, why?'

'It is about the annual performance assessments. I am a bit late doing them and now I have HR breathing down my neck, and so I thought if you have time we could do it now.'

Martin was a bit taken aback, but could not really say no. He just said 'Oh!' and nothing more.

'Let's go into Meeting Room two, we will have more privacy there.'

As they walked to the Meeting Room, Martin collected his thoughts and when they sat down he said, 'Aren't I supposed to fill out the form too before this discussion?'

'Well yes, in principle, but these were supposed to be in last week and so we need to get it done quickly.'

Martin did not like lack of due process. 'I don't want it to look as if I couldn't be bothered to fill out the form.'

'Well, alright, you can fill your part out later if you want but I need it immediately really.' David then opened the Performance Assessment Framework document that went for several pages. He handed Martin a blank copy. It included some general items and a few specific Key Performance Indicators for his job. Those KPIs that were specific to his job were supposed to have been discussed and agreed between them at the beginning of the year. But of course David had never done that.

'I think this will be relatively straightforward,' David commented. They went through the form item by item, with David saying what he thought the outcome was for each one. He did not solicit Martin's perspective. Martin was thinking that David had no way of really knowing. They were supposed to sit down once a month to discuss both Martin's work schedule and any issues that had arisen or might arise. But David was always too busy and so it didn't happen. His comments were therefore totally arbitrary, Martin thought.

For the most part Martin was prepared to go along with David's comments, reflecting that he was on top of the job and doing well. But then they came to a specific KPI about the profitability of the business area Martin was responsible for as Market Manager.

'This is probably the most important one of all,' David said seriously, 'after all it is profit that we are here to produce. And I have to say that this is a very significant fail. The profit in your area is 20% below budget.'

Martin was indignant and rather annoyed. He said, 'Well David it is hardly surprising given that reactor two blew up early in the year and there was no stock to sell for two months while they repaired it. I spent hours and hours of my own time liaising with the technical department to try and allocate product that was off spec to those customers who could still use it. As a result there were only two customers who had to stop production, and that was a considerable achievement under the circumstances.'

'Be that as it may, the fact is that this is the KPI and you did not meet it.' David said firmly.

By now Martin was quite angry but he tried hard not show it, and speaking calmly he said, 'I cannot be held responsible for things that are entirely out of my control.'

'I can't do anything but put it down as a fail.' David was standing his ground.

'It needs a note that this was due to circumstances beyond my control and that my performance should not be downgraded because of it.' Martin was adamant.

'There is no place on the form to say anything like that. For God's sake Martin it is only an appraisal form.'

'Yes and the basis for salary reviews,' Martin pointed out.

'Well let's move on.' David was uncomfortable.

When they got to the end Martin was not in a good mood. Then David suddenly asked, 'Were you a loner as a child?'

'A loner? No I don't think so, why?'

David took a deep breath. 'Well you are not really a team player, are you?'

Martin was on his guard as he was not sure where this was going. 'I wouldn't say that at all.'

'Let me put it like this, you don't go to the pub on Friday evenings with the boys. You don't turn up at events. For example you did not come to the cricket match between sales and operations where everyone turned up with their families. Many of us socialise outside work with our wives, but you never do.'

Martin had an uneasy feeling about where David was heading with this. He said nothing and just looked at David.

102

David continued. 'Do you think that the fact that you are not married and do not have children is the reason?'

Martin chose his words carefully. 'Frankly I can't see the relevance of any of this to how I perform my job, which is what this discussion is supposed to be all about.'

'Oh but it does, it's all about the team and whether you fit in. I see it as a limiting factor.' David had delivered a clear threat that had consequences for Martin's career progression within the company.

'I invite you to ask around all of my work colleagues and I think you will find that we have totally appropriate working relationships and that I am well respected and liked.' Martin was wondering whether this was true as he said it, but thought that overall it was a fair statement.

'Well just think about it,' David said.

He passed the form over to Martin and said, 'I need you to sign this.' Martin saw that under the general KPI about 'Working as part of a team.' David had written fail.

Martin said, 'I am sorry David but I am not going to sign this. I do not agree with it, and so I am not signing.'

'Up to you,' David said, 'but it will go to HR anyway.' He got up and walked out of the meeting room leaving Martin sitting there fuming.

****

Thelma opened the door cautiously. There was a general smell of paint. She noticed several easels and a few people standing in a loose group chatting. As she approached the group, they turned around to look at her. 'Hello, I'm Thelma. I am joining the art class.' She felt a bit awkward, but the members of the group smiled and murmured a welcome. She felt more at ease.

A man with grey hair swept back, tall, slim and wearing a white cotton shirt open at the neck, and designer jeans, stepped forward extending a hand. 'I am Sebastian. I run the classes, welcome.' As she took his hand in a firm but not aggressive handshake, she took in his fine features and his tanned skin. His face was lined as if he had lived life and seen many things, dominated by piercing bright blue eyes. Thelma assessed he would have been about her age.

'I am looking forward to it,' Thelma said.

Sebastian waved to a chair in front of an easel. 'Sit down here for a few minutes while I get the class underway and then we can talk about what you are looking for.'

There were just eight people in the class, six women and two men, their ages between maybe early 40s up to 70s. They had each been asked to bring a photograph of a seascape that they would paint in oils. Sebastian talked about the challenges around getting the sea right. He gave them some tips depending on what effect they wanted for the sea; whether it was cloudy or sunny, whether it was morning sun glistening on the surface or direct overhead sun with deeper blues, calm or rough. In due course he would come around and talk to them individually about how they were going.

He pulled up a chair and sat down opposite Thelma. He smiled. 'So tell me Thelma, why do you want to do this class, what do you want to get out of it, and what sort of experience have you had with painting? That will help me make sure that you get what you are looking for from the course.'

Thelma thought for a moment and then answered, 'I seem to have quite a bit of time on my hands and getting into a rut. I wanted to get out and do something creative. I did very well at art at school, but that was a long time ago. I want to feel I am doing something productive.'

'I am going to ask you to draw something for me so that we have a baseline of where you are at now.' Sebastian smiled again. 'How about a drawing in pencil of a building, something like a cottage on a hill? That way I can see how comfortable you are with perspective and shapes. Then we can get in to colours. Do you want a photograph to copy or do you think you can imagine one, or remember one?'

'I am sure I can create one,' Thelma answered. She started to draw and felt confident that this was going to be a very rewarding experience. At the end of the class she was quite pleased with her efforts.

Sebastian looked satisfied as well. 'That is very good Thelma, you have got the perspectives well. A lot of art is about observation, noticing the details and how they relate one to the other. The rest is just technique.'

'Thank you.'

Sebastian waved his hand towards the back of the room, 'Will you join us for tea or coffee? The group usually has a chat after the class.'

Thelma appreciated the chance to chat to some of the other class attendees. They all seemed very pleasant and she was very pleased that she had chosen this class. One lady had lived much of her life in Turkey, another was a retired doctor. The two men looked to be in their 40s she guessed, and seemed to be together; she wondered if they were just friends or a couple. She gave them a wide berth.

For the next three weeks Thelma went to classes and was making good progress. In particular she liked oils, and enjoyed discovering the effect of combining different pigments. After her fourth attendance she had a coffee after the class as usual. The others left and she found herself alone with Sebastian.

'I hope you are enjoying the course, you are making really good progress, Thelma,' Sebastian started the conversation.

'Yes, I am. Very much,' Thelma reassured him.

"You have never talked much about your family. Is there a husband?' Sebastian was starting to probe.

Thelma would much rather him have not known about Gordon; she quickly reflected that the fact that she felt that way was not really right. Why on earth would she want to hide Gordon? She chose her words carefully. 'Yes, my husband is a very busy man and we tend to live relatively separate lives.' She knew that was not true, at least nowadays, but she wanted to give the impression of distance between her and Gordon.

'Children?'

'Yes, just one son, Martin. Do you have children?'

'I have two daughters. One is living in London with a demanding career as a lawyer, and the other is married with two young boys of her own. A few months ago her husband was transferred to Germany and so they have gone off to live in Hamburg for a few years. She trained as a research scientist. So they have both done very well for themselves.'

'That must be very hard with both of them living overseas,' Thelma commented.

Sebastian said, 'Yes it is hard, but they have to live their lives and as long as they are happy that for me is the main thing.'

'Your wife must be very happy to have grandchildren,' Thelma observed a little enviously.

Sebastian laughed. 'I have no idea. She walked out on me over twenty years ago, and I brought up my daughters on my own. I don't even know where she is. I don't think she would even know that she is a grandmother.'

'Oh!' Thelma was genuinely taken aback. 'That must have been hard.'

'It could have been worse. As an artist I had a lot of flexibility with work times and with the help of my parents from time to time I managed quite well. My daughters are now well and truly off my hands and making their own way in the world.'

'You sound as if you are very proud of them,' Thelma commented.

'Well, yes, I guess I am. They have turned into good responsible adults. How about Martin?'

'Yes. He has done alright for himself.' Thelma did not want to go into the huge disappointment to her that he had turned out to be.

'Married with children?' Sebastian enquired.

'Not yet.' Thelma did not trust herself to say any more than that.

Sebastian decided to leave it at that as he could see that Thelma was a bit defensive, and changed the subject. 'You seem to be very fond of the arts. Are you an artistic person?'

Thelma liked the thought of being 'artistic' and she smiled coyly and said, 'Well, I have always had an appreciation of the arts. I love the performing arts and going to concerts and theatre. I love ballet, opera, plays.' She knew this was an exaggeration as she hardly went to any performances, but she would have liked to, and she felt that was close enough. Thelma was still trying to impress. 'A couple of years ago we went to Italy and I just loved all the art and history.' She remembered how Gordon had hated it and she never really did get to see what she wanted.

'I love Italy too,' Sebastian offered. 'In fact I lived there for a couple of years, in Siena.'

'That would have been wonderful,' Thelma said approvingly, 'I would love to go back again.'

'Then you should!' Sebastian smiled.

'Well, yes, you are right, maybe I should.' Thelma for a second imagined herself strolling through the Uffizi with Sebastian at her side.

'Thelma, I need to go this evening but I would love to continue this conversation. Maybe we could go for a drink after next week's class? The coffee here is absolutely awful. There is a really nice bar just down the road, and I want to talk to you more about art.'

'Oh that would be lovely. Thanks.' Thelma was wondering exactly what she should read into the invitation. Was Sebastian flirting with her?

****

Gordon started going regularly to the park in the afternoons, meeting up with Natalia and Anton. Over the course of a few meetings he found out that Natalia lived in an apartment close by which her parents had lived in and which she inherited when her mother died. She worked as a book keeper and made just about enough money to cover her day to day expenses. She had quite a few clients for whom she worked and many for whom she had worked for several years now, but she was never sure how secure the work was. The big advantage for her was that she could work from home. The only time she had to be out

107

was when she had client meetings, although often her clients would go to her. She had converted a small bedroom into a compact little office. That meant that she was able to be there for Anton as a single parent and yet at the same time be relatively independent.

Anton started to engage with Gordon, showing him his toys and asking him to play with him. Gordon was delighted and loved to talk to him and tell him things. One day Anton came up to Gordon as he and Natalia were sitting on the park bench, and addressed him as 'Yapa.' Natalia laughed and explained that he was trying to say *Nagyapa* which is the word for Grandpa in Hungarian. She hoped he was not offended. In fact Gordon was delighted and felt that it was a level of acceptance that he never imagined he would be accorded. He was chuffed!

'Has he been to the zoo?' Gordon asked one afternoon.

'No never. I just haven't had time, or to be honest the spare cash. I looked up Taronga Park Zoo online once and it was going to cost me over $70 just to get in, and then there is transport, something to eat and so on.'

'Would you let me invite you both one of these days? You must take a day off work from time to time.'

'That would be really lovely. Are you sure, I mean it is lot for the three of us?'

'Yes of course I am sure. Tell me a day that works and I am certain I can fit in. After all I am retired now.'

'Let me look at my schedule and let you know. I imagine that in the week is better because there are fewer people.'

'Yes I would suggest a weekday,' Gordon agreed.

Gordon had not mentioned Natalia and Anton to Thelma. He just felt that he wanted to keep that part of his life for himself. It was not as if he was doing something that he shouldn't, he was not having an affair and he was quite sure that however the relationship developed, it would be purely on the basis of friendship. He liked the role of 'Yapa' and it gave him some sort of purpose in his life.

****

The orchestra where Tony played was considered the finest in Sydney and one of the best in Australia. He was one of the first violins, of which there were almost twenty. As one of the more senior violinists he earned a relatively modest salary, but mostly enough to accord him the life style he wanted. In months where he was running a bit short he worked for a friend as a waiter. He had a brief fling with the owner of a restaurant, and they remained friends afterwards. The arrangement was that Tony called him if he needed some work and his friend would always find a few shifts to help him out. Tony had been calling on him less often since his salary had been increased a few months ago as he became one of the better and more experienced players, and also because he wanted to spend time with Martin when he could; he wanted to be available for Martin especially weekends when he was not working and not make it difficult to get together. He performed on average eight to ten times a month at various locations in Sydney. His favourite was the Recital Hall at Angel Place. He liked the acoustics there and the relative intimacy compared to the Opera House or the Town Hall. Sometimes there were formal rehearsals he had to attend, and then he also did practice at home. Occasionally the orchestra went on tour and then he travelled with them and was away a few weeks. He had had a couple of such trips, one to Europe and the other to the USA and Canada.

He had played around with composing a bit. But he recognised that if he wanted to develop that skill he needed more tuition. He enjoyed being creative with music but found composition challenging. The truth is that since he met Martin he had less spare time to work on composing, but he was more than happy to have it that way. Martin was more of a priority right now

One Thursday afternoon after rehearsals the concert master stopped him on the way out.

'Tony, can I just have a word with you please before you go?'

It was unusual for Andrew to want a chat with him, and he was slightly apprehensive wondering what it could be about. 'Sure,' he said.

Andrew moved over to a table with two chairs, sat down and motioned for Tony to do the same. 'Tony,' he started, 'I was just wondering where you see yourself being in say five years time and if you had thought about how you are going to advance your career?'

Tony was a little relieved. 'I suppose I had not really given it much thought. Basically I am really happy doing what I am doing. Maybe one day become a concert master, like you. I like composing as well and would quite like to develop that.'

'I think you are a very talented violinist and while I am not sure you will be a Menuhin I do think that you have the ability to develop your career a lot more.'

'Thanks.' Tony waited for Andrew to continue.

'If you want to advance however I think you need two things. One is some further study under the tutelage of a good mentor. The other is that I think it is time you had some international experience. I suggest that you try and do both of those things at the same time.'

'I don't think it is that easy. I just don't have the financial resources to do that.'

'It so happens that a good friend of mine works at the Royal London School of Music. He is going to be here in Sydney next week, and I would like you to have a chat with him. I have already spoken to him about you, and he is keen to meet. The thing is that they have some international fellowships and with Brexit happening there have been far fewer applicants from the EU which has had a special allocation for several years, but which now will stop, and that favours students from Australia. Of course I cannot promise you anything, but I think you should sit down and talk to Gareth next week about some of the options and possibilities.'

Tony's mind was racing. On the one hand he was really excited at even the chance to go to UK and advance his studies. At the same time he thought about Martin and what this would

110

mean for their relationship. He decided to cross that bridge when he came to it, after all this was just a preliminary meeting and he must at least commit to that. 'That would be wonderful, thanks so much for thinking of me and for setting up the meeting. Do you have any idea when next week?'

'Gareth is free on Tuesday and I suggest the three of us have dinner that night at my place. He is staying with me.'

Tony wondered all of a sudden just how close this friendship was between Andrew and Gareth. The way Andrew spoke about him gave Tony the impression that they were very close friends and Gareth was staying with him. It did cross his mind that they could have had an affair when Andrew had been living in London several years ago. In any case it did not matter. 'Tuesday would be fine. Thanks Andrew I really appreciate it.'

Tony decided not to mention it to Martin until after he had had the meeting with Gareth. After all, the only thing that was certain was the meeting next Tuesday. He knew Martin would worry about it and what the consequences might be, so better not to say anything until there was something to talk about.

****

Several weeks had passed since the tense dinner Martin had had with his parents following his birthday. Martin usually went round to see his parents every two weeks or so, and so this gap was unusual. It worried Martin in that he did not want to sever relationships with his parents, but at the same time the relationship was going to have to be largely on his terms. He was not going to stop being gay because they could not handle it. He needed them to accept that.

He had hoped that his parents would have called him, but they hadn't. He decided that in the interests of keeping the relationship he should call them. This time he elected to call at a time when he thought they would both be there. He thought that around 8.00 pm on a weeknight would work.

He was apprehensive as he dialled. He had set the objective of the call to arrange to go round for dinner in the hope of settling things.

'Seven six four three.' His mother's answering the phone was predictable. He ignored the slight irritation it caused him.

'Hi Ma, it's me.' He waited a bit anxiously for a response.

'Oh, Martin. At last. I thought you had died.' Thelma immediately regretted saying that. It was stupid. She had done that several times now, said something off the cuff without thinking and then regretted it.

Martin ignored her remark. 'How have you both been?' He tried to sound as normal and casual as he could. He thought that getting her talking would reveal the lay of the land.

'Oh you know, busy.' Thelma wanted to sound short and disapproving, but then she thought that at least Martin had called. She was pleased to hear his voice if truth were told. She decided not to be so difficult and trying to soften her first answer she continued, 'I have started art class and your father has been busy with his golf and whatever he does.'

'Art class? That is great. Where?'

'In Chatswood. I think it is going to be good. They seem like nice people. The teacher Sebastian is very good.'

'Have you got any work you have done to show me?'

'I only just started.' Thelma somehow felt a bit embarrassed about showing her work to Martin.

Martin decided to push the conversation towards his objective. 'If that is alright with you I thought I might drop round later in the week.'

'We are not doing anything Thursday. Would that suit?'

'Yes Thursday works for me.'

'Gordon, Thursday evening alright if Martin drops round?'

Gordon nodded his assent.

Thelma said, 'Well why don't you come for dinner?'

Martin was relieved. 'Yes, that would be nice. I will come straight from work. About 6.30 or so?'

Martin spoke to Tony that evening about the arrangement for Thursday. Tony's advice was just to go with the flow and let be what will be. He suggested that Martin should not have any great expectations at this stage. It would take his parents a while to come to terms with him being gay.

As he drove into the driveway Thursday evening, it seemed much like all the other times he had done so. He rang the bell and his mother opened it and greeted him with a peck on the cheek.

'Your father is in the sitting room. Gin and tonic?' Thelma asked. Martin felt like nothing had changed. His father was seated in his usual chair and got up as Martin went into the room and they shook hands. Nothing had changed.

'Traffic alright?' Gordon enquired.

'Yes, not bad for a Thursday being late shopping,' Martin informed him. He sat down next to his father and Thelma brought him a gin and tonic the ice tinkling gently in the glass. His parents had just started theirs he noticed. They all raised their glasses with a mumbled joint 'cheers'.

'How is work?' Thelma enquired.

It was clear that the evening was going to be cordial, superficial and would totally ignore the elephant in the room. His parents were going to cope by pretending that the conversation at the previous dinner hadn't happened. For Martin it was not ideal but he could put up with it, at least for now. He was half tempted to say that he had to go home early because Tony was waiting in bed for him, but of course he didn't. They talked about general non controversial things. Thelma talked about art classes but did not mention Sebastian, Gordon talked about the park but did not mention Natalia and Anton, Martin thought about Tony naked in his bed, but talked about climate change. They talked about local councils' greed for revenue, and possibly kickbacks to pass developments that nobody wanted; about the parlous state of public transport. They talked about the new tram system that was a year behind schedule and was costing a billion dollars more than budget. Gordon reminisced about the tram network that Sydney used to have, saying how wonderful it was and how it should never have been pulled out. Martin did not mention that the network ceased operation around the time that Gordon was born. Gordon blamed it on the financial interests of the petroleum industry and the car industry, and their greed and determination to maximise profits at the expense of the commuters of the city. Martin often mused that when talking about various issues his parents often expressed a liberal or even left leaning point of view. But they would never think of voting Labor and were dyed-in-the-wool Liberal voters. The Liberal party expressed the demographic they belonged to. They were in principle anti union, pro tax cuts, anti immigration, especially Muslims, and lamented rather than embraced multiculturalism, without ever thinking deeply about it. Just as well Tony was not Middle Eastern! In fact he was second generation Irish, and that would probably pass muster.

Thelma had not cooked his favourite steak and kidney pie, she did not want to appear overly welcoming, but instead she had made a cottage pie, which she knew he also liked. There was apple crumble with cream for dessert. Martin complimented her on it, but secretly had always thought that his grandmother did it better. Martin passed on the wine as he had had a gin and tonic and was driving; he was always responsible about drinking and driving. His parents shared a bottle of Hunter Valley red. He accepted a coffee and then took his leave about 9.30 p.m.

As he drove back down the drive and out into the tree lined street, he mused that it was all a bit unreal. It had seemed like a normal evening just as he had spent many times before with his parents, but it wasn't. Things had changed but nobody was going to acknowledge it. It reminded him of the scene in Carry On Up the Khyber, when the British gentry sat having a fine lunch while shells were bursting all around them, and yet nobody was going to acknowledge it. He felt as if his parents were forcing him into being, at least for that evening, the person they wanted him to be, and not the one that he was. He was effectively banned from being fully the person that he was while he was with them. He would put up with it for now even though he hated it. But before too long he wanted them to accept Tony as his partner and to acknowledge that Tony was an important part of his life. He was not going to give up on that.

He then started to turn those thoughts over in his mind. Yes, it was true; Tony was a very important part of his life. He missed him the evenings that they were not together. Should he ask Tony to move in? Would that work? Did he want Tony there all the time? Would that set a negative dynamic in their relationship because it was Martin's house? He turned his attention to the road as he made sure he was in the right lane for the approach to the Harbour Tunnel. Then he returned to his thoughts again.

On the one hand he wanted to cuddle up with Tony every night and wake up next to him every morning. He wanted to have sex with him whenever they both wanted it, and that was pretty often! But at the same time he was afraid that if it changed their relationship in a negative way he could lose Tony, and he certainly did not want that to happen. There were differences, Martin was pedantically, almost obsessively tidy, Tony wasn't. They had different work schedules and Tony needed to practice at home. Martin was used to a routine and inevitably given his work Tony had a far more flexible life. It was more practical to continue the current arrangement on one level. On the other hand he wanted to feel settled in a relationship. He was in his early thirties, it was time. Could you have a meaningful relationship and not live together? Surely it was more about commitment than constant physical proximity. Perhaps Martin needed to be a bit more patient. Maybe they should spend more evenings together during the week; as it was they spent most of the weekends together unless Tony was working. Tony could move some clothes and things in so he could stay several days, it would be a good stepping stone.

By this time his thoughts had occupied him right through the tunnel and Eastern Distributor, and he was only a few minutes from home. He parked the car and walked to the front door, getting his house keys out as he walked up the path. As he unlocked the front door and turned the alarm off he reflected that life was pretty good for him. His parents irritated him more than anything but he had a lot of positive things in his life.

****

'I can pick you up here at the park or outside your place, whatever is convenient.' Gordon was making arrangements for their excursion to Taronga Park Zoo. He wanted to be as discreet and accommodating as possible.

'If you don't mind picking me up from my place, that would be great. What time?'

Gordon thought and said, 'Would 9.30 be alright for you?'

'Perfect Gordon, thanks. We will be waiting outside for you on Thursday.'

It was quite a nice block of units Gordon thought as he pulled up. It was a small block in a quiet street in maybe the less sought after western part of the suburb. Natalia and Anton were waiting outside. Gordon had just said to Thelma that he was going to be out for the day with friends. He knew she would assume it was something to do with the golf club. He need not have worried because Thelma seemed to be totally disinterested and did not ask for any further information.

They parked the car at the car park by the main entrance of the zoo at the top of the steep hill. The plan was to walk down and then once at the bottom by the harbour they would take the Sky Safari cable car gondola back to the top. Natalia had brought a push chair for Anton as it was going to be a lot of walking even if most of it was downhill.

They sauntered down slowly looking at each of the animal exhibits on the way. Anton wanted to know about all the animals. Gordon was able to read the description to supplement his rather scant knowledge. Anton seemed fascinated. He was a bit scared of the Sumatran tigers and of the elephants and the gorillas. But he loved the koalas, tree kangaroos and was fascinated by the giraffes, His favourite was the meerkats that he

116

found very funny the way they darted about and stood there looking at whoever was passing by.

They had lunch at the Taronga Food Market which had a good selection of convenient foods. And later they stopped and had an ice cream; Natalia and Gordon sat on a bench while Anton was in his push chair and fell fast asleep.

'Thanks so much for bringing us here. It has been so special for Anton and I have enjoyed it too.' Natalia turned to Gordon and smiled.

'Believe me it is a real pleasure for me, I am really enjoying myself. It is ages since I was here and I am impressed with what they have done to the zoo and I still love the views over the harbour.' Gordon seemed genuinely pleased with the day.

There were a few minutes of silence between them as they took in the views across the harbour towards the city and the suburbs across the harbour. There was a constant flow of ferries and sail boats and other craft.

'Do you mind if I ask you a question?' Natalia ventured.

'Of course not,' Gordon replied.

'It is about Martin. You never talk about him. You mentioned that he is gay and that was all you have ever said about him.'

'Oh! He has done quite well for himself. He works in marketing.' Gordon was non committal.

'But do you see him? Do you have a good relationship with him?'

'As a matter of fact he came round last week.'

'And?' Natalia suspected from the way he said it that there was something to this story.

'It was a bit tense. The previous time he came was when he announced to us that he had turned homosexual, you know, gay.' Gordon felt uncomfortable using the gay word which he considered to be totally inappropriate and not an accurate description in any way whatsoever. 'When he came last week it was just not mentioned. It made the whole evening stupid really, with this huge elephant in the room that nobody was going to speak about. My wife is particularly upset about it. She just can't forgive him.'

'Oh Gordon. You know my father was gay, I told you that. I had many conversations with him about it and it gave me a far better understanding. You just said something about Martin turning gay. You don't turn gay or decide to be gay, you are gay. It is central to your identity. There is nothing that a person can or should do about it. You are born that way.'

Gordon had read that theory that day on the computer, and yet there was still part of him that till did not want to believe it because it would suggest that Martin would not and could not change. But he had to admit that the theory was well supported. He was aware that if it was correct it also meant that Martin was suffering because of something he had no influence over. He suddenly again felt sad for Martin.

'How sure are you that that is really true?' Gordon wanted proof.

'I am one hundred per cent sure. I researched it a lot. They are not quite sure how much is due to antepartum influences, possibly hormonal, versus genetic, or if there is some environmental component when children are very young. But I am convinced it is a mix of the first two. Gay people are what they are; they have no choice in the matter whatsoever. There is nothing to be forgiven in Martin.' What Natalia said was exactly what Gordon had read online.

'I did speak to Thelma about that theory and she just said it was rubbish. It was not natural and that was the end of it.' Gordon sighed slightly.

'I hope you do not mind me asking about it, I know it is not really my place, but the relationship with our children is very special. I would not like you to miss out on your relationship with Martin because of a false conception.'

'No, no. It is fine. I just find it hard when I think about what it means.' He paused and then added. 'And frankly I find it hard to think about, well, what they do.'

Natalia laughed and said, 'Oh that! Human behaviour is very diverse and surely what two people do with mutual consent is alright. What gay men do is not much different from what many straight couples do, but rarely talk about. And you can only know exactly what they do if you see or they tell you. I think what people focus on far too much is sexual expression, but being gay is much more than that. It is also about love, deeply committed love. And that is why gay people don't really like just to be called homosexual, because it is about so much more than sex.'

'Martin told us that he has a friend called Tony.'

'You must be pleased for him.' Natalia said in a way that was also a question.

Gordon did not say anything initially, and then he said, 'To be honest it was not good. We told him we never wanted to see Tony and he was not welcome in our house.'

'Poor Martin! If Tony is an important relationship for Martin that would have been so hurtful for him.'

'Yes I sort of see that now. But I just find it so hard to come to terms with.'

'Martin has not changed, he was always who he is. What has changed is that you know a bit more about him.'

'It probably explains why we did not seem to get on and have much in common when he was growing up. I guess I punished him for not being what I wanted him to be.' Gordon now sounded regretful, but all of a sudden he was looking at Martin in an entirely different way. At the same time he couldn't really accept it.

Anton woke up and wanted to see the meerkats again. It seemed so natural for him to put his hand up for Gordon to take it, and kept asking Gordon all sorts of questions.

Natalia turned to Gordon, 'It looks like Anton has found a nagyapa after all,' she said. Gordon beamed.

****

Thelma opened the door and got into the passenger's seat. She put the seat belt on, and turned and smiled at Sebastian.

'Good morning, what a beautiful day,' she said to him. She thought about the conversation in the bar two weeks ago that brought her to be sitting in his car on the way to Canberra. She went over again in her mind what had happened that afternoon.

'What would you like?' Sebastian had asked.

'A glass of Sauvignon blanc, please,' Thelma replied.

'The New Zealand one or the South Australian?' Sebastian enquired.

'The New Zealand one thanks. I love those Marlborough Sound ones.'

Sebastian ordered and paid for two Sauvignon blancs. As Sebastian had suggested they had gone to the bar close to where the art lessons were held. There were very few people there at that time of the early evening, so they took a table by the window in a little alcove that gave them more privacy.

'Your art is coming along really well,' Sebastian told Thelma.

'Do you think so?' Thelma smiled with satisfaction.

Sebastian looked at her seriously. 'Yes I do. I think you have a real talent, especially for drawing.' Thelma accepted the compliment although she was not quite sure how sincere he was really being.

'I love art, all of it, not just drawing. I just wish I had gone to lessons years ago.'

Sebastian reassured her, 'It doesn't matter when you develop your abilities as long as you do it and enjoy doing it.'

Thelma reflected that Sebastian was both gracious and diplomatic. He clearly chose his words carefully and was a confident and skilled communicator as well as a talented artist.

'Was it hard making a living from art?' Thelma asked. When Sebastian had told her how he brought up two children on his own and was able to cope though the flexibility of being an artist, she had wondered how he managed, given that most artists don't make that much money.

'I was very lucky. When I was young I had a mentor, a really accomplished artist who was very well known. We became

120

close friends. He had a gallery and when he died he left me the gallery. I used it to sell higher end art as well as my own paintings. I only had to open it a few hours a day and on weekends. That is when my parents helped me out by looking after the girls. That is how I managed.'

'Do you still have the gallery?'

'No, once the girls were independent, I decided I wanted more freedom and I sold it. That was what allowed me to go to Italy. Now I prefer to do a bit of teaching, and have time to go wherever my whim takes me.'

'That sounds wonderful.' Thelma was a bit envious.

They chatted together for an hour or so about art and about relatively non controversial things such as the way they experienced Sydney growing up and how the city had changed over the years. They each had a second glass of wine, and the time seemed to fly by. Thelma looked at her watch and was surprised that it was already 7.00 p.m. Gordon would be wondering where she had got to, even though she did tell him there was a get together after class that day.

'This has been so nice, but I really must go.' Thelma uncrossed her legs and made as if to stand up. 'The time just flew by.'

'I have enjoyed it too,' Sebastian confessed. Then he added, 'Thelma there is an exhibition of 18th century Italian art coming up at the National Gallery in Canberra starting next week. I am going to drive down for the day to see it, and I was wondering if you would like to come along as well?'

And so it was that she was in Sebastian's car that morning. She had enthusiastically, she hoped not too quickly, accepted his invitation. She had told Gordon that there was an art class excursion to the National Gallery, but she did not mention that it was just her and the teacher.

Thelma had chosen her clothes for the day carefully; she wanted to look elegant and somewhat understated wearing something that would be suitable for Canberra's reputation for capricious weather. She wore a dark brown and expensive skirt, a white blouse, and a smart burgundy jacket. She was mindful that there could be quite a lot of walking and so chose some sturdy but stylish Italian brown shoes. Thelma was well aware that she had a very good figure for her age, still a slim waist, and everything pretty much where it had been thirty years previously. Her best asset she had always felt was her legs, so the skirt she chose was designed to show enough of her legs without being considered as provocative or vulgar in any way.

Thelma felt content as she settled into the seat as they made their way through the morning traffic to the M7 and then the road to Canberra. She could see that Sebastian was concentrating on the traffic so she engaged him in only small talk conversation. They talked about the weather, the traffic and made the odd comment about other drivers' bad habits. Sebastian had put on the radio to listen to the news. He left the radio on for some political analysis following the news, then turned it off. These were rather charged political times with an election not far off, and she steered away from making any comments. To start with she had very little interest in politics and never had. She feared her views might be much further to the right than Sebastian and so it was better to remain silent about all that. She and Gordon were Liberal voters out of principle; that was what was expected of people of their standing in the northern suburbs.

Once they got past Liverpool and on the road to Canberra the traffic eased off and Sebastian seemed a bit more relaxed. He started to talk about his time in Italy and Thelma was most interested in what he said. It sounded exactly like what she would have loved to have done. But at her age it was not going to be likely that she would ever do that, especially given her current domestic arrangements and obligations. It was obvious that Sebastian had had a far more interesting life than she had and so she preferred to listen to his stories. He talked quite a bit about his daughters and what they were doing. He was obviously very fond of them and proud of them. She could not bring herself to talk about Martin, as she would have been ashamed to admit to Sebastian that her son was a homosexual.

Thelma enjoyed being out in the country and felt a kind of elation at being free of the city for a while. She looked approvingly at the low hills and the paddocks as they rolled by. They stopped at the services at Marulan for a coffee, and then continued, turning left onto the Federal Highway. As they came up to Lake George Thelma commented that when she was younger the lake came right up to the highway and that they used to stand on the lookouts and just see water for miles.

'Yes, it is really odd how it comes and goes,' Sebastian responded, 'it seems that it is not directly dependent on rainfall, and I am not sure they know why it comes and goes. But I must admit I haven't seen the lake for years and years now.'

They moved easily though the northern suburbs of Canberra, there was never any traffic problem mid morning, and shortly after they parked at the National Gallery and were at the ticket counter.

'Let me get these Sebastian, please,' Thelma asked, 'it is the least I can do after all the driving you will be doing today.'

Sebastian had intended to pay, after all, that is what men do, or used to do in his day. However he realised that Thelma was intent on paying and he politely acquiesced with thanks. It did not take them long to get to the special exhibition of 18th Century Italian art. As they walked around Sebastian started to talk about the various exhibits, and Thelma was amazed that he knew so much. He explained to her, 'The 18th century was the last period of Venice's independence, and while not producing maybe the quality of the old masters, it was an important period in the history of Italian art. This neoclassical period was about classical authenticity.'

This collection had been put together with a mix of paintings from international galleries and private collections. He explained how Tiepolo had concentrated on complex historical paintings in the rococo style. When Thelma asked how it was that Canaletto painted a lot of English scenes, Sebastian explained that after acquiring a number of English patrons, he went to live there for several years and started to paint English scenes. He then elaborated that Francesco Guardi painted scenes in Venice, smaller and simpler paintings that were at the time more affordable.

'Now, the similarity between Canaletto and Bernardo Bellotto is explained by the fact that Bellotto was Canaletto's nephew. Travel must have been in the family because he left Venice just after his uncle and went to live in Vienna and Dresden.'

'You are so knowledgeable!' Thelma said with admiration.

Sebastian smiled. 'Just bits of information that I have picked up over time. The important thing is to know what you like.'

Thelma told him, 'My favourite is really Canaletto; I love Venice and his paintings just take me there. The wonderful thing is that at first sight Venice has not really changed. It is only nowadays when you look more closely you see the hordes of tourists shuffling along the narrow streets.'

'Yes I love those paintings too. But I have a real penchant for portraits, although the 18th century in Italy was less about portraits and more about landscapes and historical scenes.'

They had a sandwich and coffee at the café and then went browsing through the rest of the National Gallery, chatting away amiably.

'How are you holding up? You aren't tired and want a break?' Sebastian suddenly sounded concerned. They had been on their feet most of the day.

'I am a bit tired yes, but I don't want to miss anything,' she replied. It was late afternoon by the time they had seen what they wanted. As they had been in the gallery they had not seen that it was raining quite hard and it looked to be set in for the whole evening. Sebastian hated driving along the Hume Highway at night in the rain with all the trucks from Melbourne already on that section of the road. It looked as if it was going to be a tedious trip back.

Sebastian pulled off the road to fill up with petrol on the outskirts of Canberra. When he went to pay, the man at the till asked if he was heading to Sydney. He said, 'There has been a huge pile up on the highway with two trucks colliding. The wet weather I suppose. The road is blocked and they say it is going to take hours for it to be opened and the traffic is already backed up several kilometres back towards Canberra. They are just talking about it on the local radio.'

'Oh thanks. That does not sound at all good. I appreciate your telling me.' Sebastian was quickly trying to think through options. When he got to the car he told Thelma what had happened.

'I know this is a real pain but honestly Thelma I think the best thing is for us to try and find accommodation in Canberra for the night and then drive back tomorrow morning. What do you think?'

'Well there does not seem to be much point in getting all tangled up in that, and it will be dark and wet. I don't think we have much option but to stay in Canberra.' Thelma was wondering what Gordon would say. She actually was quite excited about the idea of a night in Canberra.

'Let me see what I can find, there are plenty of places along Northbourne Avenue, and parliament is not sitting so it should not be too hard to find something.' Sebastian looked at Thelma. She smiled. He asked, 'Should we look for two rooms or one? Your call entirely.'

****

On Tuesday evening Tony climbed the few steps to the front door of the small terrace house in Surry Hills where Andrew lived. It was a small but very well presented house, obviously renovated and lovingly cared for. He rang the bell, and Andrew opened the door with a cheery greeting. The entrance gave straight into a living room with tasteful decor and some comfortable sofas. Gareth had been sitting on one of the sofas, and stood up when Tony walked into the room. They shook hands. Gareth was maybe late 40s, of medium height, with brown hair and sparklingly dancing brown eyes. He was wearing jeans and a woollen western style shirt with a pattern of squares, a brown corduroy jacket and brown shoes. It was anything but a fashionable look. His eyes were his most arresting feature. He had a slight Welsh accent, and quite a soft voice. Tony noticed that the interaction between Andrew and Gareth was easy; obviously they knew each other well.

Tony gave Andrew the bottle of wine he had brought, a quite expensive Coonawarra red, and Andrew offered him a drink. He said, 'A glass of wine please, anything that is open.' Andrew poured him a pinot grigio. Tony sat down on the sofa at right angles to the other sofa where Andrew and Gareth sat together. There followed polite conversation about Gareth's trip, how long he was staying and how he was managing the jetlag. Gareth explained that the trip was a work related one and his main task was to exchange thoughts and ideas with the Sydney Conservatorium of Music and the Australian Institute of Music on curriculum and other matters of mutual interest. There was the vague thought of exchange programmes, although Gareth thought that was not likely to come to anything. Tony quickly gathered that not only did Gareth work for the Royal London School of Music, but that he had a rather elevated and influential position with them.

Andrew suggested that they move to the dining table. He served a soup that was delicious, and that Andrew admitted he had bought from the local speciality supermarket, and a spaghetti Bolognese with a green side salad. Andrew opened the red wine that Tony had brought. Gareth was most impressed with the wine. Tony got the impression that Gareth was trying to check him out, find out what sort of a person he was. He encouraged Tony to tell him a bit about his life and his career to date. He questioned him about what music studies he had undertaken. Tony interpreted the questions in the context of music, but then at some point towards the end of dinner Gareth asked him if he had anyone in his life. At first Tony thought that he was being more intrusive than was appropriate but then it did cross his mind that Gareth might have been trying to see if there were any complications in him going to London for at least a few years. Or could he be assessing whether Tony was available on another

126

level; he had noticed that Gareth had been looking at him in a rather approving way. At one point Gareth had inserted the words 'a good looking young man like you' into a sentence. Was he flirting? Tony assumed not, but was careful in answering. 'Yes, there is someone I have been dating a while now.' He was careful to make the answer gender neutral although he assumed that Gareth was well aware that he was gay, and he assumed that Gareth was also gay.

At the end of the meal Gareth turned to Tony and said, 'Andrew has told me about your abilities, he sees you as one of the leading lights in the orchestra, and I trust his judgment implicitly. From what you have told me today and from what Andrew has said I really think that doing a course at the London School of Music would be exactly the right step for you, and now is the time in your career to do it. There are some full scholarships including both course fee and living allowance that had been set aside for students from the EU. With Brexit this will drop off and in any case we had already seen a drop off in interest because of the Brexit uncertainties. These scholarships certainly eventually will be taken up by students from other areas. But I am very confident that if you were to apply right now you would be accepted.' Andrew looked at Tony in a kind of knowing way and nodded.

'In fact,' Gareth continued, 'I would like to take your application back with me when I leave on Friday evening this week. The course does not start for another five months, but I would like to get it sorted out as soon as possible. What do you think?'

Tony had half expected this but he did not think it would happen so quickly. He asked, 'How long is the course?'

'The initial course would be for two years. There would most likely be opportunities to extend beyond that time and do further studies if you wanted to and depending on your results. Many students stay on and take positions with British orchestras afterwards as well.'

Andrew interjected 'You can't have him forever you know, we want him back.'

Tony was not certain what to say. On the one hand he wanted to go to London; it would be an amazing opportunity for him. Most of the people who had had successful careers in Australia had spent time overseas. It was probably a perception rather than a reality, but overseas training and experience in the performing arts was highly valued in Australia. At the same time he did not want to lose Martin. He had not even told him about any of this yet. Could he persuade Martin to go with him? He knew how set in his ways Martin was, how he likes a routine and prefers to operate within his comfort zone and not take risks. Could he get a transfer to London with the company where he worked? Would he have the courage to leave and take a risk? There could be a hope that he could persuade Martin to go with him, but it was very far from certain or even likely. Right now this was a yes no situation, he could not prevaricate. He decided that to say 'no' would be final and silly, and that if he said 'yes' he could always back out later if he absolutely had to.

'Yes I am very keen.' Tony paused. 'How does the scholarship work? Is the allowance enough to live in an expensive city like London?'

'It is quite generous, and students seem to manage reasonably well on it. Some do a bit of extra work on the side for more cash.'

Tony laughed. 'I do that now occasionally. What about visas? How does that work?'

'It gets fixed one way or another. If you do not have any other rights of residence in the UK then we would sponsor a student visa for you. Some people in Australia have patriality rights through a grandparent or parent being born in UK.'

'I just have Australian citizenship, and although I might be able to get Irish citizenship, that would take time and I am not sure how much that would help.'

'No I don't think it would help, but they will probably welcome Australians now. In any case the visa will not be an issue.'

'Let me get the application form and quickly go through a few things.' Gareth reached for his briefcase that was on the floor by the sofa and took out a folder. He handed Tony an empty form. 'Let me just suggest how you might answer some of the questions; the rest are straightforward and I will leave you to fill that part out. Can you get the form back to either me or Andrew before Friday evening?'

'Yes I can do that tomorrow and give it to Andrew at rehearsals on Thursday.'

Tony moved his chair round to sit next to Gareth and they went through the application form together. 'Andrew will fill this part out as your Australian reference.'

'Thanks, I really do appreciate you doing this for me,' Tony said when they got to the end of the form.

'It is a pleasure.' Gareth smiled. 'We always want talent at the school, you would make a very decorative addition.' Tony was still not sure about Gareth's sometimes inappropriate comments, but felt it was safer to just ignore them and try not to react.

'I think I should be going,' Tony said getting up. 'Just before I do could I use the toilet please?'

Andrew said, 'Yes by all means. Top of the stairs and at the end of the corridor straight in front.' Tony passed two bedrooms on the way to the bathroom, and he glanced casually inside as he walked past them. The larger one was obviously Andrew's with the wardrobe door open and all his clothes hanging up. But what he assumed was Gareth's suitcase was open on the floor of Andrew's bedroom, some clothes in the case, and others left a bit untidily on the floor. The other bedroom was empty and naked in comparison. The bed in that room looked as if it was not being used at all. They were sleeping together. Tony smiled to himself, had a pee and then went back downstairs.

He thanked Gareth for his interest and kindness and Andrew for making it all happen, and for dinner. He took his leave and decided to walk towards the city to clear his head and work out what he was going to say to Martin.

****

Gordon dropped Natalia and Anton off at their apartment. Anton slept all the way back from the zoo to home; he was absolutely exhausted but very happy indeed. Natalia said to him, 'Gordon you cannot imagine what a pleasure this has been. I could never have done it on my own.'

Gordon smiled at her and said, 'Actually it is I who should thank you. This is the closest I will ever be to being a Grandpa.'

Gordon drove home and let himself in. The house was quiet and empty; he supposed Thelma was off doing her art thing. It was already past six and so he felt justified in pouring himself a gin and tonic. He made it quite a stiff one, he just felt like it. He relaxed in his usual chair and looked out at the lovely garden. It was beautiful and luxuriant with the recent rain, sheltered and private, his own domain. He felt pretty good. There was just one thing nagging him a bit that he wanted to think about; it was the conversation about Martin, and what being gay was all about. He started to ponder.

All his life he had been in charge, a confident business man who operated on a stage he knew well. He was good at it. He had never really thought much about other people, such as those less well off or disadvantaged in any way. He had been comfortably middle class all his life, and felt he belonged very much to the North Shore meritocracy. Well, he thought it was a meritocracy at the time. His world view was pretty much that people were what they made of themselves, and for those who had not made it, it was generally their fault. Everyone was an individual responsible for themselves. The fewer limits on their activities the more it encouraged people to excel and the better the world was. The less well off would benefit anyway from the trickledown effect as the wealthy spent their well deserved money.

Natalia had opened his eyes to a different world, one that he had never engaged in before. He discovered that the less than ideal situation she found herself in was not generally of her own making. He realised that he had always judged people by his own values. If they did not come from his world, they were less deserving. He saw Martin through the lens of that set of values, but he had broken the rules by being homosexual. That was something that people, the right people, are not supposed to be. His own son did not fit the model that was Gordon's milieu. It had been seen by Gordon almost as an act of defiance. But what if people found themselves in situations over which they had no control? Should they be judged in the way that he had always previously judged them? What Natalia was affirming based on her knowledge of her father, is that one's sexuality is not under one's control. It contradicted the world view that Gordon had had that people are what they make of themselves, that they create their own destiny. In that case he was judging Martin for something he had no control over. No wonder Martin was distressed by their recent meetings.

Gordon reflected that following through that logic he had no right to judge Martin and that he should just accept him as he is. But in a different part of his brain there was another process happening which was totally independent of the logic. It was an emotional response and that response continued to reject Martin. He wondered why. He came to the conclusion that that was due to conditioning and his own identity as a conservative middle class man living in comfort and without concern for those who did not belong to his tribe. That homosexuality is wrong is what he had been led to think all his life, by his parents, by his schoolmates, by society. Since homosexuals are less likely to have progeny, maybe this was all to do with survival of the species, in other words an evolutionary factor to protect the species. Or had it been religions that had promoted the anti-homosexual view for political reasons, or an interpretation of the bible? He had never believed in a literal interpretation of the bible anyway. He was not even sure that he believed in God. He hardly thought about it, but certainly did not practice any religion.

It was time he thought for himself, more independently and question what he had been told throughout his life. He should allow the logic to overrule the emotional, especially since the emotional was probably more a result of conditioning than anything else. There was more to life than his own narrow tribe, and other tribes had just as much legitimacy as his own.

He came to the conclusion that he had wronged Martin. He needed to put that right.

****

While Gordon was grappling with how to apply the discipline required for his rational and logical brain to overrule his emotional brain, Thelma was just letting her emotional brain run loose. There was no doubt in her mind that Sebastian was not making an offer about splitting the costs of the hotel room in Canberra to save money; he was offering her a night of intimacy, of sex. While she was vaguely aware that there were all sorts of reasons for exercising caution in response to Sebastian's question, almost without thinking she said, 'I think we could manage with one room, don't you?' To justify her decision and not appear too eager, she added almost as an afterthought, 'It would be far less expensive and easier to find one room rather than two.' But in reality her answer was really motivated by the fact that she wanted to have sex with Sebastian.

She suddenly felt young again and for the first time in a long time she remembered Sergei. She felt the same excitement with Sebastian as she had with him. It was attenuated perhaps with age, but the flutter she felt was unmistakable.

Sebastian used an app on his phone to see what rooms were available. He found one at one of the hotels on Northbourne Avenue that would be convenient to get to and would be on the way out of Canberra for the morning. He chose a room with one Queen Size bed. He gave his credit card details to confirm the booking. Neither of them had any luggage and of course no toothbrush or toothpaste so they stopped briefly at a pharmacy and bought a few things they each thought they might need. Sebastian bought condoms and KY as well, but he did that very discreetly and Thelma had not noticed.

They arrived at the hotel and Sebastian checked in. They both laughed as they went into the room saying how weird it was to go into a hotel room and not have any luggage. If the staff had noticed they might assume that this was an illicit relationship of two lovers escaping from their partners for a quickie. Sebastian pointed out that it was already close to 8.00 p.m. and that they should go and get something to eat.

'Just a minute before we go.' Thelma hesitated a second. She did not want to say she needed to phone 'my husband,' or even 'Gordon,' so instead said, 'I need to call home just to let them know I will be back tomorrow.' She went onto the balcony and called Gordon on his mobile.

'Gordon. It's Thelma.'

'I know, your name comes up on the screen.'

'I am afraid I can't get back tonight, there has been a terrible crash on the highway and the traffic can't get through. So I am spending the night in Canberra and I will be back tomorrow late morning.'

'Yes I saw that on the evening news. It looks like a real mess. I wondered if it would affect you.'

'I left food in the fridge.'

'Don't worry; I am not going to starve.'

'Alright, see you tomorrow.' Thelma hung up. That was out of the way and now she could look forward to the evening, and the night.

Sebastian had asked the young woman on reception if she could recommend anywhere to eat. She suggested a small restaurant in one of the many local shopping centres in the suburbs of Canberra. It turned out to be ideal. The food was a mix of modern cuisines and the restaurant was licensed. They ate well and consumed a bottle of wine between them. By the time they got back to the hotel room it was after 10.00.

Sebastian excused himself and went to the bathroom and took a quick shower. He cleaned his teeth. He came out with a towel round him, and said to Thelma, 'The bathroom is all yours.'

She had no hair dryer, and had bought a cap at the pharmacy so she was able to take a shower without wrecking her hair-do. She came out of the bathroom with the towel wrapped around her. Sebastian was lying on his back on the bed, with the towel barely covering his lower trunk. He was slim and wiry, just a hint of hair on his chest. He pulled the towel a bit further down his body and smiled.

'How was the shower?' Sebastian asked.

'Great. I feel quite relaxed.' Thelma sat on the side of the bed. She put her hand on his chest. Sebastian pulled her towards him and kissed her gently on the lips. Thelma abandoned herself to a passionate kiss. Sebastian leaned over and turned the bedside light off leaving just a glimmer in the room coming from the slightly open door to the bathroom. They both threw their towels off and discovered and pleasured each other. Sebastian was surprised that despite her rather reserved exterior Thelma was a passionate lover. Thelma was surprised how skilled Sebastian was at making love; considerate, intuitive. She had never had sex before with a man who was as dedicated to her pleasure as he was to his own. They slept fitfully, neither used to sleeping with another person, Thelma and Gordon had separate rooms nowadays. But Thelma did not mind, she felt comfortable with Sebastian. When she woke up she suddenly thought of Gordon and felt as if a hollow had appeared in her stomach. What had she done? Did this mark a sudden big change in her relationship with her husband, or was it simply the culmination of changes that had been happening for a long time? She could not say she felt guilt, although she felt she should have. She rather felt a sadness and at the same time a warmth and comfort. Sebastian rolled over and put his arms round Thelma. She moved onto her side and snuggled into him. She could feel his erection again.

****

Tony wondered whether it was better to speak to Martin over dinner out somewhere in a restaurant or when they were together at home. In the end he opted for home on the basis that they would be more easily able to talk, and it would be more

134

natural. He suggested to Martin that he would pick up some food and cook dinner for him.

He said, 'I have a key so I can do all the preparation before you get home.'

Martin could smell a rat. 'So what is going on?'

'Nothing really,' he lied, not out of intention but just to put Martin's mind at rest. 'I just want to tell you what is going on at work.'

'Are you going to leave, or did you get a promotion or something?' Martin was curious now.

'No, I will tell you over dinner. So which day works best for you? I am free in the evenings every day this week.'

'Can it wait until Friday? Then we have the weekend together anyway. I was thinking on Saturday morning we could go to the market in Paddo and have lunch somewhere and then Saturday evening we have dinner with Rick and Stan, remember.'

'Oh yes, I had forgotten that. Alright make it Friday.' By then he would have put in the application form, but he needed to do that anyway. He could always back out later.

Tony did the shopping and made a Greek salad to start with and then they would have lamb cutlets with sautéed French beans, roasted cauliflower and sweet potato. All he had to do was cook the lamb cutlets and sauté the beans in butter and garlic when Martin arrived. He had already prepared dessert, a fruit salad, and had bought some panna cotta to go with it.

By six o' clock on Friday, Tony had everything prepared as far as he could. He had the gin ready and the tonic was in the fridge. Martin texted to say he was going to be a bit late because they had all of a sudden called a meeting. He was clearly pissed off from the curtness of his message. At 6.45 Tony heard the key in the door and Martin walked in. As usual he was immaculately dressed; a light beige suit, pale blue shirt and a red tie, his briefcase in hand and at least from the outside calm. Tony found him so handsome. He kissed Tony on the mouth and then sat down.

'What a lot of wankers!' Martin exclaimed.

'I take it you are talking about your work colleagues,' Tony sought to confirm.

'Yes, my work colleagues. There is a rumour of a go-slow next week by the logistics and transport department; the ones that send the goods to the customers. Some dispute over work conditions. So they wanted a meeting this evening, Friday for god's sake when nothing can be done until Monday anyway, to decide what to do. They want to avoid losing any sales and make sure the customers don't stock out. So they had this idea of getting forward orders from the customers and get them to take the stock. It is unreasonable to expect them to order and pay for goods before they need them, so we could extend the payment terms on those orders, but then it would put many of them over their credit limits and Finance will not allow that. In the end I suggested we just put the goods out there on consignment. They receive them but we don't invoice them. That all took an hour to agree, and then they wanted to go and have a drink at the pub. When I said I had to go I got the usual disapproving looks. Those straight men just don't want to go back to their families and really they don't have a life. Well, what I would call a life.'

'Do you feel better now that you have that off your chest?' Tony asked gently.

Martin laughed. 'Yes I do.'

'Want a G&T?' Tony asked.

'Let me go and change first and then we will have one.' Martin got up and went upstairs to change into shorts and a T shirt. He even looked immaculate in those, however casual they were. Tony thought again how well Martin wears clothes. Tony poured them both a gin and tonic.

'So what do you want to tell me?' Martin asked. He was always cautious and careful, and had an ability to logically think through options and assess them. This was one of the reasons he was so good at his job. He had turned over in his mind what some of the possibilities were, but obviously had reached no conclusion. It must be something to do with work he surmised. Tony was relaxed with him, but at the same time Martin could see that he was a bit anxious about something. He was not worried that it was about their relationship; Tony was too warm towards him for that to be on the cards. He was intrigued.

Tony knew Martin would be upset, and while he knew what he wanted to happen, it was quite likely that Martin would not want to leave his job and go to London with him. If that were the case it would be Tony who would have to decide between his career and his relationship. He thought it better to have the conversation after the main course. At least Martin would have eaten something by then!

'Let's have dinner and then we can chat while we eat.' Tony wanted to make it sound as non-threatening as he could.

Martin had almost finished his drink and moved to the table that Tony had already set. Tony opened a bottle of Martin's favourite red wine and poured them both a glass. He served dinner and then sat down. They ate while engaging in some small talk, Martin waiting for Tony to take the lead; it was clear he was not going to talk until he was ready, and so Martin did not want to push it too much even though he was anxious to find out what Tony had to say.

'The cutlets were delicious, thanks,' Martin said as he finished his meal and put the cutlery on the plate.

Tony looked at him and smiled.

'So?' Martin asked.

'Well, you have met Andrew, the concert master, basically my boss.' Martin nodded. 'A week or so ago he pulled me aside and asked what I was planning for my career. The bottom line is that he recommended that I go to London to further my studies for a couple of years, and he told me that the guy responsible for scholarships at the London School of Music was coming to Sydney this last week. It turns out they are very good friends, in fact I think they have had a relationship in the past when Andrew was in London. Andrew asked me over for dinner last Tuesday and during the evening this guy pretty much offered me a scholarship. There is a loophole in that with Brexit some of the places that had been reserved for EU students will not be taken up and that has left some open scholarships. He asked me to fill in an application for a scholarship, and I did.

At the same time as he automatically said, 'Wow, great!' Martin realised what the implications were and he had an awful sinking feeling in the pit of his stomach. Tony noticed as the colour drained out of his face, and he felt tortured by the look of almost panic on Martin's face.

'I had to put in the application but it doesn't mean that I am necessarily going. That is what we need to talk through.' Tony was trying to reassure Martin, and indeed he did relax a little.

'I want you to develop your career and I think London would be good for you, but I am not sure I can cope with two years of separation and I don't want to lose you.' Martin had tears in his eyes.

'I don't want to lose you either. But there is a way we could do it all.'

'How do you mean?' Martin could not see any way at all of reconciling the two.

'Just hear me out,' Tony spoke carefully and slowly, 'What if you come to London with me? You have complained quite a bit about your work, and a change might be really good right now.'

'Leave my job?' Martin was very careful and in all of his life he had not taken risks. He envisaged that one day he would leave his job and go to another one, but he would not leave until he had something else to go to. He could never understand how people could walk out on a job when they did not have another one to go to.

'Yes. I know that is not something that you would feel comfortable about. But life is for living. I would love to explore Europe with you. You would find a job in UK I am sure, and because of your grandmother you would have a patriality visa that would allow you to work.' Tony was sounding enthusiastic. 'Maybe you could even get a transfer with the company. They have an office in the UK don't they?'

'There is an office but it is just a sales office. My role there would not exist.'

'But there could be other roles maybe?' Tony was not going to give up on this idea just yet.

'I am not sure that they would give me a glowing reference, but then on the other hand they might want to get rid of me. I don't think it is likely but there could be a possibility. I have to work and earn reasonable money as the mortgage needs to be paid.'

'If you rented this place out you would get, what, at least $800 a week, probably quite a bit more?'

'A friend rented an apartment down the road, two bedrooms and he was paying around that, so maybe yes, and that would certainly cover the mortgage,' Martin conceded. He was turning things over in his mind. This had come as a great surprise to him and he was struggling to work out how he felt about it. He was really sure of one thing; he did not want to lose Tony. Neither did he want to stand in the way of Tony's career. Would their relationship survive two years apart? Maybe, but it would be painful. If it did not survive that would be terribly sad, but then again if it did survive it would seal the relationship more firmly than ever. He recognised that he was scared about unknown territory; London without a job. Yet on the other hand he did find the idea of he and Tony exploring London together sort of exciting. Thoughts were cascading through his mind.

'I might get enough rent to pay the mortgage but then there would be rent to pay in London.'

'Ah I forgot to mention that,' Tony said, 'the scholarship includes an accommodation allowance and that would cover us both as we would live together. It would not be as comfortable as this place I am sure, but it would be enough.'

Martin was running out of arguments and ended up with just the truth of his nervousness about taking risks in his life. He remembered the personality test which he had to undertake when he joined the company he worked for. When he went back for a consultation with the psychologist who had interpreted his test, she had demonstrated that the test had revealed more about him that he thought possible. In particular she talked about his aversion to risk, adding that he should guard against letting it prevent him from reaching out into new worlds.

Then he thought about the recent appraisal he had had with his boss and how unfair it had been and how much it had annoyed him. There was only one position he could be promoted to within the company and that was the one his boss occupied. His boss was in his late 50s and probably would not move unless he was himself promoted. Martin doubted that even if that position were to become available he would get it. He was not enough of what they considered a 'team player'.

'When do you have to make a final decision?' Martin was thinking that he wanted to do some research and ask around a bit.

'Tony answered, 'They have the application and as the academic year starts in September I imagine the point of no return will be a couple of months.'

'So we have a bit of time before we have to make a final decision.'

'Yes we do,' Tony agreed, 'and what I want most is for us to go and explore together. To be honest I do want to do this course but I would not feel complete without you.' He felt it had gone better than he had feared and he could see that Martin was thinking about it at least. He knew that Martin would probably have more doubts in the morning and that he would probably seesaw a bit as his natural aversion to risk battled with the opportunity.

That is exactly what happened. They went to bed quite early and Martin held Tony tight in his arms as if he did not want to let him go. Sex was the furthest thing on his mind, but as he snuggled behind Tony he could feel his erection growing and it just seemed natural to let things take their course. They fucked in a way that expressed the desire of both of them to be together and not lose each other. Just before he ejaculated Martin felt the strongest conviction that he could never let this feeling go. But he woke up before the sun crept round the edge of the heavy curtains in his bedroom. Tony had moved and was in a deep sleep on his side. Martin could hear his breath as he lay there in innocence next to him.

Suddenly Martin thought of the previous evening and he felt a horrible falling feeling in the pit of his stomach, as if his world was falling through his gut. He was scared. He just wanted so badly for this not to have happened, but it had. He drew away from Tony, and lay on his back, now wide awake. He remembered how he felt when Tony told him about the scholarship, that sinking feeling, the one he was feeling now, followed by his thinking that maybe he could go and be with Tony. But now he thought that that had been pure fantasy.

To start with he and Tony had never lived together. What would happen if he gave up everything and went with him, and then the relationship broke up? He was used to being comfortably off; if he wanted clothes he would buy them, go to the theatre when he wanted, could eat at expensive restaurants if he wanted to. How would he feel if he was again living more like a student? He recognised that he was in a bit of a rut, but it was a comfortable rut, and he was aware many people would be pleased to trade places. He had done very well for himself at the age of 34, and why would he want to throw all of that away. He could go and stay with Tony when he had holidays, maybe twice a year and Tony could come back in his holidays. The idea of them being in London together was romantic, but just not practical. He felt thoroughly dejected.

When Tony woke up he could see in Martin's face straight away that he had been rethinking it. He kissed him lightly. Martin did not react.

'Want me to get you breakfast before we go to the market?' Tony asked.

'I think that all I want really is just a coffee. We can get something at the market later. You have some if you want.'

Martin decided not to say anything right then, and Tony didn't feel it would be a good idea to start a conversation at that time in the morning either.

****

Thelma was a bit flustered as she sat down, placing shopping bags on the vacant seat.

'Sorry I am late,' she said.

Renie just looked at her and smiled. 'No, actually I was early.' Renie was always exact about such things. 'So I ordered a flat white while I waited. Do you want one?'

'I will have one after lunch I think.' Thelma picked up the menu.

'You look really well.' Renie observed.

'Thanks. I am well,' Thelma said.

'You have a kind of glow, what is all that about?' Renie was always very observant, a fact that Thelma found quite unsettling. Thelma did not respond to the question.

They perused the menu for a few minutes and then sat back ready to order. The waiter took their order and while they were waiting for their food, they engaged in the usual small talk, until Renie asked, 'So how is Martin?'

Thelma had been expecting the conversation and still had not decided how she would answer if that question came up. As a result she hesitated, and Renie seized the hesitation with her insight. 'I was right wasn't I? Did the gay thing finally come up?'

'Don't be so smug, Renie. It has been very upsetting for Gordon and me. Yes you were right as it happens, and we are not at all happy about it. I had been thinking about what you had said and then Martin missed a meal with us his birthday weekend because he went away with some friend of his and it all came to a head when he came round the week after. It was just horrible. We told him that it was just not acceptable and that if he needed help getting through this phase that Gordon and I were there to support him.'

'That would have been helpful I imagine,' Renie observed sarcastically.

'He left on very bad terms and we have only seen him a few times since and we never talk about it.'

'So he has a boyfriend. What is he like?'

'I have no idea what he is like and I told Martin that we are not interested in meeting him. And I don't like the term boyfriend, it is so sordid.'

'Really Thelma, that is terribly cruel.'

'Yes it is. How could he do this to us?'

'No that is not what I meant. It is cruel of you and Gordon. Martin is what he is, and you should just accept him and love him for the wonderful young man he is. You should be proud of him.' Renie looked intensely at Thelma.

'Well I am proud of him in some senses, but not this phase he is going through.'

'Thelma, Martin is not going through a phase. He is gay. He can't, and I am sure would not want, to do anything about it. This is not a choice that people make, it just is.'

'Gordon has been reading up about it, and that is what he says. But I don't accept that. It is just not normal.'

'Not normal in the sense that most people are straight. But there is absolutely nothing wrong with it,' Renie commented, 'just as it is not normal to have red hair. Most of us don't, but there is nothing wrong with having red hair.'

Thelma ignored the comment. 'And I don't like that word gay. How can any homosexual be gay? It suggests happy or something. Ridiculous!'

'It is what gay people prefer to be called. And that should be respected,' Renie said.

Thelma was about to respond when the waiter brought their lunch and they started to eat and then they changed the subject.

After lunch Thelma ordered a coffee and Renie a second one.

'So what have you been up to apart from torturing Martin?' Renie asked with a slight smile.

Thelma ignored the barb. 'Not much really. I started art classes.'

'Oh great. How is it going?'

'Sebastian says that I am making good progress. He seems very happy with what I am doing,' Thelma said.

143

Renie looked at her. 'Sebastian?'

'He is the person who gives the classes. He is very talented,' Thelma said quite enthusiastically.

Renie looked at her and said, 'That glow comes back again when you talk about him, Thelma. Now what is going on?'

Thelma should have remembered how observant and intuitive Renie was. Thelma was defensive. 'Nothing is going on.' She looked a bit guilty.

'Come on Thelma!' Renie said.

Thelma wanted desperately to talk to someone about Sebastian and Renie was her only sister and they had never held secrets between them. 'You are impossible Renie. But I am having a sort of a thing with Sebastian. Gordon does not know.'

'What sort of a thing? An affair?'

'Well I would hardly call it an affair.' Thelma then went on to recount what had happened in Canberra.

'And since then?' Renie pressed.

'I have been over to his place a couple of times after art classes.' Thelma bit her lip.

'Wonderful!' Renie exclaimed, 'I have been saying for ages you needed to brighten up your life.'

'I don't feel exactly guilty about it with Gordon, in fact I feel a bit sorry for him. But it is so wonderful with Sebastian, that I don't want to stop. He makes me feel wanted.' She paused a bit pensively, and then continued, 'I am a mess, Renie, I don't know where this is going and I am terrified of the future. I know that common sense dictates that I should stop it, but I don't want to.'

'Then don't. Just let it go where it goes. Life is too short not to take opportunities when they arise, just go and have some fun, but don't take it too seriously.' Renie then added, 'Just one thing, don't you think Martin has the right to do the same and follow his instincts?'

'That's different. What I am doing is normal. What he is doing is not right.'

Renie looked at her and said 'Is that so?'

****

Gordon turned the key in the lock. Thelma called from the sitting room, 'I am here, in the sitting room.'

He shut the front door and went into the sitting room. Thelma had a gin and tonic by her side and looked relaxed. 'How was golf?' she asked without any interest in his answer whatever it might have been.

'The usual I guess. Win a few, lose a few.' Gordon was non committal.

'I think I will get one of those,' Gordon said pointing to the gin and tonic. While he poured the gin, he asked Thelma, 'How was your day?'

'I had lunch with Renie in the city.'

'How is she?'

'Oh fine.' Thelma did not share the content of their conversation.

Thelma did not want to dwell on Renie and changed the conversation. 'I bought a dress.'

'Oh that's nice.' Gordon said in a voice somewhat lacking in interest. Then he realised he should be a bit more responsive. 'What's it like?'

'It's dark green, quite elegant I think. I will show you later.'

Gordon grunted. He started talking again, 'You know I have been thinking about Martin.'

Thelma was on her guard. 'Oh?'

Gordon continued 'I have done quite a bit of reading and speaking to a few people, and I think we might have taken the wrong tack with him.'

Thelma said nothing. He went on, 'I think that we have been very hard on him. I really believe that being gay is beyond his control. He just is gay and that's it. We should accept him as he is and not try and change him. I might have had ideas in my head about what I wanted for him, but fundamentally that was guided by what I thought would make him happy in his life. What I now realise is that it should be up to him to decide what that is and not us.'

Thelma interrupted him a bit scornfully, 'How can he ever be happy being like that?'

'Let me finish,' Gordon continued, 'the main reason as far as I can see that gay people are unhappy is because of how the rest of us treat them.'

'If that is an implied criticism, I entirely reject it.' Thelma was quite agitated now. 'Gordon, I don't care what you have read or who you have been talking to, it is not natural. Down the centuries it has been condemned and for very good reason. It is an act against nature, and I just can't believe that my son could get caught up in such things.' The fact that Renie had been saying more or less the same thing as Gordon caused her to become more dogmatic. This was something that she felt, not something to be argued like an abstract proposition. She knew to the core of her being that it was wrong.

'That's just not true,' Gordon countered, 'there are many cultures where it was accepted. There is ancient Japan, Greece, the Pacific Islands, even some cultures in the Middle East. It was only the church that fostered that view.'

'All foreigners with no Christian tradition!' Thelma snorted. 'All of the proper religions take the same stance, Catholics, Anglicans, Baptists. Even the Muslims, at least they got that right.'

'I didn't know you were so religious.' Gordon was irritated now.

'I am not. But this is where our value system came from. Christian values. And what about the Arabs and the Africans, they put them to death.' Thelma felt almost triumphant. 'And I am very angry that my son should go down this path. I want grandchildren!'

Gordon thought about Anton, but did not say anything. With Anton he had the closest thing to a grandchild he would ever have, and he was delighted about that. 'Surely it is about Martin's happiness, not ours.'

'How can he ever be happy living hat sort of life? Two men, it is ridiculous. Only a woman can give him the nurturing he needs, and take care of him. Women are made for that. He

146

would be fine if the right girl would come along. And he has always been good with children.'

Gordon sighed. 'I have never seen him take the slightest interest in children. Thelma I think you are making this up as you go along.'

'What would you know about him? You never bothered to have a relationship with him; you were too busy at work. It is probably your fault that he went down this path, no proper male role model to guide him. I did my best for heaven's sake, and then this is how he rewards me.'

Gordon could see that at least that evening he was not going to make any progress; Thelma was being too irrational and no amount of argument, evidence or persuasion was going to sway her view. He decided that her refusal to accept Martin as he is was not a reason for him to do the same.

****

Martin shut the door to his office and sat down at his desk. There was work he needed to attend to, but did not feel like working at all. The weekend Tony and he spent together had been excellent, apart from this sword of Damocles hanging over his head. It was Monday and he had left Tony in bed. He had not had any breakfast, he just wasn't hungry, but had bought a takeaway hot flat white at the café on the ground floor which he placed on his desk. Looking around the office he decided he hated it but felt trapped in it because of his paralysing fear of taking risks. He felt torn apart between wanting to be with Tony and losing his life style. They had been seeing each other for well over six months now, heading for a year, and Martin had been very pleased with the way their relationship was developing. Now that was all in jeopardy because of his internal conflict with no apparent resolution.

He was woken from his reverie by his mobile phone ringing. He looked at it and saw that it was his father. Surprised and wondering if something had happened, he picked it up and answered, 'Hi Dad. I didn't expect to hear from you. Is everything alright?'

'Yes son, everything is fine. Look, I am calling you because I have been doing some thinking. Martin I feel bad about how things have been going over the last couple of months since you told us you are gay.' Gordon had even managed to use the word gay almost as if it was natural to him. 'I am sorry because I don't think your mother and I have been as understanding as we could have been. I wanted to sit down and talk to you, just the two of us together over dinner some time soon.'

Martin was quite taken aback. He had never known his father to take an initiative like this and to sound so different. He was more than pleased to accept. 'Yes of course, by all means. How about tomorrow night?'

"Yes that works for me. Where?'

Martin preferred to eat in the Eastern Suburbs but did not really want his father to drive that far at night and in any case he worked on the North Shore so he suggested a French restaurant in Chatswood, one where it would be easy to park.

Gordon was more than happy with that and so Martin offered to make the booking as he knew the restaurant. 'I will make a booking for a quiet table where we can talk. Say about 6.30?'

Gordon arrived a few minutes early and was sitting at the table when Martin walked in. They shook hands, both a little on edge and apprehensive. Gordon said, 'I was about to order a drink. What would you like?'

'I'll have a Campari and soda please.'

Gordon did not see the point in engaging in small talk and got straight to the point. 'I know we have never been that close and now I have come to regret that. To be honest I really did not know much about homosexuality, just the kind of things people talk about down the pub. Sadly it is not very complimentary. So when you told us you were gay it really took me off guard. Over the last few weeks I decided to do some research and I spoke to a few people, and I think I understand it a bit better. It is taking me some time to get used to it, but I want you to know that I am trying.'

Martin was both taken aback and at the same time suddenly emotional. To hear his father's words were more than he could have hoped for. All he could say was, 'Dad!'

'Let me finish. All I ever wanted for you is your happiness. The mistake we both made is that we thought we knew better than you how to achieve that happiness.'

Martin said, 'I am happy being gay. I can't imagine being any different, it is just who I am.'

'I know that now, but I didn't realise it initially. I only want you to be very careful. With your health.'

'You mean HIV? I am not stupid, I know what I have to do,' Martin reassured his father, 'I am always careful to stay safe.'

'I just needed to know that. How long have you known?'

'That I am gay? Pretty much all my life. I knew that I was different as a child, but of course I did not know why. It was in my teens I suppose that it gradually dawned on me.' Martin did not feel like going into details about his masturbating over gay porn when he was in his teens and how he had got an erection when he was playfully wrestling with one of the other prefects at school.

'You came on your own.' Martin made a bald statement.

'Yes. Your mother and I have had several conversations about this, and frankly she is not ready as yet to see it in the same way I do.'

'You mean she is still upset and angry about it.'

'She still does not understand. She can't see it. I think for her there is some kind of emotional block about it, but I don't know what that is due to.' Gordon was trying to be as diplomatic as possible.

'I was always so close to her and now it seems like there is this gulf between us.' Martin sounded mournful.

'I am hoping I can bring her round, using Renie as well if I have to. I know from what your mother has said that your aunt Renie is on your side.'

Martin smiled. 'I always liked aunt Renie,' he said, 'she always was fun and so down to earth, almost too direct at times.'

Gordon looked at his watch. 'We should order.'

They both ordered chicken breast in some exotic sounding sauce that neither had ever heard of.

Gordon hesitated before asking Martin, 'Tell me about your friend.'

'Tony. Well, he is a violinist in the Sydney Symphony Orchestra, and I gather a very good one. He is honest, caring, good to be with and I like him a lot.

'So it is a serious relationship for you?' Gordon enquired.

'Yes, it is. The first time I have felt that I have found someone I would like to settle down with.'

The next thing Gordon said was hard for him, but he felt it was important. 'Then I should meet him, don't you think?' He dreaded to think how he would feel meeting Martin's 'boyfriend'; it seemed so alien to him. But he knew he had to get over these feelings and let logic rule the day.

'I would really like that.' Martin smiled, and Gordon could see that he was genuinely pleased.

'Maybe dinner one evening?' Gordon ventured.

'Would you like to come round to the house?'

Gordon would have preferred more neutral ground like a restaurant, but he also recognised that accepting Martin was also to do with normalising the situation.

Martin added, 'Of course Ma would be welcome too, I just get the impression that...' He stalled as he was not quite sure how to finish the sentence.

Gordon got him off the hook. 'I think the first time it would be better if it was just me. Maybe we can get your mother round the next time.' Gordon was not at all sure how easy or likely that was going to be but for the time being he felt that was the best way to leave it. It was really important to Gordon that they maintained communication even if it was only one of them. The worst thing would be if Martin shut them out of his life, and they shut him out of theirs.

Martin had not been able to talk to anyone about Tony's scholarship to London and what it meant for his relationship. He had turned it over and over in his mind and was no closer to deciding what he was going to do. Thinking it through rationally was not working. He suddenly felt that maybe he would share this dilemma with his father. He needed to get it off his chest. He thought it most likely that if he asked any of their gay friends they would tell him to go and that his father would tell him not to. But at least the conversation might reveal some other factors that would help him decide, perhaps a new way of looking at the issue.

'Dad, there is something I would like your advice on.' This was not something that Gordon was expecting, and not sure that he was going to be able to advise Martin, but he would do his best.

Martin continued, 'It is to do with Tony. I mentioned he is a violinist and a talented one. He has just been offered a scholarship in London for at least two years. He has asked me to go with him.'

'What do you want to do?' Gordon asked.

'I don't know, I have been turning it over in my mind and I just don't know what to do. You have always brought me up to be responsible and the thought of not having a job, and in another country at that, is really scary.'

'Do you want to go? I mean setting aside the work situation, would you want to go?'

'There is part of me that would really like it; a chance to visit Europe, be with Tony, discover new things. But I worry about what it would do to my career, and what would happen if I am not earning money. I would feel very vulnerable. They say that it is in your thirties that your career is made or broken. That scares me.'

Gordon wanted to steer away from the relationship aspects of this issue and was happy to stay on firmer ground such as work. 'I am not going to tell you what I think you should do, that would not be fair. But I will tell you what has been going through my mind these last months since I retired. Or was retired, to say it how it is. That might help you. While I was working I was completely absorbed by work. To be honest the way they got rid of me was very hurtful, and it made me wonder whether the time and effort I devoted to work all those years was not well placed. I let myself get so absorbed that I forgot about living. I think I neglected your mother. Of course she was happy with her part time job and her friends, but I was never the companion she really wanted. Yes I provided well for her, and she has had a very comfortable life, but it was not as complete as it should have been. Maybe if I had not spent so much time working we would not have drifted apart in the way that I sense we have.'

He paused and then he said, 'And it is even more true for my relationship with you. You grew up without me really noticing. I regret now not having taken you out, just being together.'

'I am not sure we really had that much in common. We just like doing different things,' Martin interjected, 'you know I hated the footy.'

'Yes, I know. But I regret that I did not take time to find the common ground that exists. We both like nature and it might surprise you to know that I loved theatre and plays when I was young.'

Gordon continued, 'But let me get to the point. It came as a terrible shock to me when they got rid of me under the pretext of that prostate problem I had. I was devastated. I had worked all my life with the ambition and expectation that I would take over as CEO when Reg retired. I discovered that the new regime in the US put no value on promises made, loyalty and all the hard work I had done over the years. When it came to it I discovered that it counted for nothing. I had in one sense wasted my life. Nearly forty years, my whole adult life, I had put in extra hours, put the company in front of my own family, and for what? I felt as if I had wasted the best years of my life, and suddenly when it was far too late at almost 60, I could never get back those lost years. There are times when I sit at home wondering how my life might have been if I had not been so obsessive about work.'

He paused and they both sat there in silence. Martin was stunned by his father's frank revelation and began to wonder whether he had known him at all, or whether the traumatic turn in his father's life had brought about fundamental changes in him. He said nothing but Gordon was aware that Martin was looking at him intensely.

Gordon continued, 'Maybe if I had not devoted my whole life to that bloody company your mother and I might have grown closer instead of further apart. Your mother was always more adventurous than I was, and I did not provide enough stimulation in our lives. Don't get me wrong, it is alright, but we are not close in the way that we could have been. Our life is mechanical rather than spontaneous. We tend to do things separately nowadays, she with her interests and me with mine.'

'The point of all this is that you are at a cross roads in your life and this is an important decision, so rather than drift into coming to a conclusion, you need to think it through really carefully and come to a well considered decision.'

'I know' Martin said. He realised that what Gordon was saying was true. This was not just a decision about London; it was one about what he wanted out of his life. This was going to be hard.

'I think you need to start off by asking yourself some questions.' Martin smiled. He had never really engaged with his father on any serious matter. He knew that his father must be competent otherwise he would not have risen in the company in the way he had. He had never thought about it, but he now realised that his father had a very systematic way of problem solving. Martin was all ears. Gordon continued, 'By that I mean fundamental questions, but specific enough to have meaning and help you decide. For example, what do you want out of life, three priority things you want your life to bring you? What role does money play in your life? Or relationships? Or job satisfaction? Then ask yourself how important your current job is in achieving that. Then you ask the same question about to what extent your friend is part of that.' Gordon felt that was a bit distant and so he added, 'Tony, I mean.'

'Well,' Martin started, 'that is quite a challenge. I am not sure I know how to answer.....'

Gordon interrupted, 'No, I don't mean right now, but something for you to ponder on your own. I think you need to find somewhere quiet, look into yourself and try and answer those questions. Take a few days if you need to.'

Martin sat back in his seat and looked at Gordon. 'You are right, that is what I need to do. I really appreciate your advice.' Gordon never thought that he would ever hear Martin say those words, and he felt pleased that their relationship seemed to be on a different and better footing than ever before.

They finished the chicken dish, and decided that despite the fancy name it was essentially a cream and mushroom sauce with some parsley. They chatted about a few items currently in the news and the antics of some of the neighbours, but they were both thinking about their conversation. They had coffee and Gordon paid the bill.

When they were outside the two men took their leave of each other. For the first time in a long time they hugged each other, and probably for the first time ever this time it was based on genuine affection and acceptance.

On the way back to Paddington Martin started to think about the questions Gordon had suggested he ask of himself. But he found that it was so intense that he was losing concentration on the road, so he decided to wait until he had time and a glass of wine, and instead turned on the radio.

****

A few weeks after Canberra, one afternoon when Thelma and Sebastian had gone back to his place after art class, they were just talking in bed after sex, Thelma resting her head on Sebastian's chest. Sebastian said, 'I have been thinking.'

Even though they were both very relaxed, it sounded as if this was going to be important. 'Oh?' Thelma responded, waiting to hear what he had been thinking.

'I was thinking about organising an art trip to Europe.'

'Just you or for the class?'

'No, just for you and me.'

Thelma sat up. Her immediate reaction was that she would love to go to Europe with Sebastian, but how could she square that with Gordon? Sebastian looked at her, waiting for an initial response. Thelma said, 'I would love nothing more, but there is Gordon.'

Sebastian said, 'I thought you would say that. Couldn't you tell him it is a group tour? The fact that the group is very small, like two people, only stretches the definition a little bit.'

Thelma was wondering whether she could get away with that with Gordon without him being too suspicious. 'You know I would love to go to Europe with you. That might work. Let me think about it. Where were you thinking about?'

'I had in mind Florence, Venice, Vienna and Prague. I was thinking just over two weeks.'

Thelma was delighted. 'I did not enjoy Italy the last time because Gordon just did not want to see galleries, he wasn't interested, and I have never been to either Vienna or Prague. That sounds lovely.'

'I thought maybe May or June when the evenings are longer and while reasonably warm, it is not peak season.'

'That sounds perfect. But that is only a couple of months from now.' Thelma was turning over in her mind how she could handle it with Gordon. She had pretty much made up her mind that she wanted to go. She had saved enough money from the part time job she used to have. It would not be necessary to ask Gordon if she could take the money out of their joint account. She would have felt that that would not have been right.

Over the next week Thelma gave Sebastian's proposal a lot of thought. She even discussed it with Renie at lunch, although she already knew what Renie would say. Renie had never really taken to Gordon, Thelma knew that. Renie always felt that he was too conventional, rather boring. Renie said, 'I think you have already decided Thelma. You want to go. So just do it! I would if I were in your shoes. But don't do anything silly like fall in love with him.'

They went back to Sebastian's place after art classes the next week. As soon as they got into his bedroom, Thelma said, 'I have decided. I will go with you to Europe.'

Sebastian did not ask anything about how she would handle it with Gordon. Instead he kissed her on the mouth and then undid her blouse. He whispered in her ear, 'Not only will I show you the best of Europe but we will make love in every city, and every night if you want.'

Thelma quivered slightly at the thought, and embraced Sebastian as she unzipped his pants.

She tried to sound as casual as she could a few nights later when she and Gordon sat down for their customary gin and tonic before dinner, 'Oh, they are organising an art trip to Europe in June and I thought I might go. I still have the money I saved from the part time job.'

'Oh. Just your art group?'

'I am not sure, the class leader is organising it.' Thelma was trying to tread the fine line between truth and lies, not taking into account that the moral issue was more about hiding from Gordon what this was really about. It might work in a court of law but not on judgment day.

'Where to?'

'Italy, Vienna and Prague. Just over two weeks.'

'Well you probably will enjoy this more than when we went. Likeminded people. If you want to do it, then go. When is it?'

'Early June; I haven' got exact dates yet. Should be nice weather but miss the worst of the crowds.'

Gordon said, 'It sounds nice,' and went back to reading the newspaper. He read the words on the page but was not registering them. Instead he was thinking this might be an opportunity for him to suggest to Natalia that he should take her and Anton up to the mid north coast for a little holiday.

Thelma was relieved that it seemed to be so easy. Gordon did not appear to really care, and was barely interested. That made it easier as he asked fewer questions. By the end of the week airfares were booked and hotels reserved.

****

Martin thought about driving down to the ocean at Clovelly and parking on the headland on the southern side of the inlet where he could watch the ocean and maybe get some inspiration to answer the questions Gordon had suggested he ask himself. It was a favourite place of his. Because of driving he would have to forgo the glass of wine he originally thought might have facilitated his thought processes. He did think of doing it together with Tony, but decided he should do it on his own first and then discuss it with Tony and hear what he thought about the various conclusions he would hopefully come to. Maybe he might even get Tony to think about some of the questions from his own perspective.

He decided to leave work earlier than normal the next day and headed down to Clovelly. It was close to dusk when he arrived and there was virtually nobody there, the car park was empty. He parked in the area furthest away from houses, right overlooking the rocks and the surf pounding beyond. To the right the coast stretched all the way down to the entrance to Botany Bay. The houses on the top of the hills were bathed in a warm gentle light as the setting sun cast its last rays over them. The ocean was a paler blue than in the middle of the day. It was beautiful, and he felt that wherever he went his heart would always be in Sydney.

What did he want out of life? He was sociable but also enjoyed his own company. He wanted a small group of friends around him, but not too many. He did not want to live on his own and he wanted to feel loved. But he did not want a smothering relationship. He felt it would be important for two people living together to have some separate interests and even different friends, and then some in common. He saw relationships very much as partnerships; he did not want to have a lover who was in any way dependent on him, especially emotionally. To him it was the intimacy and the company aspects of a relationship that were more important than sex, although he did enjoy sex too. But he would not describe himself as someone with a huge sexual appetite. He wanted to be comfortable but did not chase money. He wanted enough money to feel secure. In fact, he saw clearly how much security was a large need in his life. He did not like taking risks and he liked his world to be generally predictable. Beyond that he wanted to live in a nice place with beautiful things around him, and he wanted to be able to buy nice clothes.

Was he ambitious? He did not have ambition for power, he thought. But he did want status; he wanted people to respect him and what he did. He wanted to be significant if not important. For example did he want to become managing director of a company? No, not really. He would prefer to be in charge of marketing maybe, but did not want the responsibility of running a whole company. He saw what that desire had done to his father, and now his father was admitting that if he had his time over, he would have lived his life differently. He wanted a balance between work and his personal life and certainly did not want work to undermine his personal time. Added to which he was not that interested in managing people. That seemed to bring a whole load of problems with it. In marketing, there might be a few product managers to manage, but the content of the work would be mainly task oriented, technical. Yes, marketing requires good relationships with other departments like sales, production, and finance, but that was not the same as being responsible for staff and their performance.

He looked up. He had been totally absorbed in his own thoughts and now the sun had set and there were just the last lingering breaths of light clinging to the landscape before darkness crept over and day turned into night. He thought of Tony. He would be finishing rehearsals and going home to

Glebe. When Martin started to go out with Tony, he had in the back of his mind that he wanted to settle down; he was open to a relationship. Nothing had changed. Tony was an important part of his life. He feared that the decision about London was also a decision about the two of them. If he did not go with Tony, he did not give their relationship much chance of survival.

He decided to look at pros and cons as part of the exercise of deciding what to do. He started with the cons. The first big one was exactly what he had been thinking about. He would most likely lose Tony. One could argue that if Tony cared that much for Martin he would not take up that scholarship and not go to London. The fact is that one of them needed to concede, there was no meeting halfway. Either Sydney or London, the commute for holidays would be too unrealistic. He knew how important this study was for Tony's career. It would not be fair for him to ask Tony to stay. So he would have to be the one to give up his job and the security that brought. He thought about that for a second. How much security was there really with his job? The company was losing money because of cheaper imports and they had tried to initiate an antidumping action, but failed. The owners of the company were a multinational based in Germany and he was half expecting that they would close the Australian operation one of these days. He was in his mid thirties; he was not going to stay there forever anyway. It is just that he did not embrace change.

He would be a long way from his friends and his parents. The relationship with his parents had not been brilliant recently although he was getting on better with his father now, and at this stage he did not feel that their health was of a concern that should be a factor in whether he went or stayed. But he would miss his friends. On the other hand he might make new friends in London and in any case his friends would all still be in Sydney when they came back.

He would miss the concerts in Sydney, but of course the cultural programmes in London would be far more numerous and varied. So that really would be a pro.

The weather would be hard. From his previous visits he knew how depressing those monotonous featureless grey skies were that sat over North Western Europe from October to March; the constant dampness of the footpath and puddles that never went away. But the weather was not one of those things that should be a factor in making this decision. It would just be something he would have to put up with if he went.

Not being able to think of any more cons for the moment he decided to list the pros. First and foremost he would keep the relationship with Tony. He reflected that that was one of his priorities in life. He doubted that another Tony would come along in his life. He would not lose his house and the rent he could get would more than cover the mortgage. Would he have less cash in his pocket than now? It would all depend on what sort of a job he managed to get. The most worrying would be if he did not manage to get a meaningful job. What would it be like if he had to work as a waiter in a restaurant like lots of Australians in London did? Then again he was not doing the 'overseas experience' and was older than most Australians looking for work in London and he had more experience to offer. He might even get a transfer with his company, although they only had a sales office in UK, so that a job like his would be hard to replicate there. He had to discount a transfer. The job was the big unknown.

Martin had been to Europe a few times and had enjoyed it very much. But there was still so much to see. Living in London would give them the chance to really explore the UK and indeed all of Europe. Hardly anywhere was more than a three hour flight. Like Sydney to Cairns. And many places were closer than that and it could be like going to Melbourne or the Gold Coast for the weekend.

He had often been a bit concerned that if Tony moved in with him in Paddington, it would be Martin's place and although he would have to adapt to having Tony there, it would be Tony who would have to make the most changes in his life and it would remain after all Martin's place. It was not the ideal arrangement for a balanced partnership which is what Martin thought would work much better. In this case the place where they would live in London would be equally theirs. They would rent it together. He thought that was a better basis for a relationship to work, at least initially.

Looking more broadly at his life he thought that the experience of living in another country would broaden his perspectives. Much of life should be about experiences. Those people who seemed to live the fullest lives had travelled, they had taken risks. Risks! That was his weak point. He wanted a predictable world, and that was inconsistent with a fuller and more interesting life.

In the worst possible case if it didn't for some reason work out, he could always come home to his house and his life in Sydney, He was not going to be burning all his bridges. Furthermore, he hesitated to even think about this, and was ashamed of himself when he did, he was an only child and his parents were comfortably off. Unless they cut him out of their will it was reasonable to expect that he would eventually get a substantial inheritance. His mother was pissed off with him now but he thought that she would not cut him off when it came to it. He shuddered a little; he did not want to think that far into the future.

By now it was completely dark. He started the engine and headed back to Paddington. He thought that the process had been useful; at least it told him logically that he should go to London with Tony. That was what the logical part of his brain told him. But the emotional part of his brain was still nagging him about its discomfort with risk and change. He then thought that maybe, just maybe, the scholarship would not come through and he would not have to make difficult decisions. From what Tony had said it did look like a done deal, but he knew from his experience at work that you never count your chickens before they hatch.

****

It was a bright sunny day with a cool but pleasant breeze. Gordon mused at how bright colours seem to be in Sydney on days like this, the sky in particular such an intense blue. Natalia was already sitting on the usual park bench and Anton was running round with what looked like a homemade kite. As he sat they greeted each other.

'Anton looks very happy, what has he got there?'

'We made this kind of kite thing after he saw one on the television the other day. I am not sure it is ever going to fly. But he is having fun and getting some exercise.'

They chatted a while, and then Gordon asked her 'Have you ever thought of taking a break, a little holiday?'

Natalia said, 'Gordon I have often thought about it but to be honest it is a little bit beyond us at the moment.'

Gordon had anticipated her answer. 'I was thinking about that. Thelma is going to Europe in a couple of weeks, and I am not that keen on staying at home the whole time on my own. I was thinking that the three of us could go up the coast for a few days and rent a house. We would need three bedrooms of course.' Gordon wanted to clarify that he was offering friendship and nothing more. He continued, 'Natalia, I am not suggesting anything inappropriate, I feel I am like your uncle. It is just that I could do with the company and I thought it might make a nice break for you. Could you take a few days off?'

'Well, yes I suppose I could.' Natalia was trying to get her thoughts in order. She was sure that Gordon was not suggesting anything other than on the same basis as their relationship had been. He was far too much of a gentleman and she trusted him.

Gordon said, 'I did wonder whether Anton might get bored, but if we go to somewhere round Blueys Beach south of Forster there is plenty to do round there to keep him interested. And there is always the beach. I think a house would work better than a motel, and I have looked at Airbnb and there are some great places in that area, close to the beach and the shops. With a house Anton can go to bed when he wants and we do not have to worry about being confined to rooms in a motel.'

Natalia laughed. 'He never wants to go to bed, but yes a house would be so much easier. I wouldn't mind cooking.'

'I would want this to be a holiday for you too, and there is a restaurant that does takeaway, I already checked, and there are always things like pizza. Or we can go out and eat. It would be up to what we feel like.'

'It does sound nice I must admit.' Natalia was almost thinking aloud. 'It is ages since I went away and I don't think Anton ever did.'

'We would go in my car and of course I will pay for the house and everything. It won't cost you any money Natalia. It is something I would like to do and it would be far better than moping around the house on my own.'

Natalia asked 'When were you thinking of?'

'Thelma leaves in two weeks and will be away almost three, so any time during that period.'

'Work is normally quiet for me this time of year so that would fit in well. How many days were you thinking?'

Gordon said, 'I was thinking five nights. We could drive up on say a Thursday, and have five nights there and drive back on the Tuesday. Would that work for you?'

'Gordon it would be lovely.' Natalia smiled.

They agreed on dates and later that evening Gordon made a booking on the computer. He found a large house with three bedrooms and nice views right at the back of Boomerang Beach. It was perfect for what he wanted. He noticed in himself an enthusiasm he had not felt for years.

****

Thelma looked anxiously at her watch. The minibus service to the airport should be there in less than ten minutes. She had had to tell what she considered a white lie to Gordon, and that troubled her a bit. It was strange that she was going off with another man to Europe for two weeks frankly to commit adultery and yet she was troubled by a tiny white lie. Gordon had offered to take her to the airport; in fact he had assumed he

163

would. But she did not want him to in case he saw that she was going just with Sebastian. So she had told Gordon that they had arranged transport as a group so they could arrive and check in together. It had all been arranged and paid for. Gordon had seemed a bit surprised but accepted her story.

In fact Sebastian had booked a local service which would pick Thelma up from home first and then pick him up after. They had allowed plenty of time to get to the airport and check in. She was all set to go and now anxious to be on her way.

Packing had been a challenge. . She had bought a few new outfits during her shopping trips to the city when she had lunch with Renie. She shared with Renie the details of what she and Sebastian would be doing just in case something went wrong. Someone needed to know and Renie was the only person she could give that sort of detail to. She felt a bit uncomfortable about telling Renie, mostly because there was a degree of guilt about what in essence was cheating on Gordon. Renie was enthusiastic about the trip, more so than Thelma thought was appropriate.

She was pleased with her purchases, smart and youngish looking without being too youthful. She wanted to look her best for Sebastian. She had had her hair done and been to the podiatrist. She had not packed for an overseas trip in several years, and she was a bit tentative about what she needed to take. As they were staying in most places a few days she expected that laundry would be available. She made sure she had some sensible walking shoes for seeing the galleries as well as more elegant shoes to go out to dinner.

Jewellery was a problem. She did not want to take the valuable items with her just in case they were lost or stolen. At the same time she did not want to take cheap items or at least pieces that looked cheap. She carefully chose a selection that she thought would be a compromise.

She had closed the suitcase and picked it up to feel how heavy it was. Renie had loaned her a new very light weight case she had bought for her last cruise. It had wheels and handles that made it easy to manoeuvre. She was satisfied that she could manage the case given that Sebastian would have his own luggage to take care of and so she would have to take responsibility for her own bags.

She saw the minibus draw up in the street and the driver tooted lightly on the horn to let her know of his arrival. He was a few minutes early. She opened the front door and suddenly Gordon was there picking up the suitcase and carrying it down the drive. She picked up her handbag and a small leather bag she would take on board containing the few medications she was taking together with some reading material and a few things she thought she might need on the flight. The driver took the case from Gordon and put it in the back. Gordon turned to Thelma and gave her a peck on the cheek.

'Have a great trip darling, keep safe and let me know how it goes.' Gordon smiled at her.

Thelma managed to just say, 'I will. Look after yourself.' Then she climbed the two steps into the minibus and sat down in the window seat at the front. There were two other passengers in the back. Gordon would have assumed they were part of the group, but Thelma knew they were simply other passengers on their way to the airport. They pulled up in front of Sebastian's place no more than ten minutes later. Sebastian was waiting in the street for the minibus to arrive. With his case also stored in the back, he got into the minibus and sat next to Thelma. Thelma thought how worldly he looked and used to travel. He was wearing some light beige slacks, a blue open neck shirt and a sweater over his shoulders. They looked at each other without speaking and he reached over and took her hands in his.

Check in was very simple and quick. They already had booked seats together and there was virtually no queue at the Business Class check in. As they wanted to sit together they opted for the middle two seats with an aisle each side. They headed to the lounge and had a glass each of Champagne while they waited for the call to board.

Thelma had never been on an A380 before and she was astonished how large it was and how spacious the Business Class seats were. As she sat down she felt happy. This was going to be the first real adventure she had had in years.

The flight was long and at the same time as comfortable as flying could get. She and Sebastian chatted a little, both being careful not to mention anything personal, especially about Thelma's family, and then they each followed their own choices from the entertainment system. Meals came and went; the food was excellent and the wines of really good quality. Both Thelma and Sebastian slept for several hours thanks to the flatbeds. They had to change planes in Doha, but the stopover was just two hours and then they were off to Rome.

It was a beautiful morning when they landed, warm with clear blue skies. They took the high speed train *La Frecciarossa* from Rome Termini station to Florence. It took just over an hour and a half. They arrived in Florence mid afternoon, went to the hotel, had a shower and went for a brief walk. They stopped at an open air restaurant and had an aperitif, an early dinner and went to bed as they were both having difficulty keeping their eyes open. As Thelma lay in bed waiting for Sebastian to finish in the bathroom she looked around the room with approval. It was a totally modern and comfortable room, tasteful and practical, in what was a very old building that had been totally modernised inside. The bed was large and firm. Sebastian came out of the bathroom, totally naked which is the way he always slept. Thelma took in his slim lithe body, a dusting of hair on his chest. He did not attempt to hide his ample penis hanging between his legs. Thelma sighed with approval as he got into bed next to her, knowing that tonight they would just fall asleep. He turned towards her and kissed her gently on the forehead, smiling. He said, 'Welcome to Europe.' Before sleep overcame her she thought that this is where she wanted to be in every single way.

****

As he went to the drinks cupboard Martin mused that one thing he had inherited from his parents was the custom of having a gin and tonic in the early evening. He mixed the drinks and sat down on the sofa with Tony. It was Friday evening and they had purposely planned nothing in particular for the weekend.

They clinked glasses and took the first sip. Tony said in a serious tone, 'I am not sure how to broach this, it is about your mum's trip to Europe.'

'Ma's trip to Europe with the art group?'

'Yes. Let me just tell you what happened and you can make of it what you will.'

Martin looked surprised. 'Okay.'

Tony started, 'You know that my flatmate Phil works at Flight Centre Bondi Junction. Well last week after you were talking over at my place about your mum's trip, afterwards Phil said he thought that it might have been him who arranged the booking.'

'In Bondi Junction?'

'Yes. It seems that the guy organising it, Sebastian, is good friends with the manager of Flight Centre Bondi Junction and so he put the booking through him even though he lives on the North Shore, and Phil was asked to make all the arrangements. It was the itinerary that you mentioned that caused Phil to make the connection, and then when you mentioned Sebastian's name he was certain. What he booked was a flight with Qatar Airways to Rome, train to Florence and then train to Venice and after to Vienna and Prague, for Sebastian di Romano and Ms T. Grant.'

Martin said, 'The itinerary could be quite common but the fact that he mentioned Sebastian and my mother is too much of a coincidence.'

Tony continued, 'And the dates match.'

So it probably is Phil who made the booking. What a coincidence.'

'Well it is more than just that. The thing is that there was no group booking that Phil made, it was just for Sebastian and your mum. It included flights, trains and hotels. One double room all the way through.'

'Oh fuck. Are you saying that she is off with Sebastian just the two of them under pretence of it being an arts group study tour?'

'I don't know Martin, but that is what it looks like. I'm sorry but I thought I should tell you.'

Oh my god!' Martin was trying to absorb what Tony had told him. 'I just can't believe it. But thanks for telling me.' He paused to think. 'It sort of makes sense as I did feel that there was something a bit strange about this trip. It seemed to be put together very much at the last minute which is unusual for a group. Do you think I should tell my dad?'

'That is entirely up to you. I can't answer that for you. If I were in your position I honestly don't know what I would do,' Tony replied.

'My own mother having an extra marital affair with the art teacher, and at her age! And when I think about her disapproval of our relationship I can't help but feel that there is a degree of hypocrisy in that.'

****

Sebastian really knew his art! He knew exactly which galleries to go to, and knowing Thelma's tastes in art which paintings she would appreciate. He also included ones that he thought would expand her horizons. Thelma was delighted. She loved art and she loved Sebastian showing her round the various galleries and sharing his expansive knowledge with her. Sometimes her feet ached from so much walking and standing, but she did not mind in the least; it was well worth a little discomfort. To take a break from the galleries they also saw churches, palaces, Museums, the Ponte Vecchio, but her favourite was the Uffizi Gallery. She felt that man-made beauty could never get better than Florence. Her first visit with Gordon had been a disaster. They stayed only two nights and hardly saw anything. Gordon had been grumpy and difficult, and clearly did not want to be there. Sebastian was such good company, amusing, considerate. They had good breaks for a coffee and for

168

lunches outside on restaurant balconies with wondrous buildings all the way round them. The food was excellent and they enjoyed a glass or two of red wine with every meal.

They ate dinner at the same restaurant every evening. It was just round the corner from their hotel and served superb food. After dinner they would take a brief stroll through the old city. Thelma found those old areas wondrous and was in awe that people had trodden these narrow alleys for centuries before them. Sebastian assured her that despite the old external walls of the houses inside most had been modernised and were actually very comfortable. After the evening stroll they would retire to their room, and she would get into bed first, Sebastian joining her unashamedly naked and slowly removing her clothes and making love to her. Yes, she felt this was more than sex, she felt she was being honoured, courted, loved. Sebastian was a very accomplished lover, as she already knew, but this was not quick and clandestine as it seemed in Sydney, it was where time had no limits and she could be suspended in the moment and revel in every second. He would be there in the morning when she woke up.

Venice was always going to be more about soaking in the beauty of the city than galleries. Sebastian had booked a small but comfortable hotel on a canal some fifteen minutes walk from St Mark's. He chose it mainly because it was quieter and away from the hordes of tourists that never seemed to leave Venice alone. They visited galleries during the day when most of the tourists were crowding the city's sites. Then they walked around the city early in the morning or in the late evening when many tourists had left either to their cruise liners or their hotels outside the city. Thelma felt a bit conflicted in that she hated what tourists had done to Venice and wished they were not there. Yet she was a tourist herself.

On their last morning there she suddenly thought about home and Gordon. It seemed so far away and she almost had forgotten that part of her life. She had not been in touch ever since she sent him a message saying that she had arrived alright in Rome. She had made it clear before she left that she wanted only messages and not calls on the basis that calls would be too expensive, whereas the real reason was that she did not want a conversation if Sebastian were to be close by. She sent a short message to Gordon saying simply: Having a good trip, all well. There was no reply.

****

Gordon heard the phone go and glanced down and saw there was a message from Thelma. But he was driving and so did not check the message. He was happy to be out on the open road with Natalia and Anton on the way up to the mid north coast. The sun was shining, there was not that much traffic and he felt good.

He had missed Thelma he had to admit, and reflected that he was not very good at looking after himself. He just could not be bothered to cook for one, and admitted that he was not a skilled cook anyway. Thelma always looked after that. One evening, just after Thelma left, he went over to Martin's place for dinner with the aim of meeting Tony for the first time. They had agreed that he would go over on his own and while Thelma was away seemed to be the ideal opportunity.

Martin made sure that he was able to leave work on time for a change and was home at a quarter to six. Tony was already there waiting for him. Martin changed into casual clothes and they did some initial preparations for the meal. Martin placed an avocado dip and some rice crackers on the low coffee table in the sitting room. Gordon arrived at six thirty. On the way over he had been trying to remember when he had last been to Martin's place and decided that it must have been at least two years. He was a bit apprehensive about how he would feel meeting Tony but he was determined to do everything he could to be supportive. He knocked on the front door, and in a few seconds he could hear footsteps on the wooden floor and Martin opened the door and greeted his father with a hug. Gordon handed him a bottle of red wine. 'This is a nice red I found in the cellar; I think you will like it.'

Martin said, 'Thanks Dad, you always have good reds!'

'Did you manage to get a park alright?' Martin enquired of his father.

'It was easier than I expected, I got a park just down the street.'

'It is not a bad time as many people have not got back from work yet, but it is normally a nightmare. Come on in and meet Tony.' Martin closed the front door and then led the way into the sitting room.

Tony stood up and extended his hand saying, 'I am really pleased to meet you Mr Grant.'

Gordon shook his hand and said, 'Please call me Gordon.' Martin and Gordon sat on the sofa and Martin asked his father if he wanted a gin and tonic, or something else. Gordon smiled and said, 'A gin and tonic will be fine thanks.'

Tony said, 'I will get the drinks. Ice and lime Gordon?'

'Thanks Tony, yes.'

Martin asked his father, 'How are you managing without Ma?'

'It feels a bit strange. The house is very quiet. But I haven't starved to death yet. Mind you it has only been a few days.'

'Have you heard how she is getting on?'

'Actually no I haven't, but I am sure she is very busy with all that art stuff.'

Martin smiled at the words 'art stuff' knowing that it was not something that his father appreciated.

'No, I haven't heard from her either,' Martin admitted.

Tony arrived with the drinks. 'I haven't made them very strong on the basis that Gordon is driving and I am sure we will have a glass of wine with dinner.' He put the drinks down on the coffee table on some black leather coasters. They clinked glasses with the word cheers.

'So how is the baching going?' Tony asked Gordon.

'As I was just saying to Martin, at least I haven't starved to death yet. Actually I don't mind too much. I can do everything at my own pace without having to think about Thelma's

171

schedule. I have tended to eat lunch at the golf club. I managed to get a couple of rounds in as well. There are usually a few of the group around, so I am not short of company.' He thought that this might be a good time to mention he was going away for a week, but he was not going to provide any details; someone should know that he was going away. 'As a matter of fact I am going up to the mid north coast for a few days, leaving on Thursday.'

'That sounds nice,' Martin said, 'where are you going?'

'Boomerang Beach, next to Blueys Beach south of Forster.'

Martin was about to ask if he was going on his own but decided that if his father wanted to provide more details he would have. So he stayed quiet.

Martin got up and said, 'I am going to do some work in the kitchen so let me leave you two to chat.'

When he had left the room Gordon turned to Tony and said, 'Martin told me you are a violinist with the SSO.'

'Yes that's right. Even as a young child I was interested in music. It is not a profession that is easy, and I suppose I am lucky to have what in effect is a permanent position with the SSO.'

They chatted about the SSO, the Opera House and the changes Gordon had seen in Sydney. It was an easy and balanced conversation, totally non controversial.

Tony called to Martin in the kitchen, 'Are you done? I need to do the dessert.'

'Yes just coming,' he called back.

Martin came and sat down with his father and Tony went into the kitchen. Gordon realised that quite subtly the boys were manipulating the situation to give him a chance to meet Tony and for it to be as non-threatening as possible. Gordon had supposed that one of them would take the husband role and the other the wife. He was expecting Tony to be effeminate but he wasn't. Now he could see that it was not like that at all. Their relationship was not modelled on the conventional marriage paradigm, but rather they were in an equal partnership. As the

172

evening progressed Gordon relaxed and was surprised to find that he liked Tony. He seemed very sensible, expressed himself well, and was utterly direct in his responses. He noticed how comfortable Martin and Tony were with each other. It was clear from how they interacted that they were both at ease in their relationship. It actually wasn't as big a deal for him as he had feared.

Tony had made a borscht soup that was served cold, Martin had made rack of lamb with sautéed vegetables, which he knew his father liked, and Tony had made a mango and passion fruit fool dessert. They drank the red wine Gordon had brought with the lamb. They left everything on the dining table and went and sat in the sitting room where the three of them chatted together. Martin served coffee.

Gordon was surprised when he glanced at his watch to find it was well after 10.00 p.m., and took his leave. He thanked them both for dinner and said truthfully that he had a splendid evening. He hugged Martin and shook Tony's hand with enthusiasm.

As he drove home he wondered what the situation was with the London plan. He had thought about asking and then decided little steps at a time and it was just not the right time to raise the subject. That night had been all about him and Tony getting to know each other.

And now he was on his way with Natalia and Anton to the mid north coast. Gordon had picked them up around nine thirty and they stopped for a light lunch in Bulahdelah, and then took the right turn past Myall Lake and Smith Lake to arrive in Boomerang Beach. The house lived up to its description and the photos on Airbnb.

Once they had unpacked they went to the shop and bought the food they thought they would need for the next few days. When they got back Anton was keen to discover the beach and so Gordon took him over the road to the beach while Natalia prepared dinner. Anton had not spent much time at the beach in Sydney and was delighted to run in the sand and then examine a few tiny crabs scuttling down holes close to the water's edge.

Natalia's cooking was far more adventurous and interesting than Thelma's more traditional Australian meat and two veg. He enjoyed the continental menu; it made a nice change.

At night it was so quiet that all they could hear was the constant noise of the surf breaking on the beach. They all slept well after what had been a long day.

Over the next few days they followed a routine of some sightseeing in the morning and then beach in the afternoon. They went to Smith's Lake again and found a boat trip around the lakes, to the Walingat National Park and along the coast to Forster and Tuncurry. On the way they stopped at the Green Cathedral on the narrow land between the ocean and Wallis Lake. It is an *al fresco* church, a unique place with rough timbered pews and a wooden lectern, situated under a canopy of rainforest on the shores of Wallis Lake. It was deserted when they were there and Anton was totally intrigued by what he described as an 'inside out church'. They sat for a while in the cool under the trees with shafts of light filtering through the canopy taking in the serenity. Natalia pronounced that it was the most beautiful church she had ever seen and was much closer to God than the elaborate baroque churches of Europe. They did some shopping in town to top up their supplies and drove across the bridge to Tuncurry. On the way back they stopped at the oyster wholesaler of the famous Wallis Lake oysters on the Breckenridge channel. They walked through the warehouse and a man explained how the oysters were farmed. Anton was captivated but when it came to tasting them he was not so keen. Natalia was ambivalent but Gordon loved oysters and so he bought three dozen to eat back at the house.

The last night of their stay, after Anton had gone to bed Natalia and Gordon were chatting over a red wine and Natalia asked, 'Gordon you never talk much about Thelma, or Martin for that matter. I know it is none of my business, but I just wondered why?'

It was an intrusive question, but Gordon felt relaxed and he did not mind. 'No I suppose I don't,' he said. He reflected a moment or two, and then continued, 'I don't think there is any particular reason it's just that my friendship with you and Anton seems very separate from my family. It is my friendship and not theirs; perhaps it is my escape in a strange way.'

'What is Thelma like?' Natalia asked.

'You have to go back to what the world was like in the 1980's. It may not seem a long time ago, but we were a lot more conventional then. Thelma and I met at a party. We got on really well and we drifted into a pretty conventional relationship. I guess she thought that I would be good at providing for her and that I would be a reasonable father to her children. We had planned on having more than one, but her pregnancy with Martin was so difficult that we decided not to have any more. She was beautiful as a young woman; she still is a fine looking woman now. She has a tremendous figure for her age. Most of my friends were either engaged or married and it just seemed that that was the thing to do. She ticked all my boxes, she was intelligent, interesting, from a good family, we had similar backgrounds and I could see myself with her in front of my friends and with work colleagues. And she has always lived up to those expectations. She has always been supportive and we never have really argued.'

He paused a few seconds as if he was thinking, and then continued, 'Overall I think it is a good marriage. But I focused a lot on work and maybe neglected the relationship a bit. I now realise that one really has to work at a relationship to get the best out of it. While I was working and late home most evenings, Thelma built a life for herself. In the early days there was Martin to bring up, and then after that she got a part time job, and she saw a few friends socially. She sees quite a lot of her sister Renie. In hindsight it was probably Martin who suffered most from my absence from the household as I threw myself into work. We did not spend time together as he was growing up, especially when he was a teenager, and I have recently discovered that I did not really know him. I am pleased to say that is changing now. Over the years the relationship between Thelma and me became a habit, more mechanical than spontaneous. I think it worked well for us both on a practical level. And then my world fell apart and that has changed a lot of things.'

'What happened?'

'I had spent my whole life serving a company. And they shafted me. I was supposed to become CEO, and instead they just got rid of me. There was a change in the ownership of the whole international group, and a totally new team of people came in. They were all American, and I suppose I did not fit in with their corporate culture or something. They used a health issue I had at the time as an excuse for paying me out. It meant that I was thrust into retirement long before I had intended, and I was just not prepared for it, either mentally or emotionally. My pride was hurt and I felt a failure and lost my confidence and self esteem. I was at a loose end, and I could see that it changed life for Thelma too. She gave up her job because she thought she was going to have to look after me, whereas in fact she didn't need to.'

'As I said, over the years our relationship had lost its lustre anyway. We had grown apart. I had my work and Thelma had her life and it sort of worked. We would rarely go out together and there was no real sparkle as there had been in earlier days. And then suddenly we were both at home and I think we started to get on each other's nerves. I was glad when Thelma started the art classes and I think this trip away with the Art Group will do her good. But the bottom line is that frankly I can't imagine life apart from her. We have created most of our history together and our lives are too intertwined to separate them, especially given the pain that would be involved. There is no practical alternative than to work it out. We have to find a way of living together that gives us both harmony in our golden years.'

'And then all this stuff started with Martin. We were both shocked, disappointed and we rejected him. He must have been so upset at our reaction when he told us. I can now see it was very hurtful, and really based on our ignorance. I have to thank you for causing me to question my feelings about it. I read loads and loads of articles about homosexuality; it is amazing what is on the net nowadays. I tried to talk to Thelma about it but she just would not listen, would not read any of the articles and is still furious with Martin. In some ways this is not like her and I wonder what is behind her stance. She tended if anything to be more liberal and progressive than me; well that is what I thought. She was always close to Martin, much closer than me. They are quite alike in some ways, even in looks.'

Natalia said, 'Could it be because she is disappointed about grandchildren or fear that he will not be happy?'

Gordon answered, 'That could be part of it, but somehow I think there is more to it than that, but I have no idea what. I went round to Martin's for dinner a couple of nights before we came up here. Martin invited me to dinner to meet Tony. I was so apprehensive and did not really want to go on one level, but I am glad I went. I did not expect to, but I liked Tony. He was nothing like I expected. In fact I am not sure what I did expect but I had this vague idea of a rather effeminate man with very feminine mannerisms, like the stereotypes that we all know. But he was nothing like that. He is a very pleasant young man. Neither of them looks odd, they are like any other young men, maybe more tidy and careful with their appearance, and a bit more sort of refined, if you know what I mean.'

'Yes I do know what you mean. My father was the same, and he was more intuitive and considerate than most men,' Natalia reinforced what Gordon had said.

'I could see that they are both happy together, they work so well as a team. I knew in a subtle way they had orchestrated the evening so that Tony and I could get to know each other without it being awkward. I had never seen Martin with anyone and it just seemed to me that his relationship with Tony is very natural. I think Martin is happy, and after all as a parent that is what we want for our children. The problems start when we define for them what it is that will make them happy rather than letting them decide themselves, and that is what Thelma is doing. The irony is that Thelma would never have followed what her parents told her if she wanted something different when she was young; she was always stridently independent. Yet that is what she is doing now with Martin.'

'Do you think she will come to accept him as he is?'

'I have no idea. I have tried to explain to her, even pleaded with her. I have tried logical arguments and emotional ones. But she just seems intransigent on this issue. It is not even as if it is through religious belief. She was born an Anglican but her parents did not go to church and she was never interested in it either.'

'What happened about London?' Gordon had told Natalia about Tony's scholarship and the decision Martin had to make.

'He hasn't heard yet as far as I know, but I am pretty sure he will get it, and then Martin is going to have to make his decision,' Gordon responded.

'Do you think he will go?'

Gordon paused. 'I don't know. I hope so but I have stopped short of telling him what I think he should do. I have tried to gently push him in that direction by telling him of my own experiences of investing too much in a job that wasn't worth it. He is rather risk averse and I suppose a bit like me in that regard. But in my view his job is not going to lead anywhere, and he is financially secure. He already has his house he can rent out, and let's face it, he is an only child and will inherit a lot of money when we both go. He needs to go and discover the world beyond his comfortable current life.'

'Let's drink to Martin,' Natalia said as she raised her glass.

'To Martin!' they said in chorus and clinked glasses.

'And thank you Gordon for what has been a really lovely break that both Anton and I have enjoyed and appreciated immensely.'

****

Tony saw the envelope as soon as he shut the front door. It must have come in the mail that morning, and his flatmate had put it on the table in the hall. It was a large envelope and had foreign stamps on it. He knew it was from London. He knew that the chances were extremely high that he would be accepted; Gareth had been very confident. But even so his heart missed a beat and then raced. As he picked up the envelope he told himself that if he had not been accepted, that was alright. After all this had all come along unexpectedly and if it all fell apart he would have lost nothing. He slit the envelope open and withdrew the contents carefully. He could see there was a covering letter and then a whole lot of forms. There was also an envelope addressed to the Royal London School of Music. Surely this meant good news. He took the cover letter. It congratulated him on being offered a two year scholarship. He sighed with relief. But what might have been elation was tempered with concern over whether Martin would come with him. He knew he was asking a lot of Martin, and he did not relish being in the position of having to choose between his scholarship and Martin. If only Martin would say yes, it would be perfect. He knew Martin had been turning this over in his mind ever since he found out about the scholarship, and that had been causing him some angst to the point where he was not sleeping as well as he usually did. Martin normally fell asleep and stayed in the same position all night long, but recently he had been tossing and turning a lot in the night.

He read the covering letter again. To accept he had to fill out the forms and return them. They had to be back in London in three weeks time. Given the mail system could sometimes be slow, that meant that he had about a week to make the final decision. He and Martin would have to talk about it the coming weekend.

Martin got home first on Friday night. Tony arrived only half an hour later. Martin had already changed from his work clothes into a more casual light grey slacks and a deep blue shirt. He had socks that matched his shirt, and had taken off his Italian leather shoes upstairs when he got changed. Tony never commented on Martin's clothes, but he always noticed how good he looked in them. Tony was not very focused on clothes and as usual was dressed in jeans and a favourite but not very new T-shirt.

They kissed and gave each other a long hug. They had not seen each other all week as Tony had been busy with rehearsals.

'Do you want a drink?' Martin enquired as Tony kicked off his sand shoes and came into the sitting room.

'Yes please. Gin and Tonic.'

'Me too!' Martin made the drinks, and got some pâté and biscuits from the kitchen. They sat together on the sofa.

'So, how was your week?' Martin asked. Even though they spoke several times a day Tony had not told him about the letter from London that had arrived two days before. He thought it was better to have that conversation face to face.

'I got the offer from London in the mail on Wednesday. I have been accepted.'

Martin was expecting this and so it did not surprise him, but at least it made things more concrete now. 'Congratulations!' Martin said, and raised his glass to clink with Tony's. 'I thought it would come through for you.'

'I have to let them know definitely one way or the other in a week or so.'

'Surely you will go,' Martin said with a clear edge to his voice.'

Tony looked him straight in the eyes and said, 'I want to, but I want you there with me.'

Martin sighed. 'I know, and part of me wants to go and at the same time I am scared about giving everything up here.'

'The only thing you are really giving up is your job. You will have your house, we will manage financially alright in London, and if everything turns turtle you have everything back here.'

"Yes maybe.' Martin was non committal

'Don't you think that job has served its purpose for you? You have gained experience and done well. But it is not going to lead to anything else. You have said many times that they don't think you fit in. And maybe you don't. It is a very family man's club. Remember the bad appraisal they gave you? And there is not going to be any prospect of a promotion. Your boss is not competent to go anywhere else and in any case they probably would not promote you if he did. It is time to move on anyway.'

'I am not even sure they will continue to manufacture here. Their supply of raw materials is under threat and they are losing money. It would not surprise me that Head Office shuts it down. The plant is almost at the end of its intended life anyway.'

'So just tell me that you will come with me!' Tony was anxious and frustrated at the same time. He had more or less decided that if Martin would not go, he would go all the same.

'Give me the weekend,' Martin said.

That was going to be hard for Tony, but he had no alternative but to accept Martin's timeline. He had watched Martin agonise over this for weeks, and it was getting him down a bit. He understood that Martin was finding it hard to let go of what he saw as security, and although on the one hand Tony found it frustrating, on the other he accepted that was the way Martin was. He decided that while he waited anxiously for Martin to make up his mind he would try and make it the most pleasant and normal weekend he could. He would make sure that they did things together and try and demonstrate what Martin would be missing if he said no.

Saturday morning they had a leisurely breakfast and then wandered around Paddington Market and dropped into the pub for lunch. In the afternoon they drove to Tamarama and went for a walk along the coastal path to Bondi and back.

Saturday night Tony had a concert and Martin said he would stay home and have some quiet time. They both knew that it was for Martin to finally make a decision.

'I will be back quite late, so don't wait up for me,' Tony said on his way out.

Martin watched television after Tony had left for work, but was not really concentrating on the content. All this was doing his head in. He remembered the conversation with his father, and he knew what Tony said about his work was right. It really was time to move on. But he liked certainty in his life. He had no guarantees that Tony and he would stay together for always even if he went to London. That scared him too. He was much happier in a relationship. He was aware that there were two processes going on his brain; the logical one and the emotional one. They were not necessarily in synch as they were processed in different parts of the brain.

In the end Martin went to bed exhausted from thinking about it; Tony was not back yet. He thought about what it would be like going to bed on his own every night and knowing that Tony would not be coming home late and crawling into bed beside him and holding him in his arms and falling asleep all cuddled up together.

He drifted off and then heard the front door lock. In a few minutes Tony was naked in bed with him. Tony kissed him gently on the neck. Martin put his hand behind him and felt Tony was hard, and he felt his own erection stirring; they just melted into each other. Martin knew he could not give that up. He had decided.

****

There was a heavy thump and then a roaring of the engines as the captain put them into reverse to slow the A380 to a sedate walking pace as the aircraft slipped off the runway towards the terminal. Thelma was pleased to be home in Australia but at the same time sad. She had had a wonderful holiday with Sebastian. He had been the perfect companion, guide and lover, all in one. Sebastian had fallen into a deep sleep after dinner whereas Thelma had been awake most of the flight despite the comfortable flat bed. She had been thinking about the last few weeks. She felt so alive with Sebastian, so wanted and valued. At almost 60 years of age she had fallen for him.

Vienna had been quite different from Italy, grand and more structured. She had quite liked that. They went to the Opera House twice and she was pleased to see that the Austrians dressed up for the occasion, so unlike Sydney where people turned up even in T shirts, jeans and trainers. She could imagine herself in Vienna's heyday, being there at the centre of a great empire surrounded by culture. At the Mayerling Hunting Lodge she was particularly affected by the story of Crown Prince Rudolph's suicide pact with his mistress Baroness Marie Freiin von Vetsera. A comparison with her affair with Sebastian was a bit of a stretch given Rudolph's mistress was only 17 years old, but she could not help but imagine that it could have been her and Sebastian together in that lodge with the world against them.

Prague had been their last stop and she was aware that their time together was limited, and that took the edge off the magic of that city. Some parts she found were like a Disney set, and it was amazing what a beautifully intact baroque city it was. It had been spared the destruction of most European cities, and the only damage was from an American air raid on the city in 1945 which they later claimed was the result of a navigational error. The bottom line however is that Prague is perhaps the best preserved capital in Europe. Apart from the wonderful architecture and gothic churches, the city was fun. She did not find the cuisine as fine as Italy but she really enjoyed the several concerts they went to, the old churches and strolling across the Charles Bridge. She was just a bit disappointed that there were so many tourists. But frankly that had been the case wherever they went.

Apart from everything she had seen, she had relished the time she and Sebastian had spent together. That was really the best part, to have his company totally for the whole three weeks; every minute of every day, every meal and every night together in bed. He made love to her exactly the way she wanted.

And now she was back in Sydney. The doors of the aircraft were open, the engines winding down, and the other passengers were getting their hand baggage down from the overhead lockers. Sebastian reached up for Thelma's bag and handed it down to her and then retrieved his own. He looked at her a bit anxiously.

'Are you alright?' he enquired. Sebastian was really sensitive to the moods of others.

'Oh just a bit tired from the flight.' Thelma was not telling him what really was going on in her mind..

She had told Gordon that because the flight got in so early it would be ridiculous for him to pick her up and she would take the same shuttle service and be home in time for breakfast. The arrivals process was straightforward and they located their shuttle bus easily. They sat mostly in silence as they wove their way through the early morning traffic to the north shore. As they got close to where Sebastian got out he turned to Thelma and said 'Thanks you so much for coming with me. I had a wonderful time, far better than I ever expected, and most of that was due to your company.'

Thelma was too emotional to say much. But she looked at Sebastian and said, 'I have had the time of my life. I am so very grateful.'

As he got out of the van Sebastian kissed her gently on the lips, a kiss that lasted longer than a simple kiss between friends, but rather one between lovers. He did not speak and picked up his hand luggage, lifted his suitcase out of the back of the van and waved as the van pulled away.

In a few minutes they were in the drive to the house and Gordon must have heard the tyres on the grit. He opened the front door, and then as Thelma picked up her hand luggage, Gordon took her suitcase from the back of the van.

'Welcome home, darling,' he said as he gave her a peck on the cheek, 'have you had a good trip?'

'It was wonderful,' she said and smiled a rather forced smile. They went inside the house.

'Shall I put the kettle on? Are you hungry?' Gordon asked.

'Yes a cup of tea would be nice. I had breakfast on the plane so I am not hungry at the moment. What I would like to do is take a shower and then get a couple of hours sleep.'

'Is it nice to be home?' Gordon asked looking for some assurance.

'Yes of course,' she said. But her tone of voice was not very convincing.

The day after Thelma got home Martin called the house from his office at work. Thelma picked up the phone 'Seven six four three, hello.'

'Hi Ma it's Martin!'

She replied with a simple 'Oh!'

Martin was not sure how this call was going to go. He tried to sound as natural as he could. 'So how was the trip?'

'Absolutely fantastic,' she said, 'I had a wonderful time. The weather was perfect and the art is amazing.'

'Oh good! Is dad there?'

'No, he's out at golf. How's work?'

'Actually talking about work there is something I wanted to tell you both. I am going to put my notice in. I have decided to go to London with Tony.'

There was a pause; obviously Thelma was thinking what she was going to say. 'Why on earth would you do something so silly and irresponsible? Why give up a good job to go off on a whim?' Thelma was angry, partly with Martin but mainly with herself. She knew she was being unkind and unreasonable, but that is what she felt like doing. And she asked the question knowing what Martin would say, and knowing that his answer would provoke her more.

'Because I love him.'

'Don't be ridiculous, I am over all this nonsense with you.' Her voice was sharp as she intended it to be.

Martin had been turning over in his mind whether to tell his father about what he had discovered about his mother's trip to Europe. He had decided it would be very hurtful to him, and that it was really an issue between them that they would have to sort out. He could feel a certain resentment rising from his stomach. Martin was normally very even tempered, it was his nature. But when something really riled him he could get as angry as anyone else. He decided it was time to bite back.

'Ma, I think it is a bit hypocritical of you to pretend you are taking the moral high ground and accuse me of being irresponsible.'

Thelma had rarely heard Martin sound as angry as he clearly was. She asked, 'Exactly what do you mean by that?'

'I mean that going away on a trip for two with Sebastian pretending it was a group art trip is a rather deceitful thing to do.' Martin's voice was terse and precise,

Thelma was completely thrown. Had she misheard what he had said? How could he possibly know? She thought the best thing was to deny it.

'Martin, I don't know where you got....' Thelma sounded indignant, but Martin interrupted her.

'Ma, Tony's flatmate works for Flight Centre Bondi Junction and he did the bookings. Sebastian arranged it all through him, and it came to light by chance one night when we were talking. And it was one double room for the whole trip.'

Thelma was floored. She did not know how to respond. There was quite a long silence. There was really no point in denying it; she knew that Sebastian had booked through Flight Centre Bondi Junction and it would have been clear that it was just the two of them travelling.

She was more contrite. 'Does your father know?'

'No, I haven't told him. That is something between you and your conscience. But the point is that it is a bit rich for you to make judgments about me when you have been cheating on Dad in a pretty massive way.' Martin hung up. He felt there was nothing more he wanted to say right then.

Thelma placed the phone back on the charger, sat down in the chair next to the desk and burst into tears. She was overtaken by a kind of panic. She had tried so hard to keep her affair with Sebastian a secret and now by this awful turn of fate Martin had found out about it. He had said he would not tell Gordon, but what if he did? What would Gordon do? Would it be the end of her marriage and her life for the past nearly forty years? She suddenly felt very insecure. Until then she had managed to block out of her thoughts what the consequences of her affair with Sebastian might be. As the reality of what she had done sank in she was ridden with both guilt, and at the same time exceptional anxiety. Apart from Gordon, how was she going to repair her relationship with Martin? She knew deep down inside that she was being purposefully nasty to him, and yet at the same time she adored him. It was not really that she had any issue with gay men; she had known several in her lifetime and liked them all. She just did not want her only son to be gay. But he was and she knew that he could not change however much she wanted him to. He was going to go to London and would be on the other side of the world. She regretted that the conversation had unravelled so quickly that she had not found out when he was going or how long he was going to be away. Her life had changed from a comfortable if not exciting existence to a real mess with no certainty.

She was still in a shocked state when she heard Gordon's car on the grit drive. The car door closed and she heard his key turn in the door. He looked at Thelma as he walked into the sitting room.

'What on earth is the matter?' he said looking very concerned. He could see from her face that she had been crying and she looked very drawn and tense.

Thelma was not going to tell him the whole reason and said, 'Martin called to say he is going to London, together with that man.'

'Tony! Oh good!'

Thelma looked shocked. 'What do mean, good?'

Gordon said, 'Let's sit down and have a drink, it will do you good.'

Thelma did not answer but Gordon mixed two strong gin and tonics and they moved to the comfortable arm chairs in the sitting room.

'So you knew about this London thing?' Thelma asked as she took a good sized sip.

'Yes I did as a matter of fact. Martin discussed it with me a few weeks ago. I honestly think it is the right decision to go.'

'With that Tony?'

Gordon looked at her seriously and said, 'Yes, with Tony. He is a very nice man.'

'What? You met him?' Thelma felt she was in a whirlwind of turmoil that was carrying her along like out of control flood water.

'Yes, while you were away I went over there for dinner. Martin had previously asked me what I thought about going to London. I did not tell him what I thought he should do but I did give him some ways of looking at it, and I told him about some of the regrets I have about dedicating myself to a job for most of my life.'

'I just don't believe what I am hearing. Why did you not tell me all of this?' Thelma was indignant.

'Firstly you were away and secondly I wanted to have a chat with you about Martin anyway.'

'You seem to have accepted what he is doing.' Thelma was almost accusatory.

'Yes, I suppose I have. I have talked to people, done research, and I came to the conclusion that this is not something Martin has chosen, it is part of who he is. He has no control over it, and all attempts to change a person's gender identity fail and are very destructive.'

Thelma just looked at him.

He continued, 'I know this is not what either of us wanted or expected. But this is the way it is. We can't change it, and it is wrong and useless for us to tell him to change. There are all sorts of theories, some saying there is a genetic bias, some say it is due to hormone levels in pregnancy. Most specialists tend to say it is nature rather than nurture.'

Somewhat alarmed Thelma said, 'Are you suggesting it is our fault, my fault?'

Gordon reassured her, 'Thelma it is nobody's fault, it just is. We should not take blame for it and neither should we blame him.'

Thelma was about to say that that is what Sebastian had told her, but she stopped herself in time. She did not want Sebastian's name mentioned at all.

Gordon changed tack. 'I think we both agree that what we want for him is to have a happy, healthy life that brings him satisfaction, peace, contentment and love. We want him to be financially comfortable but I don't think lots of money is essential to achieve most things in life.'

Thelma took another sip of her gin and tonic. 'Well, go on then,' she said.

Gordon continued, 'We can't relate to it, don't understand what it feels like, but I saw that night how happy Martin is with Tony. They just seemed like a really well adjusted couple. It is just that they are both men.'

'But why would he give up a good job and ruin his career and go to London? He has had a good start in life; he has his own home and a good job for his age. It seems so irresponsible for him to give that up.' Thelma's voice was calmer now, almost resigned.

'This job he has is not going to lead anywhere, you know that. In any case it is time he discovered a bit more of the world. He has had a pretty sheltered life. And look at what happened to me. I devoted all that time to work and then they ditched me. If I had my time over again I would have done much more with my life and I think it would have been better for our marriage.'

Suddenly the paranoia set in and Thelma asked defensively, 'Are you saying that our marriage is in trouble?' It clearly had its problems but she saw very clearly that she did not want it to finish.

'No, I am not saying that. But I do think that because I spent so much time at work I neglected doing things as a family. We have grown apart slowly over the years; just like most couples do I think.'

Thelma knew that in part that was the reason she got involved with Sebastian. She was non-committal. 'Maybe,' she said.

Gordon continued, 'There is something that I don't understand though. I know we were both shocked when Martin told us he was gay and to be honest our reaction must have been very hurtful to him. But you are intelligent, normally open minded, and yet your reaction was vicious, and even now after

189

having had a lot of time to think about it, you still seem angry about it. Why? Can't you see the truth in what I am saying?'

'Could you get me another drink please?' she asked Gordon.

He finished his own and poured them both another.

Thelma seemed to be thinking deeply about something and so Gordon said nothing and left his question hanging.

Thelma started, 'When I was 18 years old and just discovering sexuality I had a horrible experience. It is something that I put out of my mind but I don't think I ever resolved it.' Gordon was terrified she was going to say she had been sexually abused or raped. But he said nothing and let her continue at her own pace.

'The first man I had ever fallen for was a boy the same age as me called Jonathan. We would have been about 18 I suppose. He was so handsome and charming, loved art and had a real sense of taste, and I fell head over heels in love with him. He was the first man I ever had sex with. I was young, inexperienced and when I think back I suppose it was infatuation rather than love. All I remember is that I felt I could not live a day without him. I used to fret if he did not call, in fact I would not go out in case I might miss his call. We dated for about two months. Then one day he told me he had been trying to explore his sexuality and he had decided that he was gay. He had been dating a guy at the same time as he was dating me, and decided that he liked him more than me. In fact he moved in with him just after he dumped me. I was devastated. I blamed myself thinking that if I had been more attractive or more experienced sexually I could have changed his mind, and kept him. He had had sex with me so how could he possibly be gay? I felt wretched, angry and depressed, all at once. I felt I had been taken advantage of, and that he had not been honest with me from the start. That hurt even more.' Thelma was quite emotional by this time and tears were rolling down her cheeks.

Gordon got up and put his arm round her shoulders. 'I had no idea,' he said.

'I coped by putting it out of my mind and had not thought about it in years and then when Martin said he was gay it brought it all up again. It seemed like it is a plague on my life.'

Gordon said, 'I can see that, and I understand why it feels like that. But Martin has been honest and he has not ruined the life of a woman, and his own, by marrying. And in the end neither did Jonathan. There is such a pressure to be what is considered normal and get married.'

Thelma said, 'What Jonathan did was unforgivable.' She still sounded angry.

Gordon could see that while it was just as well Jonathan played with Thelma's emotions for a short time only, it had had a profound effect on her. Jonathan had been insensitive to Thelma's emotions and what he had done was understandable but wrong. Martin being gay had brought all that pain back. He was wondering what the best way to approach it would be. He tried some gentle logic, 'Yes, nobody should play with the emotions of other people, it is very selfish.'

Thelma shuddered slightly thinking about whether what she was doing with Sebastian fell into that category. She decided not to pursue that line of thought right now.

Gordon continued, 'Not all gay men are the same, and you can't hold Martin responsible for the hurt that guy caused you.'

'But what about the hurt that Martin is causing me?' Thelma snapped back.

Gordon sighed and then said very gently, 'Thelma. Thelma, don't you think that you are causing your own hurt?'

Thelma sat still but did not reply. Gordon continued, 'Martin told us because he did not want to lie to us. We were putting pressure on him to get a girlfriend and marry, and then Tony appeared in his life so he decided to be up front with us. It must have taken a lot of courage, and what he was hoping for was our understanding and support. And he did not get it.'

'Was it my fault? Did I cosset him too much?' Thelma was now feeling the guilt.

Gordon reassured her, 'No, no, it is not like that. I told you what the research says. It isn't helpful to blame ourselves.'

Thelma said rather forlornly, 'Do you think our reaction has caused him to want to go to London?'

'Not at all. It was all because Tony got this scholarship and Martin had to decide whether to give up Tony or his job, and he decided it would be the job. And frankly he needed to move on anyway. So honestly I think he has made the right decision. It will do him good to have broader experiences. I wish now I had done something like that at his age. We will miss him of course but he will be back.'

'I just feel that I might have pushed him away.' Thelma was not going to let go of the guilt trip.

Gordon said, 'It was clear to me that evening I went over for dinner that they are both very keen to have a good relationship with us. I think we should have them over for dinner, both of them, before they leave. And we still don't know when that is.'

Thelma sighed. 'I suppose you are right. I guess we have to accept it, even though frankly I still don't really understand it.'

****

A few days after they had returned from their trip Sebastian called Thelma.

'How was the homecoming?' he enquired.

'A lot has been going on. Life was so much easier when we were travelling and did not seem to have a care in the world,' Thelma responded.

'I am sorry to hear that, what happened?'

'Oh all this stuff with Martin came to a head. He is going to London with his friend.'

Sebastian always seemed to be able to strike the right note, 'How do you feel about that?'

'I am upset on several levels. I suppose I have been hard on him for reasons that were more to do with me than him. I just have to accept the situation as it is, even if I don't like it.'

'Life is like that,' Sebastian observed. He changed the subject, 'There is something I want to talk to you about, and was wondering if you want to come over?'

Thelma was intrigued but knew better than to ask him what it was over the phone. 'Yes by all means. Does this afternoon work?'

They agreed on 4.00 p.m. Thelma was trying to work out what it might be. He had said 'something I want to talk to you about'. Was he going to suggest some sort of change in their relationship? Was he going to ask her to move in with him? It would not surprise her as she knew he was lonely and they had got on so well together on their trip. On the one hand she could not think of anything more wonderful than living with Sebastian, but being on a holiday is different from day to day life, and she doubted that she could bring herself to leave Gordon. She and Gordon got on alright in the sense that they never argued or had tensions, but they were more like friends who had known each other a long time. Was this enough for her, or did she still want romance and excitement, not to mention sex? The other issue was finances. It would mean a divorce. She shuddered at the thought. She would lose her house and as she thought that Gordon would not really be able to buy her out, he would lose it too. It would have to be sold. If they split the assets into two there would be enough money for them both especially as Gordon got a very substantial pay out and superannuation from his company. But what would Gordon do? He would be totally lost. He had never looked after himself; she had provided during the whole time they were married, and he had lived at home with his parents before that. But should she be expected to sacrifice her own life and happiness because of a sense of duty to him? It was almost like making the decision to be young or old. She would prefer not to have to decide and just continue with their affair.

She pulled up in front of Sebastian's place. She reflected how for years she had had a stable and easy life with no issues or conflicts and then in the past year her life had been turned upside down; it was a roller coaster. She felt a bit calmer thinking that she would have time to think about whatever Sebastian was about to propose; she would not have to decide there and then.

Sebastian opened the door and smiled. He was wearing just a tank top and shorts reinforcing his slim and firm, well proportioned body that even a younger man could have been proud of. For Thelma he just oozed sensuality. Sebastian kissed her on the lips and held her in a tight hug.

'Come on in. I have opened a bottle of red, is that alright?'

'Yes, lovely!' Thelma sat on the sofa and Sebastian sat next to her. She was wondering if they were going to have sex. But Sebastian was not making any such moves. Thelma was aware that her heart was racing a bit, and she was far from relaxed.

'Over the jetlag?' Sebastian asked.

'Pretty much I think. But the first few nights I kept waking up at 4.00 a.m. and then couldn't get back to sleep again.'

'Same here,' Sebastian said, 'then I had a whole load of things to sort out and so it has been a busy few days.'

Thelma was wondering how long this small talk was going to go on, and she felt like telling him to get to the point.

After some further general conversation Sebastian leant forward and said, 'Thelma there is something I need to tell you.'

This was it. Thelma felt anxious.

Sebastian started, 'You remember me telling you that my younger daughter Monica went to live in Germany with the two children when her husband got a transfer with work?'

Thelma was not expecting this lead in to the conversation. 'Yes!' she said.

Sebastian continued, 'It seems that after they got there the marriage started to break down. There were fights and it got quite nasty and to cut a long story short they have separated. Monica has started divorce proceedings. She will ask for custody of the children but wants to stay in Germany so that her husband will get access. She has managed to get a research job at the university in Hamburg and financially she says she will manage quite well.'

'Oh dear!' Thelma said wondering where all of this was leading.

'The thing is that Monica finds it hard to cope with bringing up two children and a full time job when she has no support there. So she has asked me if I will go and live with her and the boys to provide some help to her. And to be honest I think she is a bit lonely too.

Thelma simply said, 'Oh!'

'I will get my own place but close to her so that I can be there for her and the children but also have my own space. That will allow me to paint as well.'

Thelma thought that maybe he was about to ask her if she would go with him.

Sebastian said, 'I leave in ten days time, so as you can imagine I have a huge amount to do here. To start with I want to rent the house out which means that I have to pack everything up.'

Thelma pointed out the obvious, half in a daze, 'So that means that we....' Her voice trailed off.

Sebastian interrupted, 'You know how much I have enjoyed the time we have spent together and I hope we will remain in contact, and there is always Skype or WhatsApp.'

He is not even inviting me to visit him, she thought. She felt hurt, a little angry and at the same time frightened. Her immediate reaction was that she wanted to get out of Sebastian's place.

Thelma tried to not sound rude or petulant saying, 'I can imagine how much you have to do so I should leave you to get on with it.'

Sebastian could see she was very upset, and he had anticipated that. It was easier to just let Thelma leave; he had sincerely enjoyed the time they had spent together, but he had never wanted to take it further than that. Had he remained in Sydney he could have envisaged that they would have continued their affair, but for him it had never been more than that. It was better to bring it to a close now.

'Yes, I do have a lot to do, and I should get on with it,' Sebastian said as he stood up. Thelma stood up as well and she walked to the front door and opened it. She knew Sebastian was right behind her but she did not turn round, she went out and down the path without saying anything or looking back. Almost in a daze she went to the car, got in and burst into tears.

She felt stupid, betrayed and annoyed for having allowed herself to get involved in such a profound way. On another level she felt relieved that she did not have to make decisions that would have been very difficult and painful. The cruelty was that being with Sebastian had shown her what her life might have been like. It was cruel that she had had that fragment of fulfilment that demonstrated how mundane her real life was in contrast. It would have been better if it had never happened. But regrets cannot change history.

****

'Then you had better start the application process right now,' Tony said.

Martin had explained that he had investigated the Ancestry visa that would give him the right to work and reside in the UK. He felt it would give them more flexibility than a partner visa in that such a visa would be tied to Tony's ability to reside there. If they wanted to stay after Tony's student visa ran out then Martin's Ancestry visa would come in handy. All he had to do was to show that one of his grandparents was born in the UK. It would take three weeks, they said. There were still about six weeks before they were going to leave. Martin would hand in his notice in two weeks time. He was actually now looking forward to doing that.

'Oh a couple of things,' Martin said, 'Ma called me today. She seemed quite different, relaxed and friendly as if nothing had happened. Firstly she said that her art classes had stopped because Sebastian was going to move to Germany permanently. I suppose I am meant to assume that the affair with him is over. Then she issued a dinner invitation for next week, for both of us! She said that given we were going to London she should get to meet you. I accepted.'

Tony smiled. 'So I need to be on my best behaviour. But that is really good news. When?'

Martin said, 'Next Wednesday if that suits. And then there was one more thing she said. She had been talking about me going to London to one of her friends whose son has been living in London for a couple of years. He is back here on holiday to see the family and wondered if I want to catch up with him just to get the lowdown on London. I know him quite well as we are about the same age and since our mothers are friends we got to know each other growing up. I never kept in touch with him, but it could be useful to have someone there that we know, a familiar face. So I agreed to do that too. Do you want to come along?'

'Maybe you should go on your own if you have not seen him for a while, but yes, it could be useful to know another Aussie there,' Tony agreed.

'I have his phone number so I will call him later,' Martin said.

'Dave speaking,' the voice at the other end of the phone said.

'Hi Dave, it is Martin Grant here. My mum told me that you are back in Sydney and were suggesting we catch up. We are off to London in six weeks as I think you know. So, yes, it would be great to catch up.'

They arranged to meet a couple of days later for a drink after Martin left work. They chose to meet at The Lord Dudley in Woollahra. Dave was already there when Martin arrived. They shook hands and Dave, who already had a beer, ordered one for Martin. Dave said, 'I gather that you are going to London to be with your girlfriend who has some sort of scholarship, is that right?'

Martin laughed, 'I guess my mother was a bit misleading, almost certainly on purpose. Actually I am going with my boyfriend, he has a scholarship at the London School of Music for two years.

'Oh cool.' Dave did not seem to be the least interested whether Martin had a girlfriend or a boyfriend.

Dave talked a bit about life in London in general. He liked it but found the British more reserved and less straightforward socially. He tended to befriend Australians, who were quite numerous in London.

Dave changed the subject with the question, 'What sort of a visa are you on?'

Martin replied, 'An ancestry visa. Well, I haven't got it yet, I have applied. I can't see any reason why it would not be granted.'

'That is a good visa to get if you can. Unfortunately I couldn't, my ancestors all came from Eastern Europe. So with me it was a bit more complicated but I got there in the end.' Dave did not elaborate, but then asked what Martin was intending to do for work.

Martin explained that he would ask his current employer if there were any opportunities with their UK office, but that he doubted it and in any case he felt like a bit of a change. Other than that he would look around when he got there. There were a few other companies that were in the same industry he could try, but he knew it was going to be difficult He was prepared to do pretty much anything for a while. But he would rather have something that either advanced his career or enhanced his skill set. He was more concerned about doing something useful that he enjoyed than making lots of money.

Dave asked if they had any thoughts on where they would live. Martin said that the London School of Music was in the East End and the nearest tube station was Bethnal Green on the Central Line. He supposed that rents in that area would be high and so maybe somewhere on the Central Line a bit further out might work. They would love Notting Hill Gate or Holland Park, but suspected they might be pushed further out to Acton because of high rents. They would stay in a cheap hotel for a week or so until they found something. The Music School said they would help them find a place as well.

Dave said, 'I have a mate who has been living in a one bedroom flat between Camden Town and Chalk Farm. He is leaving to come back home. It might be possible if you are interested to see if you could take that over. It is quite a nice garden flat in a converted house and I know it is reasonably priced. It is not on the Central Line, but you can take the Northern Line and change either at Tottenham Court Road or Bank.'

Martin was keen to investigate that possibility, partly because it would give him more peace of mind knowing they had a place to live, and partly because he knew how hard it was to find a decent place at a reasonable price. The thought of going round looking at tragic places to rent did not appeal at all.

Dave continued, 'There is something else I want to talk to you about. Can we chat over a quick dinner, I am starving. They have food here.'

Martin was surprised but happy to go with the suggestion. So far the meeting had been very useful and it was good to catch up with Dave again. They moved into the restaurant and ordered just a main; Dave took the fish and chips and Martin the lamb's fry. They ordered a glass of red each.

While they waited for their food Dave explained, 'Apart from my normal job in London I have also been working with two other guys in establishing a chain of gyms. We have four and we are negotiating for a fifth. None of us works full time in the gyms as we all have other jobs. They have been pretty successful, there is a high demand in London and we have a formula that tends to appeal to the young trendier clientele who don't have much free time. There are two issues. One is that as it gets larger it needs more supervision, and none of us really has the time or inclination to do that. The other is that while they are doing well, I think they could do much better with a bit of marketing and a bit more discipline in the way the gyms are run. Each gym has a manager but they tend to be a bit lazy. I mean they are alright, but we need something better than just alright.'

'It sounds as if you need an overall manager,' Martin observed.

'That is exactly what we need,' Dave agreed, 'in fact we have tried but it did not work out very well. Because none of the three of us can spend enough time, we found that people were trying to take advantage of us. We need someone we can trust, and to be honest we would prefer an Australian. Communication is just that bit easier. The manager we hired just didn't perform and I think he was ripping us off.'

Martin wondered if he was following where Dave was going with this. He had thought it was a bit odd when he asked him about his visa, but perhaps he wanted to check whether he was legally allowed to work in the UK. He listened intently.

'When I heard you were heading over to London it crossed my mind that you might be interested in taking over the manager's job. I have known you for years and I trust you, and that is a major issue with us not being around much. You have the right training in that you know how organisations work and you are involved in marketing. You are the right age.'

Martin was of course very interested but wondered if he really was suitable for that job. He would not want to stuff it up for Dave. He wanted to make sure that Dave understood that the sort of workplace where he had been working was very different from a gym. He said, 'Wow, that would be amazing, and thanks for the confidence, but a chain of gyms is a very different business from a multinational in the manufacturing sector. The culture would be different; the business itself is totally different. The marketing would also be nothing like what I have been doing, even though I was in marketing.'

Dave smiled and said, 'I would have been a bit concerned if you had not brought that up, because it is true. Superficially. But what I look at is the basic core competencies, like for example the ability to analyse problems and come up with a solution. It is about having systems in place and making people accountable, and about interpersonal relationships to get the best out of people. The industry you apply that to is secondary in my book. You will learn what the issues are fairly quickly I am sure. Much of it is about managing people.'

'I have not had direct reports in my job, but I have a very clear idea of what works and what doesn't having been on the receiving end. Is my being gay an issue?' He did not want to have a job where he had to hide his life as he had had to in his last one.

Dave laughed. 'In some gyms I reckon half of the clientele is gay so it might be an advantage. And as for the staff, this is London in the 21st century and they are all young. It is not an issue.'

'Makes a change from my current job,' Martin observed.

'In terms of compensation I suggest a starting salary of £38,000 and then a bonus scheme dependent on the gross profit we make. I estimate but can't promise that might be another £5,000. It all depends on how we go. So, are you interested?'

Martin did not need to think too long and hard about it. Having a job would be a huge relief for him; the thing he was most apprehensive about was finding work. He thought that it might not contribute to the career he had envisaged but on the other hand it would be both good and very different experience and it sounded like fun. He had no idea whether that was a good salary or not as he had not really investigated salaries. Even though using the current exchange rate with the Aussie dollar it was quite a bit less than he had been paid, he knew UK salaries were somewhat lower and he considered it was probably fair enough. Tony and he would manage.

'Yes I am interested,' Martin confirmed.

'Good! Alright. The gyms we have at the moment are spread around London a bit; there is one in Fulham, one in Hammersmith, then there's Wimbledon and Finchley. The fifth one we are negotiating right now, and I am pretty sure we will get it, is in Acton. I suggest we give you a travel allowance of £2,000 rather than process daily travel costs. You can get an annual oyster card for all zones for about £1,200 and then if we assume you might need to take taxis sometimes, then that would cover it. I really don't recommend you get a car. Honestly in

London it is a pain in the arse. If you want to go away for a weekend or something just hire one.'

Martin had been looking at the tube map and was more or less aware of where those locations were. 'Yes, we are not planning on having a car.'

Dave said, 'So where do we take it from here?'

Martin said, 'I have just one more question, it is about hours. I am assuming I would need to spend a lot of time in the gyms. I also imagine that sometimes it would need me to see what is going on in the evenings and over weekends?'

Dave answered, 'Yes. The gyms are open from 6.00 in the morning until 10.00 at night including weekends. Normally you would work around thirty five hours a week, and it is up to you how you spread that over the week. And yes you are right, it is important to be at the gyms at odd hours, and it is always better not to have a regular schedule so that they never know when you are going to be there.'

Martin said, 'That makes sense. Would I work from home when I am not at the gyms or is there an office I can use?'

'There is an office that you can use at the Hammersmith gym, but if it suits you to work from home as well, that is fine.'

'Well, I am definitely interested. Your offer has a lot to commend itself for me right now. I would just like to discuss it with Tony, but I suspect he will be keen on me taking it.'

Dave said, 'I am going back to London early next week so if you can just confirm in the next day or so, that would be good. Then I can get a contract to you. Nothing too fancy but you will need some kind of documentation that sets out what we have agreed.'

The food came and they reminisced about their childhood and the times they had spent together in Sydney getting on for fifteen years before.

Before they parted Dave said that he would chase up the flat he had been talking about to see if it was still free. They agreed to talk again in the next day or so.

Tony was at home waiting for Martin. Martin had sent him an SMS to let him know he was having dinner with Dave. 'So what had Dave got to say?' he asked when Martin sat down.

Martin was very animated, 'You will never guess what!'

Tony rolled his eyes, 'No probably not. Did you pull his pants down and have your way with him in the public bar?'

'No! He offered me a job managing a chain of gyms!' Martin recounted their conversation.

'Wow, that is fantastic. Are you going to take it?'

'Well I just wanted to discuss it with you before giving a final answer, but yes I was thinking of accepting.'

'It sounds really good. Any misgivings?'

'I think it is just not going to be that easy to get a job in London as a foreigner unless I want to do waitering or something equally awful, so this is a real godsend. I doubt that there will be any offer of a transfer from work, and I am not sure that is really what I want to do anyway. This does not help in the career that I embarked on, but that was never the purpose of us going to London. I think it would be a fun job. I am sure it will have its problems, like trying to manage the people who run the gyms. But it has so much going for it. And by the way he might know of a flat becoming available that an Aussie mate of his was renting. It is between Chalk Farm and Camden Town, one bedroom.'

Tony smiled. 'Does that mean you will be all buffed up and will crush me in your arms rippling with muscles?'

'Yes, nothing will change!' Martin countered. He slapped Tony on the arse, they pretended to wrestle a bit, and they went to bed.

****

'It seems like ages since we did this,' Renie said as Thelma arrived with several bags of shopping and sat down.

'It is ages and frankly it might have been a lifetime with everything that has happened,' Thelma agreed. She and Renie had spoken briefly on the phone when Thelma had just got back,

203

but when Renie asked how the trip was, all Thelma had said was that it had been marvellous and she would tell her when she saw her face to face.

They were having lunch at their usual venue of David Jones. 'What did you buy?' Renie enquired indicating the bags that Thelma had placed on the spare seat between them.

'I bought myself a dress, a couple of blouses and a skirt!' Thelma said with a certain amount of satisfaction. 'I felt as if I needed cheering up. Retail therapy.'

'Oh dear!' Renie said, 'what has been going on?'

'It is a very long story. I am not sure where to start.' Thelma clearly had a lot to talk about, and Renie was really the only person to whom she could tell everything so the list was quite long.

'Start with the trip,' Renie suggested.

'The trip was fantastic.' Thelma described some of the places they went to and what she had seen, galleries, the concerts, the restaurants.

'You have not really said anything about Sebastian. How was that?' Renie went straight to the point.

Thelma sighed deeply. 'He was wonderful, but it's over.'

'Oh?' Renie was keen to hear more.

'Yes, he is going to live in Germany for the foreseeable future to be close to his daughter and help look after his grandsons. It seems she and the husband split up, and she needs someone around to help now she has a full time job there. And what is most hurtful is that he did not invite me to go with him either to live or even just for a holiday.'

Renie could see that Thelma was very distressed by this. She said, 'To live with him? I can hardly believe what I am hearing. My god Thelma you haven't fallen for him have you?'

Thelma did not say anything but Renie could see she was on the verge of tears. She said, 'For god's sake Thelma, I said have an affair I did not say go and fall in love. In fact I specifically warned you against falling for him. That is a complication at our time of life that we don't need. Much as I think Gordon is boring the last thing you want to do is lose the house and possibly end up high and dry on your own. It sounds to me as if you have had a lucky escape. It's just as well he is going overseas.'

That was not what Thelma wanted to hear and she had been hoping for some understanding and sympathy from Renie. She was still looking for sympathy, 'And Martin found out I was having an affair with Sebastian.'

'How did he find out?'

'By an amazing set of coincidences; Sebastian booked through Flight Centre Bondi Junction and the guy who did the booking turned out to be the house mate of Tony, Martin's friend.'

'Does Gordon know?'

'Martin says he has not told him and I don't think he will. As far as I know Gordon has no idea but I can't be sure.'

Renie said, 'Well just as well. And if it is over even more reason to keep it from him.'

'The problem is that Martin hung up on me. We had words. He called me a hypocrite for judging him when I was having an affair with Sebastian.'

Renie responded, 'Don't you think he has a point? One thing I have never understood is why you have been so hard on Martin for being gay.'

Thelma explained further, 'While I was away it seems that Gordon has made his peace with Martin and he went over for dinner and met this Tony person. He says that he did a lot of reading and research and realised that that is just the way Martin is and that he can't change what he is and he has come to accept it.'

'It is true, and I am sure deep down you know that too,' Renie observed.

Thelma said, 'Yes I know I have been hard on him, but it just seems that this gay thing is destined to wreck my life. I realised that I never resolved that stuff with Jonathan; do you remember him?'

'Yes of course I remember him, and I also remember that he was your first infatuation and you cried for days when he dropped you for a man.' Renie was always blunt. 'The thing that puzzled us all is that you could not see he was gay. It was so obvious. And I think it was that gay side of him that you liked. It was his sensitivity, his love of art, as well as the fact that he was very good looking that attracted you to him in the first place. And I think he wanted to try and see if he could be straight; given you got on well together it was an obvious choice for him to put his sexuality to the test with you. You were his experiment, and it did not work because he really was only attracted to men.'

'And then Martin being gay, it was just too much.' Thelma was still looking for sympathy.

Renie was not going to give her any though. 'That's life Thelma, you can't change it. You have to play the set of cards you are dealt and stop feeling sorry for yourself.'

'Sometimes Renie, you are so hard,' Thelma observed.

'Yes I know. It is because I love you,' Renie smiled and put her hand on top of Thelma's and squeezed it. 'I mean that,' she said.

'And now Martin is going to London to live. Tony got a music scholarship for a couple of years and Martin gave up his job and is going with him.'

Renie looked pleased. 'Excellent! That must have been a hard decision for him, he was always far too serious and responsible; I think it will do him the world of good.'

'I need to repair our relationship before he goes, and that is in just a few weeks.' Thelma sounded anxious.

'It's not that hard. He was screaming for your acceptance, and you were always so close. All you have to do is apologise and embrace Tony as his partner.'

'Actually they are both coming over for dinner next Wednesday.' Thelma paused just a second or so and then continued, 'It is not going to be easy meeting Tony. I am not sure how I will react.'

Renie said, 'Let me give you some advice. Just be yourself and focus on the fact that he is Martin's partner.'

'Gordon said he is very nice,' Thelma said.

'If Martin is happy with him, isn't that enough?'

'Yes I suppose it is.' Thelma sounded resigned if not enthusiastic.

****

'So what did you think of Tony?' Gordon asked as they sat down in the sitting room. Martin and Tony had just left after the dinner.

'He was actually nothing like I imagined,' Thelma declared.

'In what way?' Gordon enquired.

'I suppose I thought that he would be kind of small and a bit passive. And he is nothing like that. I have to admit that I like him. He is personable, very polite, actually engaging.

Despite Martin and Tony's apprehension it had been a very successful evening. Martin had handed in his notice a few days before. He asked if he could take his remaining holiday entitlement which would then give him a few days after he left work before they left to London. He was not sure what he expected, but his boss seemed almost disinterested in his leaving. The leave was granted and there was no mention of how or if Martin would be replaced. His boss had simply asked Martin if he had another job, and Martin just said that he was looking for a change in his life and he was going to London for a couple of years. His boss did not suggest that he contact their UK office to see if they had any jobs, but Martin asked for contacts there just in case. There was no suggestion of any formal farewell dinner or get together, but he supposed they would probably go to the pub with some of his colleagues after work on his last day. Since he handed in his notice Martin had left right on time at 5.00 p.m. sharp. He felt he did not owe the company any more than that; he would just tie up loose ends the best he could. In some ways it reinforced for him that he had made the right decision. There was neither affection nor appreciation or loyalty from his company. He was just another cog in the wheel, and one that did not really fit in.

Martin had time to go to Glebe to pick Tony up on the way back to the North Shore to his parents' place that evening for dinner. As they drove through the front gates and up the drive Tony said, 'So this is where you grew up!'

'Yes, I lived here all my life until I left home when I bought Paddington.'

'It must have lots of memories for you,' Tony said thoughtfully.

'Yes, I suppose it does. In some ways this still seems to be home even though I have my own place.' He put his hand on Tony's thigh, looked at him and said, 'I never thought I would drive through these gates with my boyfriend at my side.'

They got out of the car and Martin knocked on the front door. Thelma opened the door with Gordon right behind her. Martin stepped forward and she kissed him saying, 'Hello Darling.'

Martin stood to the side and said, 'This is Tony.'

Thelma had thought long and hard about this, and she had decided that whatever she felt, she had to be welcoming. Tony offered his hand saying, 'I am pleased to meet you Mrs Grant.' Thelma ignored the hand and put her arm on his shoulder, leaned towards him and kissed him lightly on the cheek. She said, 'Thelma, call me Thelma Tony, come on in.'

Gordon shook hands with Martin and then with Tony, a warm and welcoming handshake accompanied by, 'Nice to see you again Tony.' As they walked in to the lounge, Tony and Martin exchanged glances. The ice seemed to have been broken.

'Gin and tonics?' Gordon enquired.

Gordon made the drinks and they all sat down around the low coffee table.

'Well boys, how are the plans going?' Gordon started the conversation.

Martin had already told them about the job offer in London. He updated them on his notice at work and their lack of reaction. Gordon commented, 'Yes I know what you mean. We put so much energy into work and the company and in the end the truth is that they do not care a fuck.'

'Really, Gordon!' Thelma exclaimed with a very disapproving look.

She turned towards Martin. 'Did you get the visa yet?' Thelma asked.

'In fact I heard today that it is ready and they will mail it to me and I should get it next week.'

To include Tony more in the conversation Gordon asked him about the course and the London School of Music. Tony told them about the course and talked about the importance of it for his career. Thelma asked Tony if he had been to London before. Tony explained that he had travelled a little outside Australia including London, mainly with the orchestra, but less than Martin, and that was one of the reasons he was looking forward to London. Martin and he hoped to use it as a base for visiting other places in Europe, possibly for long weekends. Thelma and Gordon made suggestions as to which might be interesting destinations as well as suggesting places they should visit in the UK.

Thelma served dinner, the usual pumpkin soup and steak and kidney pie. 'I know this is your favourite,' she said to Martin. Martin smiled; she often served it, and while Martin quite liked it, in fact it wasn't his favourite at all, but he never said anything. They asked Tony about his family and his childhood. He talked about what it was like growing up in Tamworth, and how his parents were very modest country folk who never had much money, but how they had coped and in the end supported him to develop his skills as a violinist. He talked about his two elder brothers, and how they got on alright even if they did not get together very often. They both still lived in the Tamworth area and were married, with two children each. Thelma was struck by how he expressed himself easily and thoughtfully, and how different his upbringing had been compared to Martin who always had virtually anything he wanted as a child; money had never been an issue for them as a family.

She observed how he and Martin interacted with each other and she felt she was seeing a side of Martin she had never seen before. He as an only child had always been a bit of a loner, almost selfish and aloof if she was honest. But she now saw how considerate Tony and Martin were to each other, how natural they were. She did not feel the discomfort she had expected. She sensed that they were being careful not to show affection to each other in front of them, but she felt it all the same. It seemed odd because it was between two men, and at the same it seemed totally natural. She reflected that Martin had become an adult with his own life and identity, and she hadn't really realised before then.

The conversation flowed easily and then it was time for Martin and Tony to leave. Thelma was going to miss Martin while he was away. Just before the boys left, to Gordon's surprise she said, 'If you have to leave the house before you get on the plane you can always come and stay here for a few days. We kept the double bed in Martin's room and so you could have that room.' She wanted to make it clear that she was expecting Tony to stay as well. They both thanked her and said they would let them know when they had worked out the details. As they said goodbye there were hugs and kisses for both of them from Thelma and enthusiastic handshakes from Gordon.

Gordon continued the conversation as they sat and contemplated how the evening had gone, 'You have certainly changed your tune. I was quite taken aback when you invited them to stay. But I think it is a good idea. How will you feel with them being in the same bed together?'

'They sleep together at home.'

'Yes but in our house?' Gordon commented as much as asked.

'I admit it might feel a bit strange the thought of Martin in bed with Tony, but that is how it is and that is how it is going to be,' Thelma said quite firmly.

'I totally agree,' Gordon said.

Gordon wondered what had caused Thelma to have the change of heart, thinking that maybe confronting the pain and hurt from the breakup with Jonathan all those years ago had been cathartic. He was not game to ask; it was just good that she had.

He commented, 'I did initially wonder if Tony was interested in Martin's money.'

'He doesn't have that much money,' Thelma countered.

'Not now maybe, but he will be quite comfortably off once we are gone.'

Thelma had not thought about that. 'Do you think he is?'

'Actually no I don't. He doesn't seem very focussed on money at all, and do you remember that at one point he said that one of the good things about going to London will be that it will be more balanced between them, that instead of them living in Martin's house they will be more like partners together in the place they both rent?'

Thelma agreed, 'Yes I did notice that at the time, and it struck me as being quite insightful.'

Gordon got up and went to the drinks cabinet. 'Do you feel like a port?'

'Yes, that would be nice, thanks,' Thelma said.

'I was thinking that maybe we could go up to London while they are there, what do you think?' Thelma asked pensively.

'I was thinking exactly the same. We could go up there in late spring for them, and then travel around a bit while we are there.'

'I would quite like to see Scandinavia,' Thelma said while thinking that she would not want to repeat Italy and central Europe. She added, 'I am not sure if I told you that the art classes have finished.'

'No you didn't. Really? What happened?' Gordon looked surprised.

'The art teacher is going to live overseas and there is nobody to take over. I think it was making a loss anyway. So, I was thinking that I might look around for another little job; something local and part-time.'

'I think that is a good idea.' Gordon was pleased. He thought that it would give Thelma something to do and an outside interest. 'What were you thinking of?' he asked.

'Maybe a receptionist at a medical practice, or something like that.'

'I was also thinking that maybe we should think about a cruise; so many of our friends are doing them.' Thelma was using the opportunity to see if she could reset her life. She had changed through all of the recent events in her life, and she sensed Gordon had too. This was going to the best shot she would have at trying to redefine their relationship and build something that they both valued. 'I would love to go to Japan for example. We have never really travelled in Asia. I am not talking about those huge mega boats, but one with just a few hundred people.'

Gordon would not have thought about cruises; he did not particularly like to feel that he was being organised. The idea of those ships with two thousand or more people just did not appeal to him. But on the other hand Thelma and he needed to start doing more things together and Japan did appeal to him and a smaller more exclusive cruise sounded like something he might enjoy.'

'That sounds nice. Let's investigate what is available. We could stay on a few days after if we wanted to; somewhere like Kyoto and maybe Tokyo as well.'

They both agreed it had been a successful evening.

'So what did you think of Ma?' Martin asked as he drove out of the gate and onto the street.

'It is just so hard to imagine that she was so difficult about you being gay; she now seems to be okay with it,' Tony observed

'Yes it is a huge change and I wonder what brought it about. I suspect that some of it was due to Auntie Renie. I speak to her every now and again and last time we spoke she said she needed to have a heart to heart talk with Ma about me. Anyway whatever it was I am really pleased. She clearly liked you.'

'She was really nice to me. You are a lot like her in looks.'

'Do you think so?' Martin seemed a bit surprised.

'Yes I do!' Tony said.

'I couldn't help thinking of her with Sebastian. I can't believe that she did that; my own mother cavorting around Europe with the art teacher.'

'Well she is a very good looking woman especially for her age, and you both have the same sense of style,' Tony observed.

'I think the biggest changes are actually with Dad,' Martin said, 'he was so distant and buried in his work when I was growing up, and we seemed to have nothing in common. It is as if he has had some sort of epiphany, and is looking at the world in a different way. I think his illness and the company dumping him has made him think through a lot of things.'

'It was very nice of your mum to invite us to stay before we leave. I must admit that I had not even thought about that. We will have put everything in storage and we will not even have a bed to sleep on,' Tony said.

'Yes, I was quite shocked. I think she is trying to make amends. But I am not sure that is really what I want to do. It will only be a couple of nights and we could either ask Frank and Bill if we could stay there or else just take a hotel. In fact a hotel would give us a lot more flexibility'

Tony said, 'It is a pity that I will have left my place by then or otherwise we could have stayed there.' In fact Tony was going to move into Martin's place in a couple of day's time until they left. After a bit of reflection Tony added, 'You know, if she really is serious about us staying there it might be politically a good thing to do. And it will only be for a couple of nights.'

'You are right.' Martin had been absorbed in the conversation and now suddenly realised he had to decide between the Western Distributor for Glebe, or the Cahill Expressway for Paddington and get in the correct lane. 'Are you coming to Paddo tonight or do you want me to drop you in Glebe?'

'Well it depends on whether you want to get fucked tonight?'

'Paddo!' Martin pronounced.

****

The next two weeks were a whirl. It was just as well Martin had the last two weeks as holiday leave from work. As he

213

was still actually employed but on holiday he could keep the company car until the day before they left. Martin had asked his father if he wanted to manage the renting of his house. His rationale was that Gordon would be far more diligent than any managing agent, and that it would find him something to do. Martin had offered Gordon the fee he would have paid an agent but he would hear nothing of it. Gordon was delighted to have the opportunity to get involved. They would put it on the rental market as soon as Martin and Tony left. There would be no problems in renting it, the Sydney market was overheated. It was a question of getting the right tenants.

Martin started packing up with Tony's help. He was going to put all the house contents into storage. There were boxes all over the house, and Martin, methodical as ever, was careful to label each box so that he would know where everything was. The hard thing was to decide what to take with them. Tony had a few pieces of furniture which they put in storage together with Martin's. The big question was whether it was worth sending a box to London by freight with some of their familiar and best loved items. It was going to cost well over a thousand dollars for just a relatively small box, so in the end they decided to take just clothes and what they could get into their suitcases. Usually in London flats were rented furnished and so they would not need to buy a lot of furniture or kitchenware. He assumed they would need to buy sheets and towels.

Tony wanted to see his parents before they left and so he suggested that they both drive up to Tamworth for a few days. Tony's parents were just a few years older than Martin's but they did not have such good health, Tony's mother was riddled with arthritis and his father had had a heart attack a few years ago. Retirement had been forced on them but it was not a retirement with a lot of spare cash. Tony's father had his superannuation from the mill where he worked so many years, but it was not a large sum, and then they relied on the disability pension until they qualified for the age pension.

They lived in an old two storey red brick house that had belonged to Tony's paternal grandparents. It needed more attention than it was accorded, and Martin could see that Tony's parents had neither the will to fix it themselves nor the cash to pay someone else to do the work.

Tony's parents were welcoming, down to earth, open and kind. They greeted Martin with enthusiasm and obviously adored Tony. They were very proud of him and his accomplishments as a violinist, and told Martin the story of his progress from a small child, revealing a lot of satisfaction about their own role. The central room of the house was the huge kitchen where they sat and where Tony's mother served wholesome and generous Australian fare. She had made up the double bed in what was now called the guest room although hardly anyone ever came to stay nowadays. Martin surmised that Tony was their favourite son and they were anxious about him being so far away; they had only been to New Zealand outside of Australia. Tony's middle brother was away in Brisbane for work but the eldest brother dropped in one evening but did not stay long. He and Tony resembled each other, Martin thought, but Tony was far better looking. He was pleasant enough and Martin could see that while they got on alright, they were not very close. Martin suspected that their lives were so different that it really could not be otherwise. His brother seemed comfortable with Tony's homosexuality and was pleasant and cordial with Martin.

Tony took Martin round the area where he grew up; the school, the local sports ground, the places where he used to play down by the river. Martin reflected that he had had a very different upbringing from Tony. Tony's had been far simpler and yet it seems to have been a much happier childhood than his. Having two brothers would have made a difference. Martin had had a far more comfortable childhood but Tony had been brought up with love and affection that had been easily given and shown. In a way he envied him that. He also understood why Tony found it easy to express his feelings and in particular his affection for Martin as he saw how easily affection was given in his family. He could not imagine Tony's mum going off round

Europe with an art teacher! Martin and Tony came from different worlds and yet fitted so well together now.

When they left both Tony and his mother cried, and his Dad was pretty emotional too. His parting words to Martin were, 'Take care of each other.' Tony hugged both of his parents and Martin felt sad, partly because of the moment and partly because he saw how very close they were as a family.

As they headed back to Sydney along the New England Highway Martin said to Tony, 'I think your parents' relationship is a better model for us to aspire to than mine.'

Tony was still upset and he just said, 'Yes, they are really wonderful parents, I have a lot to thank them for.'

Apart from the mechanical things they had to do there was a series of social goodbyes. As Martin surmised his work farewell was just a get together in the pub. His boss came for ten minutes and then said he had to leave. Martin's assistant was trying to push him on why he was going to London and with whom? Martin evaded the cross questioning through non committal statements. Martin got away as soon as he felt he could. He took an Uber home and as he got into the car he felt relief and no regrets.

There had been the orchestra farewell for Tony which had been a much happier affair. Martin was invited; there was no way he would have invited Tony to his work's get together. They met for drinks at the pub and then went out to a Vietnamese restaurant in Surry Hills. It was obvious to Martin how popular Tony was with the other members of the orchestra. Andrew the concert master had taken Martin aside and said, 'I am so pleased that you decided to go to London with Tony. If he had had to choose between his music and you it would have torn him apart.'

They caught up with Tony's flatmate Philip and they had dinners the last week with a few other friends, and Tony had dinner with Simon, his first sexual encounter from so many years ago. Martin had a conversation with his mother. Thelma had been quite insistent that they stay with them before they went to London. Tony observed that it was often like a battle of wills between the two of them. Finally at Tony's suggestion they

216

stayed there the night after the removalists came. They came on Thursday and took everything to the storage depot. They supervised the whole removal at both the house and the storage place, and were both so exhausted that they were glad in the end to be able to just go to Martin's parents place, have dinner and go to bed. Conversation over dinner was mainly about the mechanics of getting ready for their departure. Both boys confirmed that they had their visas. Martin had set up with his father all the direct payments and banking to handle the rental of his house. Thelma wanted to know where they were going to stay when they first got to London. Because London is so expensive they had booked a week in a Gaybnb place in Fulham. They had a room and ensuite for a fraction of what a hotel would have cost. Thelma was not sure she was that keen on the arrangement but let it pass. When would Martin start work? Once they were settled. When did Tony's course start? A couple of weeks after they arrived. Would they still use their Australian mobiles? No, they would get British sims and communicate mainly through web based apps. Would they get a car? Very doubtful. When would they come back to Australia for a holiday? They will not be rushing to do that as they want to do more local travel in Europe or close by while they are there. Istanbul and Marrakech are on the list, together with St Petersburg and the Greek Islands.

On Friday it seemed almost an anticlimax. They had been so busy and now pretty much everything was done. They did not hurry to get up and had a leisurely breakfast together; Gordon and Thelma had had their breakfast much earlier. Gordon drove them all to the house in Paddington and Martin showed Gordon a few eccentricities that all houses have and are annoying if you don't know about them. Martin was surprised that he did not feel sad at seeing his house empty. He rather felt dispassionate about it, more concerned with getting the right rental arrangements. Wondering what was going through his mind Tony took his hand and squeezed it, for reassurance mainly. Thelma noticed. While she thought it was sensitive of Tony she also felt it just looked 'odd.'

They went out the front door and Martin turned the key in the lock and gave it to Gordon. They dropped into the local pub for a sandwich and a beer. It was a tense meal knowing that shortly the boys would go to the hotel they had booked for their last night and Thelma and Gordon would go back to their home.

Thelma asked a bit tentatively, 'Gordon and I were talking and we thought it would be nice if we came up to UK to see you next year. Would that be alright?'

'Of course,' Martin said. He could hardly not have said that but in fact he thought it might be nice for his parents to visit – for a short stay. He added, 'I doubt we will have room to put you up, I think we will end up with a one bedroom flat because of the costs in London.'

Tony wanted to show a united front. He said, 'Of course you would be welcome.'

Gordon added to the conversation, 'We have never been to Scandinavia and so we thought we could combine the two.' That was a relief to both Martin and Tony assuming that it would therefore not be a lengthy stay in London.

Gordon drove them to the hotel they had booked very close to the airport. It was not a hotel with much character; it served the airport transit trade mainly and had an air of constant movement about it. The shuttle ran to the airport regularly bringing and taking guests for a brief stop between flights. Martin mused that this hotel was not one where anyone really wanted to stay, it was purely functional. They checked in at reception and took their luggage up to the room, and then came down to say goodbye to Gordon and Thelma. They sat in the very pedestrian lounge close to the large windows looking out on the car park. Martin reflected on how ordinary everything appeared, and yet it wasn't. They all seemed as if they were itching to move on; the moment of goodbyes was looming imminently yet nobody seemed to want to embrace it. Gordon, feeling that this was just prolonging the agony made the move and said, 'Thelma we should get going and let these boys settle in.'

'Yes,' she said, and they all got up. Thelma kissed Tony while Gordon hugged Martin. Martin said, 'Thanks so much Dad for all the support, I really appreciate it.'

Gordon said, 'Martin go and live your life, you have made the right decision.' While Gordon shook hands with Tony, Thelma put her arms round Martin. By now she was in tears.'

She whispered in Martin's ear. 'I am so sorry; I know I have been horrible to you. It is hard for me to adjust. But I like Tony very much and I hope you have a wonderful time. You are always my son and I love you.'

Martin was close to tears himself and just said, 'It's alright Ma. It is okay now.'

Thelma then said, 'That other business is all over. Dead.'

Martin knew what she meant and decided not to comment.

Gordon walked towards the door and Thelma turned and followed. At the door Gordon said, 'Have a great journey and let us know when you arrive.'

Thelma added, 'Be safe.'

The two boys waved and Gordon and Thelma went through the large glass swing door into the car park and were gone.

'What now said Tony? It is a quarter past three.'

'It's going to be a long journey tomorrow, let's have a nap.'

They went up to their room, took off their clothes except their underpants and got into bed. As Martin half expected Tony reached down and put his hands down the front of Martin's underpants.

'Aha, is this what you call a nap?' Martin asked, by which time he was hard.

They ended up having sex. When they both had orgasmed they curled up together Tony with his arms round Martin's chest, both lying on their sides.

'You okay?' Tony questioned.

'Never better,' was Martin's response.

****

Thelma and Gordon walked to the car in silence. They headed out of the hotel grounds and towards the North Shore and home.

Thelma said, 'I feel sad. This has not turned out the way I wanted. I know we have to accept there will be no wedding and grandchildren, and don't get me wrong, Tony is a nice enough young man, but I did not really want Martin to go to the other side of the world like that.'

Gordon responded, 'It is exactly what he needs. He was getting into a rut, just like I did, like we did.'

Thelma said, 'What do you mean when you say like we did?'

Gordon put his hand on her thigh. 'We have been doing the same things for thirty years, both of us. If I had not been so married to work, life could have been so different. I did not want him to fall into the same trap and wake up at 60 and ask what the hell he had done with his life. It is too easy when things are comfortable to just stay in that comfort zone and in the end not achieve anything. Life is about experiences, it is about people, it is about seeing and doing as much as you can. Martin was too much like us, living a comfortable life and getting into a rut. He had a job that did not challenge him, he owns his own home, he has no money problems. It was all a bit too easy for him. The world should be at his feet and he needs to explore it'

'Is that why you encouraged him to go while I was away?'

'I did not tell him what he should do, but I did tell him how I feel about the opportunities that I wasted in my life. It's funny how often good comes out of adversity. If they had not thrown me out form work in the way they did I might never have seen it this way.'

'I know what you mean,' Thelma said trying not to think about Sebastian too much. 'So what do we do about our rut?'

'We are lucky Thelma, we are not short of money and that gives us lots of options. We are both in pretty good health and we should learn from this whole experience and get on with our lives. We should travel more, go out more, do things.'

'Yes the cruise to Japan we talked about and London and Scandinavia. But to be honest we do have different interests. You hated it when we went to Italy together.'

'Over the years we have both changed I suppose. There are things we will enjoy doing together, and then again we can have separate interests, even friendships, which we should be prepared to pursue. I think you have done that already.'

Thelma was on guard. Did Gordon know about Sebastian? His comment could have been about her interest in art, but he did mention friendships. She was fairly sure Martin would not have told him; he was always true to his word and highly principled. So if Gordon knew, how did he know? She decided to leave it there and hope it did not come up again. She said, 'Let's start with the cruise. But I do see what you mean.'

****

Martin and Tony went down to the restaurant for a light dinner. They had a beer each. Martin said, 'Well for our last night in Australia for a while this is about as un-noteworthy as you can get.'

Tony commented, 'Yes I know. I think we are now just keen to get going and get there. It is almost as if we are already in the funnel of that long journey, just waiting for time to pass.'

They went to bed and watched some television before going to sleep. Neither of them slept that well.

In the morning they were driven by the timetable. Their flight was due to take off at 11.30 so they had breakfast at 8.30 and then checked out of the hotel, caught the shuttle to the airport and went to the check-in counter. They had already checked in on the internet and had boarding passes. They had chosen two seats together on the left hand side of the aircraft by the window about half way back. All they had to do was check in their luggage. The check-in agent was young and acted very gay. He said, 'You boys are a couple of kilos over.'

221

Tony said, 'We are off for a couple of years to live in London, so you can imagine.....'

The agent winked and said 'Oh. That sounds wonderful. I will just pretend it is on the limit.'

The boys took their immigration forms to fill out and walked away. 'The gay mafia at work, I think,' Martin observed.

'Just as well, even two kilos excess to London would be expensive!' Tony said.

They went through security and immigration without much of a delay and waited in the lounge for about 45 minutes before their flight boarded. They boarded early to make sure they could get their hand luggage stored in the overhead lockers. Martin took the aisle seat and Tony the window seat.

'They should make people take their back packs off at the door,' Martin grumbled, 'people turn round to look at the seat numbers forgetting that they have all that bulk behind them which smacks passengers who are already seated in the face.'

Getting everyone seated and the flight under way seemed an interminable process, but eventually they were taxiing and announcements were made. The aircraft reached the end of the long runway and after a wait of a few minutes turned onto the runway and the engines revved until the plane vibrated slightly, and then the brakes were released. Martin had always enjoyed the thrill of the acceleration as the giant machine picked up speed and then reaching the right speed slowly lifted off the ground.

Tony squeezed Martin's hand. 'Too late to go back now!' he said.

As they reached cruising altitude the flight attendant took orders for a drink; two gin and tonics; some things in their lives never changed.

The two boys clinked glasses. Tony said, 'I am so very glad you are coming with me. I would have been gutted to go without you. I just don't know what I would have done.

Martin said, 'It was a no-brainer. If I had not come with you I know I would have regretted it for the rest of my life. There was no other decision to make.'

Also written by John Rock:

Paseando, "Out" for a walk.
ISBN 978-1-4466-8167-1
In Paseando John recounts the colourful characters and evocative locations of his global adventures with a keen eye for detail and provocative observations about the universalities and idiosyncrasies of the human condition. His thoughtful narrative weaves culture, travelogue, personal experience, personal journey to 155 countries, and one man's wryly hilarious and often moving perspective into an utterly engaging tapestry.

Demons
ISBN 978-0-6484388-0-9
Demons is an anthology of ten short stories that insightfully explore, with wit and compassion, the existential challenges of life, relationships, and how the demons we all carry with us from childhood affect our ability to deal with them. From injustices of power and corruption to handling marriage breakdowns; from financially and sexually discordant relationships to love that inevitably is unrequited, and the role of trust, these keenly observed stories provide an insight, with an unerring sense of nuance and clarity, into issues we all face but rarely want to talk about.

CPSIA information can be obtained
at www.ICGtesting.com
Printed in the USA
FSHW012217270621
82735FS